W9-BSG-399

THE HUMAN ZOO

Also by Sabina Murray

Valiant Gentlemen

Tales of the New World

Forgery

A Carnivore's Inquiry

The Caprices

Slow Burn

THE HUMAN ZOO

A NOVEL

SABINA MURRAY

Grove Press
New York

FIRST EDITION

Published simultaneously in Canada
Printed in the United States of America

First Grove Atlantic hardcover edition: August 2021

This book was set in 12-point Goudy
by Alpha Design & Composition in Pittsfield, NH.

Library of Congress Cataloging-in-Publication data is available for this title.

ISBN 978-0-8021-5750-8
eISBN 978-0-8021-5752-2

Grove Press
an imprint of Grove Atlantic
154 West 14th Street
New York, NY 10011

Distributed by Publishers Group West

groveatlantic.com

21 22 23 24 10 9 8 7 6 5 4 3 2 1

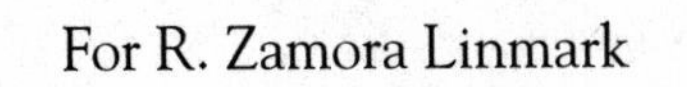

For R. Zamora Linmark

I fain would be an Igorrote,
Without a stitch of clothes,
And dwell up the sandy beach
Where the cooling sea-breeze blows.
Iron-jointed, supple-sinewed,
I would walk—would almost fly,
Catch the stray dog by the hair,
And work him into pie.

There I'd live the life idyllic,
Caring naught for Summer suns,
Caring naught for scorching cities,
Where the perspiration runs.
Dressed alone in my complexion,
With a palm-leaf fan, perchance,
I would rather be a savage
Than a magnate wearing "pants."

New York Morning Telegraph,
July 19, 1905

THE HUMAN ZOO

I

I

The plane had been delayed departing Seoul and, on reaching Manila, was at first unable to land. For over an hour we circled in the heavy, gray air. Suspended like this, I wondered why I had been so determined to return to the Philippines and was not altogether sure, beyond knowing that my aunts would be happy to see me. In the darkness below, I could sense Manila's ever-expanding hive, its choked highways, teeming tenements, and raucous babble. When the plane finally touched down, it was with an alarming shuddering of the overhead compartments, vibrations I could almost feel in the roots of my teeth. I found the possibility that one might crash on landing comforting, in a darkly humorous way, because my life had become chaotic. I did not want to crash, but it was a prospect that offered resolution. The outer edge of an early-season typhoon was dropping impressive amounts of rain and glazed the windows with thick, sheeting water. Contorted in the aisles, we waited to disembark. Lines through immigration were long. There was a band playing somewhere in the terminal's bowels, and traditional Filipino songs—cheerful guitar, love-soaked lyrics—echoed from the source.

The crowd at the baggage carousel was composed largely of overseas workers in bright sneakers and flashy clothing, but the girl blocking my access to the carousel, who had walked to stand directly in front of me, was a well-fed, solitary blonde. She was wearing a sleeveless plaid shirt that exposed a tattoo on her right bicep, an outline of a circle in black. Doubtless she was waiting for a backpack. A stream of boxes thudded down the chute, the girl's backpack, which she quickly shouldered, and, finally, my yellow suitcase.

There was no one to meet me because my family didn't know that I had returned. I hesitated by the sim card booths before exiting the terminal, put off by the thundering rain. A pair of children—boys, brothers—were shoving a wheeled suitcase at each other, back and forth, laughing like maniacs, until their frazzled mother yelled at them. When the sliding doors released me, it was through a wall of heavy heat and the dim flicker of fluorescent bulbs into a black night shot through with headlights. Horns sounded all around as if a force of nature.

At the taxi stand, the girl with the circle tattoo was looking into a battered Hyundai, speaking to the driver. "Cocoon Boutique Hotel?" she asked. "Do you know where it is?" The taxi driver did not seem to understand. "Kyoozon City?" she said, consulting a piece of paper. Leaving the girl to flounder had its appeal, but I did not feel up to being so callous.

"Excuse me," I said, interrupting. "It's Quezon City." I pronounced it in the acceptable Spanish way. "You're going to the Cocoon Hotel? Let's share a cab. It's not far from where I'm headed."

Together, we slid into the taxi's rear seat. "Cocoon Hotel," I said. "Alam mo ba yon? Dumaan ka sa Timog."

"You speak the language," the girl said.

"Enough." I smiled. "I'm from here."

"You don't look like it."

I was too tall and too light skinned to be recognized as a Filipino by this girl, but my mother had been Filipino, and this is how I thought of myself. "Some Filipinos look like me," I said. I caught the cab driver checking me out in the rearview mirror. "And what brings you here? Are you traveling alone?"

"I'm meeting my boyfriend in Cebu, but I have two days in Manila," the girl replied. "We were on the same flight, but you were in Traveler Plus."

"Yes, that's right," I said.

"Do you travel a lot?"

"I do." The taxi had made it off the curb and was slowly easing its way into the traffic. The driver wiped at the windshield with a sodden tissue, clearing a porthole through the condensation. "And you, do you travel much?"

"I was in Machu Picchu in January." The girl was proud of this.

"Really?" I said. "I was in Peru last November."

"Isn't Machu Picchu amazing?"

"I wouldn't know." I smiled. "I spent all my time in Iquitos, except for a brief foray up the Amazon."

"Why didn't you go?"

"There wasn't time. I was doing a piece for a travel magazine and my assignment was to cover the Amazon River International Raft Race." November was dry season in Iquitos, and the city, built on stilts but currently without benefit of flooding, had seemed to float above the packed dirt. Vultures dropped heavily into the shadows without warning. The town hall had reminded me of an old Manila building: the broad staircase, the heavy wood, the unchecked decay. The race itself did not intrigue me; it presented a predictable challenge, a victory—as with all races—given to whoever was fastest, assuming that speed was a universally valued thing. "Competitors come from all over the world," I added.

"Who won?"

"Who won? Oh, some Peruvians, of course. Although one year, the Americans had it."

The girl was looking out the window, her mouth agape, the bright lights slowly dragging across her face. Pedestrians rushed along the underpasses of Edsa. A jeepney stopped abruptly, releasing a number of people. The women had taken off their shoes, which were tucked under their arms, and they stepped cautiously into the ankle-deep water like socialites closing the final yards to the beach after a day spent yachting.

"Is it always this bad?" the girl asked.

"The flooding? Often worse, actually. Although if this continues, much of the city will be shut down tomorrow."

The girl nodded as if registering something, but she remained openmouthed.

"Timog will be clear. Where your hotel is located is actually at a higher elevation."

"I hope the weather's better on Cebu," the girl said. "I want to go to the beach."

"Yes. Cebu's known for its beaches. And for its mangos and beef."

"Weird," the girl said. "What else do I need to know?"

Perhaps I should have told her about pakikasama, social empathy, and amor proprio, personal dignity, which were the two tenets that Filipinos lived by, but I was discouraged by her large, wet eyes that seemed hopeful for things to be simplified rather than complicated. "The balut, the fertilized duck eggs? They're not for everyone. Many Filipinos don't eat them, including me. Try the bagnet, which is fried pork belly. And make sure the water you're drinking is filtered."

I lifted my chin to the driver in the rearview mirror. "Nasa corner ng Scout Tobias at Timog ang Cocoon. Okay?"

The driver nodded.

"You must excuse me," I said to the girl. "I have a bit of a headache. I'm going to close my eyes for a few minutes, if you don't mind."

The girl nodded in response and I, duty fulfilled, pretended to nap.

Nearly a year had passed since I had last visited Manila. I had been on assignment from *Vice*, covering newly sworn-in president Procopio "Copo" Gumboc, who had swept the elections in an upset and was now governing the nation in state-run terror. Under his rule, police had carte blanche to execute anyone suspected of dealing or using drugs, mostly shabu, a form of crack cocaine. The policy had been embraced by a corrupt police force, whose officers were gunning down anyone they felt like. I wondered if this girl knew, if she was aware that close to ten thousand people had lost their lives.

Vice had sent me to explain why, despite the killings, the president's popularity rating had held at an astounding eighty percent. I had set up interviews with people that I found interesting—college-age socialists, a radical nun who had been active when the former dictator, Batac, was ousted in the eighties, a community leader whose neighborhood of Mandaluyong had lost many lives. *Vice* ran it as a centerpiece to an issue on populism. Since then, Gumboc had managed to insult an assortment of people that included the president of the United States and an Australian nun, who had, improbably, inspired his sexual fantasies. As I wrote the article, I felt as if I were inventing things, but it was all verifiable and, when it appeared, fact-checked, as if reality were something that earned its name through verification rather than by just being real. Barreling along the night streets, the taxi wrapped in an aqueous blanket, the driver constantly clearing the tiny porthole through the fogged windscreen amid the thump and screech of the faulty wipers, it was hard to feel that I was in anything but a dream.

It must have been close to 1:00 a.m. when we reached the hotel. As we pulled in beneath the concrete overhang, the sudden relief from the water created a degree of silence. The girl asked, "How much do I owe you?"

"This trip is on me," I said. "Consider it local hospitality."

The girl thanked me and got out of the cab. The driver handed her the backpack from the trunk of the taxi and the girl returned to tap on the window. "I didn't get your name. That seems weird."

"Christina," I said. "And you?"

"Martha."

"Martha, it was a pleasure to meet you. I hope you have a wonderful time in the Philippines."

From the hotel, it was just over a mile to my aunt's house on Twelfth Street in New Manila, a ten-minute drive along familiar streets. When my aunt's house was first built, right after the war, it had stood alone on a hill, a symbol that the Filipinos had survived, that wealth still existed. Over the years, the gate stayed the same deep green it had always been, resisting change—although across the street, where once had been a series of smaller houses, a towering apartment building now stood, the whole area having been aggressively developed in the last twenty years.

"Busino ho kayo," I said, indicating that the driver should use his horn. A few short blasts sent a sleepy security guard beneath a deteriorating pink umbrella into the street. He peered suspiciously into the taxi and I presented my face as explanation. The guard unbolted the gates and swung them open, holding the umbrella in the crook of his neck, and we continued in and up the circular drive. By the way the taxi bumped along, I knew that some repaving was in order, and I could see the plants were overgrown. The headlights picked up a thin dog, who lifted a paw questioningly and then ran around the back of the house. I paid the driver, thanking him and tipping him well, although the look he gave the money seemed disappointed. As I stood with my yellow suitcase at the bottom of the tall steps that led to the front door, I wondered if anyone was awake, if it would be difficult to rouse the maid. Just then, the door swung open. Leaning against its frame, silhouetted by the dim light glowing behind her, was my tita Rosa, an old woman made stout by her age. My aunt looked out suspiciously at first, then swooned back dramatically, her hand on her breast.

"Ay, Ting," she said. "Thank God it's you."

I laughed. "Tita, why 'thank God'?" I picked up my suitcase and started up the steep set of steps that led to the front door.

"For a second I thought you were your mother."

I reached the top of the landing and hugged my aunt, who peered closely into my face, as if I might be hiding something, and then released me.

"You don't seem surprised to see me," I said.

"I'm not." Tita Rosa waved for me to follow her into the library, which was through a doorway by the front entrance. "Why shouldn't you be here?"

"Because I live in New York."

"Well, you know how things are." Tita Rosa lowered herself carefully into a rocker. "Sometimes people are in one place, and then they're in another. Is it true you're divorcing your husband?"

"Yes, that is true." I sat on the low couch, which my aunt had chosen over a bed for the last three years.

"He is a charming man," the old woman said. "And you know, I don't like charming men. But he is your husband. I feel I have to say that. Still, if God didn't make annulments, who did?"

"Lucifer?" I ventured.

"We are Lucifer." My aunt laughed. The maid, Beng, placed a tray with a bowl of ice, a bottle of Coke, and some glasses on the small table. "Aren't you thirsty?"

I nodded, and my aunt nodded to Beng, who dropped some cubes in the glass and poured the Coke. Tita Rosa instructed Beng to make up the guest bed and to make sure there was a towel and some filtered water and a glass in the room.

My aunt's long white hair was down around her shoulders, a rare sight, as in the day she always had it pinned into a bun. She was wearing a floral shift and beaded, black velvet slippers.

"Why are you still awake?" I asked.

"Me? I don't really sleep. An hour here, an hour there." My aunt reached over and began rubbing my arm. "It is so good to see you. I was worried about you. I love you so much. You know that. I pray for you every day, after my great-grandchildren and before your cousin Gina."

"You pray for me before Gina?" I gave a wary laugh. "I really must be in trouble."

"Yes," my aunt said calmly. "Yes, you are."

My aunt's house was sliding into indolent decay, but its elegant symmetry and high ceilings and staircase made of wood felled from giant trees cast a spell that was deeply tied to its history.

Its rooms had no air-conditioning and no screens, a testimony to its age, and the plumbing, which had been a wonder in the late forties, was challenged by the years, though there was still water running in the pipes. A full bucket was in the shower stall, and a tabo with which to bathe. If I had waited until morning, I could have asked Beng to heat water, which usually she did in a large kettle that she added to the bucket, but the idea of dousing myself with cold water was actually appealing.

Tita Rosa was the eldest survivor of my mother's siblings. Her role in the family was that of matriarch, a self-created title that she'd claimed as young woman and held for over sixty years. She was now ninety. Shortly after the end of the Second World War, my aunt had married a man who had been a friend of her father's, one of the old Konyos, or Spaniards, whose money had survived. At the time of their wedding, Tita Rosa was seventeen and Tito Iñigo thirty years her senior. Tito Iñigo had died in the eighties, but I remembered him well. He had a narrow face and a long, hooked Spanish nose. His expression had always been composed in a sort of regal withdrawal, but he had loved low Filipino culture: bad TV, junky food. Tito Iñigo had often traveled to the province for cockfighting, boxing matches, local fiestas with native dancing—things that people in Manila disdained. He had been loved by the peasants who worked his lands, where rice and peanuts were grown, and at his funeral, bus after bus had pulled up outside the church, disgorging what seemed to be the entire village of San Isidro. That day it had felt to me that we were burying not only my uncle but also an era of Philippine life that had been lost with land reform and the rise of the city.

Of Tita Rosa's four children, two now lived in the States. Charlie was a doctor, and all his children were also doctors. Carmi had built a house behind my aunt's and ran a series of businesses but seemed to spend six months out of the year in Spain. Baby was in New Jersey and had made some money flipping houses. But Tita Rosa's oldest son, Jim, had built an empire with tentacles in every sector of the Makati business district. He owned houses in the wealthiest neighborhoods of Forbes Park and Dasmariñas, in which his children and their wives and children lived. There was also a vacation compound in Batangas that in addition to the impressive holiday home had a twelve-room guesthouse, a horizon pool, a freestanding chapel, a helipad, and, most interestingly, its own museum built to honor his and his father's dynasty. Much of the artwork that had once filled my aunt's house had been moved to the family museum, including the life-size oil portraits of Tita Rosa and Tito Iñigo. The chandeliers that Tita Rosa had carried back from her honeymoon in Spain were also gone, now in one of my cousin's houses. Even the great mirror from the foyer had been switched with a newer version, and your reflection—so much clearer than before—now greeted you with a superfluous abundance of information.

I faced my bath and the bucket of cold water. I could feel the heat rising off my body as I completed my ablutions and fell on the hard bed with its stiff, clean sheets. The bottle of water was sweating on the nightstand. I switched on the fan and off the light, wondering if I was too tired to actually fall asleep, if I should take a lorazepam, if one of my dead relatives whose spirits I could feel animating the humid air of the house would actually manifest, how long I would stay—all these things—when I fell into a deep sleep.

II

My aunt's voice, shouting in the hallway, had entered my dream and woken me up. The matter of the dream itself had evaporated instantly, leaving me with an uninflected anxiety prickling through a fog of jet lag. I managed to roll over and pour myself a glass of water. As I'd slept, someone had placed a floral shift, like the one worn by my aunt, on the chair beside my bed, also a pair of slippers. I drank the water and poured myself another glass, then pulled myself out of bed. The shift was stiff but slipped easily over my head. It was tight around the sleeves, boxy, and hit two inches above my knee. I wondered who it belonged to.

In the hallway, Tita Rosa was scolding two maids and a grinning houseboy.

"He's not my husband," she said. She threw up her hands.

"Who's not your husband?" I asked sleepily, standing at the door of my room.

Tita Rosa gestured at the floor where, sitting with a quizzical look on its face, there was a small white dog, a puppy, with sharp ears and a pink nose. "It is now weaned, and they want me to bring it in the house."

"Why?"

"They say it's your tito Iñigo, reincarnated."

"Why would they think that?" I looked at the dog, who also seemed curious to know.

"Because he's white, some sort of albino."

Tita Rosa shook her head and gestured for me to follow her to the dining room. At the near end of a table that could seat twenty people, there was a plate of fried eggs, one of longanisa sausages, a bowl of pan de sal rolls, and two cut mangos. "There's your breakfast. Eat."

I chose a seat, ready to eat, but unsure of where to start. "Is there coffee?"

"Beng!" my aunt called. "Kapé!"

I took a roll and one of the mangos and put it on my plate. An ancient fan that looked like a propeller was set high in the crook of ceiling and room divider, grinding a circuit, creating a powerful punch of air as its orbit picked out spots around the table.

"Listen," said Tita Rosa as she settled into a chair. "One of Remi's granddaughters just got engaged and her fiancé is here for a visit."

"Remi? In California?" This was my mother's first cousin, who I'd met a few times in the Philippines but who had been a fixture of my mother's childhood.

"Yes. Anyway, I'm hoping you can introduce him to some writing types. You know these people, don't you?"

"He's a writer? What's his name?"

"Laird Bontotot."

"Laird Bontotot? I've never heard of him." There were many writers now. Anyone who managed to post an online article was now a writer, but had I seen that name, I would have remembered it. "What kind of name is *Laird Bontotot?*"

"Laird, isn't that an American name?"

"I meant, what kind of name is Bontotot? Are they Manila people? Because it doesn't sound like it." I gestured for Beng to top up my coffee. "I don't know any Bontotots. Do you?"

"No. Maybe it's a Mindanao name," said Tita Rosa. Mindanao, the largest southernmost island, was the scapegoat for anything unfamiliar.

"He's not staying here, is he?"

"No," said Tita Rosa. "He'll be with your tita Remi, in Malate."

"How long is he intending to be here?"

"It can't be too long," she said. "He's getting married in August."

"Tita Rosa, I know you like to help people, but this Laird isn't even a relative." My aunt had a tendency to involve herself in things and, having done so, to involve anyone else who happened to be in the vicinity. "He's marrying Tita Remi's granddaughter. Do you even know her name? When was the last time you saw Remi?" Remi was most often in California, but she and my aunt would see each other on Remi's sporadic visits home.

"I told Remi you would help him out."

"You did? How does she even know I'm here?"

"Remi called and I told her." My aunt furrowed her brow. "Why are you so hotheaded? Am I supposed to be hiding you? Because you didn't say to keep it a secret."

This was true.

"So Remi's visiting and she called me, and I said, 'Ting is here too.' And she said, 'Which one is Ting?' And I said, 'The one who married the banker and lives in New York and teaches at

Columbia.' And that you were the writer in the family. And Laird knew who you were and wanted to meet you."

"He's probably just bored and trying to escape his in-laws."

"Maybe he is."

And Remi likely wanted to get him out of the house, wearied of entertaining and feeding him.

"He's apparently very interested in political things. He read your article in *Voice*."

"That's *Vice*." I knew who Laird was, a recently awakened Fil-Am, the type I encountered at various literary functions. They liked microphones and Spam. America's streets and classrooms had instilled in many a sense of inferiority and in some a seething resentment at being brown in a white world. The Fil-Ams suffered from the shame of otherness, while Filipinos born and educated in the Philippines struggled with disdain for gauche American culture. In the States, we were all seen as being of the same tribe, but it was, at times, a flawed taxonomy.

The dog had smelled the food and was nosing my leg. I cut the end off of one of the longanisas and fed it to him.

"I can't have a dog in the house," said Tita Rosa. "He'll urinate everywhere."

"He's cute."

"That's how I know it's not your tito Iñigo."

There was a clamor at the front door and it swung open as if of its own accord. Tita Dom stepped into the foyer, followed by the driver, Mannie, who was carrying two heavy shopping bags.

"Dom!" said Tita Rosa. "Look who's here."

"My God," she said. "Ting! Why didn't you say that you were coming?"

"I wasn't really sure until I was on the plane." I got up and went to hug her.

Tita Dom gave me an appraising look, somehow both critical and impressed. "You're so thin."

"Am I supposed to be fat?"

"Is it one or the other?"

I sat back down at the table and my tita Dom took the seat beside me. Beng hustled out of the kitchen with another plate.

"How are my cousins?" I asked.

"They're okay." Tita Dom would not go into detail with her sister sitting there. "For how long are you here? Rikki will want to see you." Rikki and I were close in age. He was at heart a philosopher, although he worked at a bank. "I am so glad you're here, but why now? These are dangerous times."

"It's always dangerous here," I said. "What's new?"

"Don't you write this stuff yourself?" Tita Dom took a sausage and a fried egg. "Didn't you hear about the Korean businessman?"

"I did. The story was breaking when I started traveling." The Korean businessman had been kidnapped from his house and murdered.

"They accused him of dealing drugs," said Tita Dom.

"Who accused him?" I asked.

"Some scallywags, you know. The police. Anyway, they picked him up in his house in Laguna and dragged him off to Crame. His wife paid the ransom, but he was already dead. They cut him up and flushed him down the toilet."

"Did they find the people responsible?" I asked.

"Yes. The guys who cut him up were paid off with a set of fancy Korean golf clubs, and they got nabbed." My aunt waggled her eyebrows with a dark humor. "What did those hoodlums want with golf clubs? Are these people going to all of a sudden start playing golf?"

"Maybe they thought they could sell them."

"This is gruesome talk for the breakfast table," Tita Rosa interjected. "We don't want to put Ting off her food."

Sitting with my aunts made me feel my mother's absence. When my mother was still alive, she and her sisters had formed a trinity: Rosa the Wise, Benedicta the Beautiful, and Dominica the Adventurer. My mother was Benedicta, a woman who loved abstractions and therefore study, but her scholarly pursuits had been overshadowed by her fine features and stately bearing. She had met my father, an American, in graduate school in Boston (he was studying law). Then she settled into raising their children—there were four of us, an even split of boys and girls—in the town of Concord. In the grip of a fury against "the West," my mother had moved me and my younger sister to Manila when I was thirteen and my sister eleven. The West was a conglomerate of corrupt and soulless cultures populated by selfish, materialistic people. The West was any nation that didn't abide by amor proprio and pakikasama. The West was the States when my mother was missing home. My brothers remained in the West, because males needed profitable careers, or so she said, but she also felt that males were a lost cause. My father had acquiesced because it was pointless to oppose my mother and also because he knew that by letting her leave, he had avoided her splitting the family in ways both permanent and legal. My sister and I had not wanted to go, but then we had not been consulted.

I spent all of high school and two years of college in Manila, while my younger sister, who, miraculously, had never learned a word of Tagalog and managed to hang out with the few foreigners available the whole time in school, had decided that she was going to college in the States. For reasons known only to her, my mother had taken this as her signal to return, and she did, to my father and younger brother (the older one was already in law school), and my parents picked up as if the last six years had never happened.

I could have stayed in Manila, but I returned with my mother, although at that point the Philippines was more familiar. Visits to Concord, where I would see my childhood friends—who were obsessed with *The Official Preppy Handbook* and asked me why I hung out with my cousins—had made me see, a bit, what my mother's "West" was all about. But I thought myself less articulate in the Philippines, not only in the language, but somehow in my being. I had transferred to Boston College, but the return was not without difficulty. During my years in the Philippines, I felt American, but back in the United States, I felt alien. Later, my husband would introduce me as an American, my whiteness assumed. And I had gone along with it, managing a good impression, until "good" became "effortless" and then morphed into a variety of being.

The morning had wasted itself and now the day was settling into luxuriant heat. My aunts had finished their breakfast and were sitting with their coffee. The conversation drifted to the sale of a piece of property in the province, which was fetching a surprisingly high price. In the year since I'd been here, cousin Jim's youngest daughter had finally gotten engaged, businesses had been started and abandoned. There had been births, pregnancies, affairs, et cetera, that my aunts related with a varying degree of detail. Neither of them pressed me on my separation: they seemed happy to have me back and free of that American man. They had probably given my mother the same treatment when she'd taken the six-year vacation from her American man. That was their attitude, despite the fact that my mother and her siblings were a solid quarter American. My great-grandfather, Benjamin Klein, had been a Texan, a leftover from the Spanish-American War, who had settled in Manila and grown rich working with the railroads. His son, my grandfather, I never met, because he died during the Second World War.

Tita Dom rose from the table. "Ting, call me tomorrow," she said. "We can have lunch."

I agreed to the plan, and my younger aunt left to make her weekly pilgrimage to the bank.

"It's good that you're here," said Tita Rosa. "It is just good."

"Why?" I asked. The statement was intriguingly vague.

"Because your mother cannot care for you, and I feel that she has brought you to me." This was, of course, nice, but my mother, although an amazing woman—exciting—had most often let me fend for myself. There was the urge to state this truth, but I felt the smallness of it and let it be. Beng was rushing around, clearing the last of the cups. She whispered something in Tita Rosa's ear and gave me an expectant look.

Tita Rosa said, "Beng would like to know if you would like her to unpack your things."

"Unpack my things? She doesn't need to do that."

"But she wants to. She saw someone doing it on *Downton Abbey*."

"Beng watches *Downton Abbey*?"

"She watches it with me."

"Talaga?" I looked at Beng, who was probably sixteen years old. She was thin with doleful eyes. Her mouth had trouble closing over her large teeth, but she was still pretty. "Sige. That would be very nice." I hadn't brought much with me and it would not take her long. My aunt was looking sleepy, ready for her nap, one of the many she took throughout the day, like a cat.

"Tita Rosa," I said, to catch her before she nodded off. "Do you have Wi-Fi?" She didn't but happily informed me that from the third floor, I could pick up the Wi-Fi signal from Cousin Baby's apartment, currently rented to a Dutch embassy worker, which was in the new high-rise across the road. The signal carried, and although it was no good for streaming movies, it was functional for email.

When I returned to my room, Beng was neatly folding my underwear into little squares and color coding it in a drawer of the great cabinet, which was otherwise filled with clothes of long-grown children and babies. Beng closed the drawer with a careful reverence. My pink fake-fur coat, which had taken up half the room in my suitcase, was sprawled across the bed like an improbably hued dead animal. The coat had no purpose in the Philippines, but I had forgotten it hanging on the coat stand in the hallway when packing to leave New York. My other things had already been boxed and sent to storage. I could have left it, but the coat—ridiculously expensive and too young for me—had been an extravagant birthday gift bought by my husband as he tried to convince me to stay, even as the finer details of the last six months had been exposed. If I had left it there for him to find, it would have made a statement that did not express how I felt. Beng picked the coat up and stroked it like a cat. "Ang ganda namaan nito." She thought it was pretty.

I said, "Try it on."

Beng slid into the fur, which reached her ankles. Her hands were hidden by the sleeves. Smiling, she went to the mirror.

"Very nice," I said. "When you get too hot, just hang it in the closet."

III

I spent the next few days recovering from jet lag, comforted by its lack of focus. I didn't know how long I would be in Manila. I might stay until my money ran out, but as I wasn't paying for rent and I was living in an economy where it was not unusual to make 150 dollars a month, the money would stretch.

I had proposed a follow-up article to *Vice*, one that focused on Gumboc's repeated threats to reinstate martial law, but he had gone quiet on the issue. Even a Muslim uprising in the southern city of Marawi, which had resulted in a locally imposed army rule and suspension of civil rights, had failed to expand beyond the region. What money I possessed was the result of a book proposal that Ann, my longtime editor, had felt moved to fund because my marriage had fallen apart, even though she was concerned that the book might not sell. I had won a National Book Award ten years ago and Ann's constant hope was that my next book might perform equally. The advance was small but adequate. I had been able to let go of my teaching appointment at Columbia, one class, where the students asked questions like: "Are there still jobs for journalists?"

To which I'd thought: *This job, teaching journalism to people who will never find work.*

For my book, I was researching the plight of Timicheg, a chief of the Bontoc tribe of Northern Luzon. Timicheg had lived his short life in the early part of the twentieth century, first among the fierce peaks and diving ravines of the Ifugao region. He and his tribespeople had been discovered by an American businessman, Richard Schneidewind, and brought to America to entertain the throngs of visitors that flocked to Coney Island, visitors in search of something new. The Bontoc were novel, naked but for loincloths and wraps and intricate tattoos. They formed their village in an enclosure in the shadow of the Wonder Wheel, on display for whoever might stop by. At precise times throughout the day, they would perform a ritual slaughter on an unfortunate dog procured from the local pound, butcher it, cook it in a pot over an open fire, and eat it. The Bontoc took their sleep on mats in the chilly air. The next day, they would awake and begin it all again. They could no longer stalk deer through the forests and mists of the Cordilleras, but, as they were promised money and safe passage home after a time, they consented to the yapping dog, the banal ogling of the tourists, and this strange diet. At home, dog was rarely on the menu. The Bontoc were headhunters, although this practice—the most intriguing—was only ever described. Schneidewind provided each bloody detail with a booming voice that competed with the organ-grinders and carousel music and reveling crowds. Timicheg's tribe was not the only one on display in the United States. Other headhunting groups were touring in the Midwest and California. This was to illustrate the colorful ways of the backward Filipinos and justify America's occupation of the islands. Why exterminate all the brutes when you could display them and make a profit?

The Philippines was not the perfect place for me to research the story. Timicheg and his people had merely been of ethnographic interest until they'd left, and it would have made more sense to be in Ghent, where they were abandoned by Schneidewind and where the Bontoc chief had died from pneumonia. If I'd stayed in the States, I would have had access to extensive archives. But I wasn't yet sure what shape the book would take. I wasn't sure of anything, other than the fact that I'd wanted to get out of New York.

I again slept late, and when I reached the dining room, all the breakfast offerings had already been cleared. Beng was nowhere in sight. I made myself a cup of instant coffee from the packets and thermos on the side table and cast a cursory glance at the book proposal. The sections seemed to flow naturally. There would be a chapter on the Bontoc Igorot, region, hunting practices—Rousseauian tripe necessary to get the piece going. And then a chapter on Schneidewind and where he'd come from. The next chapter would segue into the Coney Island midway, followed by a chapter on the world's fair in Ghent. I had written the proposal as an exercise and was now faced with writing the book. It was a sort of joke. The opening sentence seemed an impossibility. I checked my phone to see if there was Wi-Fi, which there was not, and stood from the dining table to take the broad steps that led upstairs.

The second floor had largely been abandoned not only because of my aunt's compromised mobility but also because the space was not needed. Half of the floor plan was taken up with an immense master bedroom, now filled with boxes. I suspected that they belonged to my cousin Jim, because he often stored things in his mother's house. I could hear the cook snapping at Beng in the kitchen, but the sound reached me through a filter of silence. My uncle had died in this room, but I felt that his spirit had never left and was hovering in the high corners of the ceiling or maybe behind the oval mirror, framed in heavy wood, that had startled me before I realized the other presence in the room was actually my reflection.

There was a verandah off to the side, and I crossed to the door passing the canopied bed, covered with stacks of paper, to go outside. What had once been an impressive view was now largely obscured by high-rises, but I could still look into the garden, where a houseboy was trimming the lawn with a set of shears. The traffic passing on nearby E. Rodriguez created a cacophony of blaring horns and occasional spurts of music. It had rained all morning and now that it had stopped, the heat was generating a cloud of steam that the city was steeping in.

I lit a cigarette and checked that the Wi-Fi on my phone was on. The news was full of shootings and the investigation of the slaughtered Korean, but Gumboc took no responsibility. Instead, he had assembled an assortment of police officers for an orchestrated dressing down. He had placed the blame for all the killings on their corruption, instructing them that should they not improve their behavior, he would have them cleaning the Pasig River—the polluted waterway that bisected the city—or send them to fight the Muslim insurgents in the south, who had gained notoriety for beheading more than one unlucky tourist. I thought, *These are dangerous times.* And then: *It is always dangerous here.* In the street, a passing vendor was calling, "mais, mais," as he circuited the neighborhood. The wall surrounding my aunt's house was topped with broken glass to discourage thieves, and, looking past this glittering menace, I was following the vendor as he pushed his cart of steamed corn when my phone pinged with a message.

You're back.

It was Inchoy, sending a text through WhatsApp. I had requested a library pass from the University of Santo Tomas, where Inchoy taught philosophy, and it was only a matter of time before he learned that I was in Manila.

You're still here, I replied.

Pick you up 7. Dinner in Tondo. Bibo wants to see you.

Inchoy had hired a GrabCar, a treat for me as he most often took jeepneys. We were lucky that the rain had taken a hiatus because the streets were clear, although still glutted with the traffic that would not let up until deep into the night. Inchoy taught five classes at the university and was always short on time. He had brought a shopping bag of papers to grade on the ride to Bibo's house, but just his presence, even if he was preoccupied, settled me. I hadn't seen him in a year, but our friendship always picked up where it left off, with little ceremony, a friendship cemented in a shared sense of what was interesting—of what deserved attention—although we often disagreed on why. In the street, a pair of children was weaving through the cars with garlands of sampaguita. Two of these garlands, no doubt purchased from a similar pair of children, hung on the rearview mirror of the car, scenting the air. Inchoy watched me watching the children, and I felt my perspective slowly shift from mine to his: from my joy at the beauty of the children to Inchoy's perception of forced child labor. He flicked his eyebrows at me to drive home the point. And maybe I was reading too much into his gesture, but after many years of similar exchanges—we had been friends since college—the words did not seem necessary.

Inchoy was a staunch socialist and quietly active in gay circles but still lived with his mother, who knew about neither aspect of his identity. His house was around the corner from Tita Dom's, although Bibo—the great love of his life after Lacan—lived in Tondo. I did not know all the particulars of their financial situation, but Inchoy must have been paying for Bibo's tiny apartment and had likely set Bibo up in the sari sari store that sold cigarettes, snacks, and Coke.

Inchoy delivered a frank look in my direction and sighed heavily. "So you're leaving your husband," he said. "I never understood this marriage of yours. No kids? Why bother?"

I considered. I knew he would give me time to respond because he wanted the truth, but I wasn't sure how to present that. In reality, I was having difficulty believing that I had actually been a wife. It was my Manila mindset. It was as if, as the time theorists proposed, the ordering of things only happened in one's consciousness and without this ordering, the matter of life floated around as event signatures simultaneously. From where I sat, in this GrabCar with the street flashing by, it seemed possible that I never had married my husband. He could just have been one destiny, one option that, if I chose to ignore it, would simply go away. Maybe my husband was in the future or in some other present and not in the past. Maybe I could decide to not have been married.

"Well?" Inchoy asked.

"You wouldn't understand."

"When you say that," Inchoy said, "it usually means that you don't understand."

He began to grab sheaves of paper from the shopping bag, dumping them on the seat between us. "You can correct the quizzes," he said, handing me a stack. "This one has no mistakes." He passed me a quiz that was already graded.

There were ten questions on the quiz and I read through the responses. 1. Hobbes, 2. Free Will, 3. Head of State, 4. First Cause, 5. The Social Contract, 6. The Phenomenon of Man, 7. Spinoza, 8. Hegelian Dialectic, 9. Critique of Pure Reason, 10. The City of God. Uncertain of the questions but sure of the answers, I took the red pen and started marking.

By the time we reached Bibo's apartment, it was almost nine. We had stopped on the way to buy some crispy pata, and Bibo was making sinigang and would have rice. Bibo's apartment was right above the sari sari store, which was, at this hour, manned by Chok-Chok, one of Bibo's friends. We stood in the dark, deeply hot stairwell and Inchoy knocked. The sound of three locks being opened quickly followed.

Bibo wasn't conventionally beautiful, but she had strong cheekbones and a small, well-formed mouth. Her long, straight hair was down around her shoulders despite the heat. She smiled, and the smile settled in her eyes.

"Welcome," she said. "Welcome, welcome."

The local term for people like Bibo was *binabae*, or "womanly." There was also the broader term *bakla*, which just meant gay. Regardless, gender here was simplified by *siya*, Tagalog's gender-neutral third-person pronoun.

I had been in the States when Bibo and Inchoy got together, and Inchoy had never shared how, exactly, they had become romantically involved. What I did know was that there had been a hole in Inchoy, an anger that Bibo had settled. Or maybe Inchoy had just mellowed with age. Or maybe it was a combination of the two. Inchoy had rescued Bibo when she was just a teenager and still dressing as a boy. Bibo had been a small-time drug dealer and a distant relative of one of the maids at Inchoy's house. There was secrecy around the relationship. Not even Inchoy's mother knew of Bibo, although the two had been together for a decade. Only three of Inchoy's friends were aware of the relationship, which I felt was excessive, but Inchoy was a private person, private for the sake of being private.

The apartment was just one room with a kitchenette and a small sink. The walls were crowded with wood carvings from the mountain provinces, Bontoc masks and shields, and Kalinga woven drapes. Inchoy was enamored with Ifugao culture, although his family was from Cebu in the Visayas. A small table was set by the window, which gave a view to the street. The other window was filled with an air conditioner that was working hard. The room felt deliciously cold, although it couldn't have been cooler than eighty degrees. Inchoy set the crispy pata on the counter and Bibo waved me over to the table. Bibo said little and performed all her tasks with an exquisite sense of purpose. Even the ladling of sinigang into bowls seemed a performance in Bibo's hands. Bibo was from Negros and her first language was Cebuano. She spoke some English and her Tagalog was fluent, but she and Inchoy seldom used these languages with each other. They spoke in Cebuano, even with me there. Cebuano was not a secret language, but they used it with each other as some kind of affectionate code, translating what they thought I should know. The food now served, I began to eat, but Bibo and Inchoy were gossiping. Bibo said something, then hid a knowing smile behind her manicured hand.

"She wants to know if you really left your husband," said Inchoy.

"Yes, I did, Bibo, but don't get any ideas. Inchoy would be destroyed if you ever left him."

Bibo gave Inchoy a frank look and waved a cautioning finger at him. We talked about the weather and the business at the sari sari store, which was doing well, as the other store around the corner had closed. The owner had been killed by the police and the family had moved back to the province. This was not a safe area, but Bibo's family were close by and if Bibo could not live with Inchoy, this is where she wanted to be. Inchoy broke into a pleading tone. I couldn't follow all of what was said, but the word "baril" was repeated several times. Inchoy must have been urging Bibo to keep a gun, but Bibo waved him off.

After we had finished eating and the plates were cleared and washed, Inchoy and I moved to the small couch. Bibo sat on the mattress on the floor, her legs swung gracefully to the side, and began to pack a pipe with marijuana. This was one of Inchoy's few vices, and he indulged only when he was with Bibo. There was a seventies turntable on the lone bookshelf, and Bibo, still sitting, reached for an old record and put it on. It was a recording of Kalinga tribal music. I gestured for Bibo to hand me the battered sleeve with its image of naked tribesmen in sleek bowl cuts holding spears. A three-column explanation of its cultural significance remained alien because I couldn't read it without my glasses and was too lazy to reach for them.

Inchoy was moved by this northern music, the gongs and drums and fright of it. It was the music playing near the end of *Apocalypse Now* and had seemed well suited for that. But it also seemed to fit this: the cool air, the slowing time, the heavy perfumed smoke entering my lungs. Bibo held the pipe and took a small, birdlike drag. She then got up and began to dance in the Kalinga way, flicking her wrists outward and stiffening her shoulders, moving in a small circle around the apartment. I watched her through the long minutes, my mind wandering. I thought of Timicheg, whose tribe was neighbor to the Kalinga, hearing the drums coming over the rib of mountains as he and his warriors left to hunt heads.

Suddenly there were two loud bangs. They sounded like bawang firecrackers, but maybe gunshots. The lights were dim inside and the sounds were muted by the air conditioner. Outside a siren went off and then another. Flashing lights danced around the walls of the apartment. There was shouting on the street, but Bibo kept dancing, her palms now flat and open, arms wide to the sky, the gongs answering each other, each ring echoed by a softer response, the cacophony rising in a sharp crescendo of tempo and volume. Inchoy lazily raised his eyes to me and I knew he was wondering, as was I, if someone had just been murdered.

An hour later, when we made our way back down the stairs and into the car that would take us back to Quezon City, the police had already left, and if someone was indeed dead, it was as if they had never lived.

IV

Several days later, I found myself at the library at the University of Santo Tomas. The air-conditioning felt brutal and unnatural and made the sound travel with a crispness that the usual humidity softened. Here, I felt pleasantly ignored. I could have been trawling through the stacks but instead was making use of the internet. Online, there was an account of the Bontoc Igorot written in 1903 by an American, Albert Ernest Jenks. Jenks had lived among the Bontoc for five months, in which time he had developed an admiration for them. He found them an intelligent people, hardworking, and physically attractive. I wondered if Jenks had known Timicheg and decided that they must have crossed paths. Even if it wasn't written in history, this white man, Jenks, had probably paved the way for the other white man, Schneidewind—less sympathetic to Bontoc well-being, although just as in thrall to their culture—who had been the chief's undoing.

The Bontoc had lived unaware of Western society until the 1850s, when the Spaniards finally penetrated the mountain provinces. They were taxed heavily by the Spaniards, paying in palay, or unthreshed rice. Despite this subjugation, the Bontoc managed to hold on to their original beliefs, a system of animism in which everything—rice, rivers, axes—possessed a spirit. They believed their departed ancestors lived a ghost life in the neighboring mountains, that a supreme Lumawig governed nature and protected crops, that thunder was the result of a bellowing wild boar. The Spaniards did not convert the Bontoc to Catholicism, although a few did take native wives.

Just as Magellan had used the Cebuanos to wage war on the Mactanese, the Spaniards used the Bontoc to subdue neighboring tribes. In his account, Jenks did not include whatever spoils the Spaniards received in these battles, but he did list the tribute permitted for the Bontoc to take, and the unit used was heads. Sometimes the warriors returned with just a few, but in one battle of the 1890s against the rebellious Sagada, led by a ruthless Comandante Saldero, the tribute was listed as one hundred heads. When the Filipino nationalist revolutionaries, the insurrectos, showed up in the months after the Sagada massacre, the Bontoc were eager to switch sides. Some Spanish heads were scored. Comandante Saldero escaped to the north, where he boarded a ship in Vigan and sailed for Spain, away from the islands that held such a singular danger.

When Schneidewind showed up in 1911, Timicheg had not been a prelapsarian savage. He had already served as mercenary for the Spaniards and encountered several Americans. Although he could not have pictured the particulars of Coney Island, he was a man who had struck a bargain with a recognized foe. He must have been suspicious, concerned, but in the end felt that he was doing what was best for himself and his tribe. Timicheg would learn the ways of men who had the power to demand taxes, who had weapons that made one's ax—no matter where the blade landed—seem futile.

The reading for this book was fascinating, yet I still felt no desire to write. I had received an email from Ann asking how it was progressing, even though I had been in the Philippines only a few weeks and the trip was largely conceived around research. My editor had caught wind of another book in progress by a more established writer, Kent J. Baxter. The subject of Baxter's book was world's fairs and would likely address the topic of human zoos. Ann was concerned that my book might not get much coverage if published in the shadow of this other. She had recommended that I get the book done as soon as could be managed, which seemed wise but also impossible.

I had only gone to the Santo Tomas library because my aunt had generously offered car and driver and I could not refuse without admitting to a lack of inspiration, although my aunt would likely not have cared. I knew that although my family admired my being a writer, none of them had read anything I'd written. I found it funny that this didn't bother me, but it really didn't. Still, once at the library, I felt it would be dishonest not to attempt a little research. Most often it was easy to procrastinate. For the last month, I had avoided writing with trips to visit relatives, trips to church, trips to the neighbors, and the three daily time-consuming meals. I joined Inchoy for his meetings with the Philosophy Club. I bathed the dog when he had fleas. I went to Tita Dom's house to watch *Probinsyano* and insisted on accompanying her to the market, although Tita Dom didn't like it because she was concerned that the price went up when they saw my light skin. I eagerly joined the seasonal trip to Nueva Ecija to collect the tribute from the kasamas, which would have given me a day alone in the house. I had spent the three hours in the car getting there, driven past the ancestral home, walked along a rice paddy, waited as the farmers assembled, watched their sun-lined faces crease with concern as they paid my aunt, and then gotten back into the car. I had tried to convince myself that this had something to do with my book, but it didn't. Each word I put down seemed false and each sentence a plea for both approval and money, which meant that my style was too glib, too desperate.

The rain eased up and I took the opportunity to leave the library before it started again. I wasn't sure where Mannie had parked the car, but I would present myself wherever the driver had most recently dropped me off, and he would reappear, as if by magic. Mannie was younger than me and for years had looked young, but, as if overnight, he had aged dramatically. I scanned the cars, reminding myself that I was looking for a white van driven by a white-haired driver.

An unrelenting stream of jeepneys with their singing horns zoomed and halted unpredictably in the street. When traffic brought the entire parade to a standstill, pedestrians wove their way in and around, filling any vacant space. Across the street, a restaurant offered kare kare, sisig, and ojos de vaca, traditional food, the last of these items being the boiled eyes of cows. The sleek, glass cube of an air-conditioned bubble tea shop occupied the space next door. Students swarmed the sidewalks and filled the restaurants, all in their neat uniforms and tidy black shoes. A few trees struggled upward between the buildings, waving their feathery leaves, as if trying to fan themselves against the heavy air. At the corner, a team of construction workers, their chests bare and T-shirts wrapped around their heads, was desperately trying to clear a drain in anticipation of yet another deluge. The rain was just beginning to get going when my aunt's white minivan pulled up.

"Mannie, are we picking up Tito Ben?" It was Wednesday, the day of my uncle's weekly visit.

"Oo po," he said. But first we had to stop by my cousin's son's house to drop off some tools and then collect Tita Dom. If I wanted to join my aunts and uncle, they would be attending five o'clock Mass at Christ the King, as they did every Wednesday, despite not being obligated to do so.

Mannie began to navigate through the streets as I sat lost in my own thoughts in the back seat. The air-conditioning in the van was working hard, but it was still warm, and the interior of the van smelled of a bubblegum-scented perfume, a result of the bouncing-cat air freshener fastened to the dash. Weeks had passed, and I had not heard from my husband, which seemed a variety of mercy. I thought, indulgently, that my mother had never liked him, but that was not true. She had liked him but not for me. Was that it? Or was it rather that she hadn't wanted me to get married? No, that also was not true. What she'd wanted was for women to not to have to be wives, and if we could pull that off *and* be married, all would be fine.

Despite her conviction that men were sadly inferior, my mother's relentless and often-remarked-on low-grade anger was deeply tied to her being a woman. She felt trapped in her womanhood, although she was accepting of all the degradations: that anything anyone didn't want to do would fall to her, from washing dishes to listening to problems. When I pointed this out, she would get even angrier. Did I not think she was proud of this role? Despite her prickliness, she was very good at being a woman, a cook, a wife, a comforter of babies, a brilliant student—although one who'd abandoned her studies. Any sympathy from me over what she'd given up she took as condescension. What I felt acutely as I watched my unspooling divorce with the same detachment I reserved for a Netflix documentary, was that she would have been a friend through this. My mother, whose advice had always struck me as bizarre and unusable (friends are usually stupid, don't have friends) would have understood. She would have sat me down and explained it all with a clarity made just for me, in a language all our own. But she wasn't in Manila. Here I felt the vacuum of her absence more keenly, but sometimes, when for example I was looking at my tita Rosa napping in her rocker, the rosary beads held loosely in her lap, I would think that had my mother been here, this is what she would have been seeing. She would have gazed at her aging sister and begun to grieve, worried at the long years she would spend alone after her ate had died. In these moments, I felt that we held the same space, as if I were not feeling *my* anticipation of grief at Tita Rosa's death, but my mother's. Or maybe this was just more magical thinking, my little way of keeping her alive.

V

I awoke with the heat of the day flung over me like a blanket. The previous night I'd had difficulty sleeping and resorted to my dwindling supply of lorazepam at three. It was now eleven thirty. I rose from the bed and went to the bathroom to splash some water on my face. There was no water in the pipes, which responded to my turning of the tap with an angry rattle, but at least the bucket in shower stall was full.

Tito Iñigo greeted me at the door of my room, wagging his tail. A puddle on the parquet near the phone table attested to some earlier activity. I wandered across the sala, to where Beng was sitting at the dining table. She said that Tita Rosa had just gone into the library to pray the rosary and asked if I wanted breakfast.

"Kapé lang," I said and helped myself to the thermos and the coffee packet.

Beng was picking unhusked grains and bits of rock out of the rice, a task she accomplished by putting it on a cookie sheet and raking through the grains with her nails. The grains made a pleasing sound as she sifted through them. I sat down beside her and began to help. The activity was almost a meditation, yogic, which struck me as funny.

"Beng," I asked, "what do you want to do with your life?"

"I want to go overseas and make money, but your tita says I'll end up in a refrigerator in Dubai."

It was a distinct possibility.

The telephone by the front door began to ring and Beng rose from the table and ran over to answer it. Beng seemed to like answering the phone. When she said hello, she lowered her voice to make herself sound older or maybe more formal, something else she might have picked up from watching *Downton Abbey*.

"Ate Ting," said Beng, gently waving to me.

I got up from the table. No one called me on the landline except for Tita Dom, and that's who I thought it was until Beng, handing me the phone, mouthed the word "lalaki": it was a man.

"Hello?" I said.

"Ting, let's go for lunch."

It was Chet Rey, my old boyfriend. I'd been wondering when he'd call. "Lunch?"

"Yeah, like now. I'm here."

"In Quezon City?"

"No. I'm here." There was a sudden, loud knocking, Beng opened the door, and Chet walked in. I put the phone down. Chet was wearing an immaculate white shirt, open at the collar, and a pair of perfectly tailored black pants. I was wearing the floral housedress. "Okay," he said. "Where should we go?"

"I'm not ready," I said.

He put his cell phone in his pocket, looking me up and down. "Not ready for what?"

"All right, fine," I said. "I'll go like this."

"Fine," he said.

Tita Rosa exited out the library. She too was wearing a floral housedress and slippers. We looked like twins. "Chet!" she said. "What a pleasant surprise." She gave me a sympathetic, wary look.

"Tita!" Chet took her hand and raised it to his forehead in the traditional, polite way. "Okay. Ting, come on."

I shrugged at my aunt and followed Chet out of the house.

His car was pulled up directly in front of the stairs. Top Gun, his driver, was leaning against the hood, arms folded, the focus of his gaze some distant target. I smiled at him and he smiled back. The car, a Toyota, was big, black, and very shiny.

I asked, "What happened to the BMW?"

"Asia First," Chet said. He opened the passenger door and I got in. Top Gun slid into the rear seat. Chet did not trust anyone's driving except his own. Top Gun, ostensibly a driver, only drove when Chet was not in the car. When Chet had to be somewhere, Top Gun would park it and keep watch. Like many drivers of a certain group of Filipinos, Top Gun was actually a bodyguard. He had been in special ops in the Philippine Army and had worked for Chet for over ten years now. None of this was responsible for his nickname, which instead came from "Top Gone," a merciless pun about his premature balding that had stuck and whose origins were now largely forgotten given his role in Chet's life.

"Why are you dressed like a lola?" Chet asked.

"Why are you dressed like some asshole businessman neck-deep in corruption who doesn't give a shit about anyone but himself?" I was flirting in my haughty way because this was the only way I knew how to speak to Chet.

He smiled. "But you're not a lola."

Chet took a right on E. Rodriguez and started working his way in the direction of Morato, where all the restaurants were. "Don't worry," he said. "I won't take you somewhere nice, just one of those shitholes you love so much."

He pulled over in front of a narrow restaurant squeezed between a Korean barbecue and a Max's Fried Chicken. Top Gun was already standing at the driver's side. When Chet got out, he got in. Chet opened the door for me and gallantly extended his hand. "My provincial maiden." He was still teasing me about the dress.

The restaurant was half full, populated mostly with uniformed college students and uniformed call center workers. Chet pulled a chair out for me at a small table by the window and I sat down. I felt this had to be one of his regular restaurants. Chet was about to take his seat when his phone went off. He stood by the door and said a few abrupt, affirmative things and then hung up. I was about to ask for a menu when he barked at the waitress.

"For her, fried bangus, some laing, and a kalamansi juice. I'll have a Coke." The waitress made an about-face. "Okay," he said, sitting down. "How long are you here for?"

"Not sure," I said.

"And are you writing one of your crazy stories? Because I'm telling you right now that you should stay away from Gumboc."

"Why?"

He shrugged and looked out the window, then turned back to me, delivering a penetrating look. "Do whatever you want. You always do anyway."

"I'm not writing about Gumboc this time," I said. "I'm working on a book."

"Good."

"Don't you want to know what it's about?"

"Sure," he said. His phone went off again. Chet got up and, after a moment's patience, yelled something into the phone and hung up. "Your book?"

"Forget my book," I said. "Tell me what's happening with Gumboc."

"Me tell you? Aren't you the great journalist who's telling everyone else?"

"Aren't you going to tell me I have it all wrong?"

"Not all of it. Some of it. I don't like the guy, but he's right on a few things."

"Like what?"

"So now you're giving me the third degree?" He pushed his chair back and leveled another look in my direction. "I don't like that they're killing all the drug dealers, or so-called drug dealers, okay? That's not good. It makes the Philippines look like a backwater. And I hate that. But Gumboc is working on the traffic, he's working on infrastructure. Business is good. Obviously, there are problems." He ran his thumb along the edge of the table. "It's wrong that there's a bounty offered on the dealers. It's turned the police into headhunters. They're underpaid. If shooting people on the street helps them make ends meet, they're going to do it."

"How much are they paying them?"

"The killers?" Chet delivered a dispassionate look. "Rumor, Ting, unquotable rumor, is seven thousand pesos."

"And what's the motive?"

"How should I know? Shit, Ting, I'm in business. I go to Korea. I go to China. I sell stuff. I buy stuff. I fix up some buildings. I work and I like working. Maybe in the past, I was involved in different kinds of deals, but now it's all legitimate. You're offending me."

"I'm offending you?"

"Yes, you are."

I had heard from others that Gumboc's vendetta against the drug dealers was largely personal, that the ten thousand dead were some sort of performative revenge, the result of a brother who'd been an addict and had died. It made sense, and then it didn't. Another possibility was that it kept the Philippines in a constant state of fear, making it easier to govern. Yet another possibility was that the iron fist of Gumboc appealed to many voters, who liked his swagger. If the Philippines were overrun with drug dealers, that would be an incentive for bringing back martial law. It all seemed plausible and could well have been all there was to know—and all I needed to know—but Chet's casual arrogance annoyed me. I wanted to get under his skin. I didn't know why Gumboc rattled Chet, but he did.

The waitress brought the drinks, set them gingerly on the table, and hustled off.

"How's C. G.?"

Chet narrowed his eyes at the mention of his wife. "She's fine."

"And the kids?"

"Good." Chet drummed his fingers on the table. "I know about your husband."

Now we were playing. "What do you know?"

"Maybe I don't know." He was quiet. "Why are you hiding from everyone?"

"I'm not hiding. I've seen Inchoy."

"Inchoy? He won't be happy you're hanging out with me."

"That's because you're a capitalist pig and he's a socialist."

"Inchoy isn't a socialist," said Chet. "Inchoy is poor."

I had met Chet through Inchoy when we were in college. Inchoy hadn't wanted us to get together. He'd warned me that Chet was trouble. He'd said the same thing to Chet about me, which convinced me that Chet and I were fated for love. Chet and Inchoy's profound differences had created in them a wary admiration for each other, one they both denied but that did explain their enduring friendship, although they rarely got together. Occasionally, Inchoy would need Chet to make a phone call to ensure his mother's building permit got approved or find a job for some smart young relative who was otherwise doomed by lack of connection, and Chet always complied. He didn't ask for thanks, and he knew Inchoy disdained everything he did, but Chet was one of the few who knew about Bibo.

What I had always liked about Chet was his ability to get things done. He had been a big figure on campus, known for being able to accomplish his goals when the inability to accomplish anything was almost a national trait, a resignation borne with such fortitude that it created a feeling analogous to pride. In his time in college, Chet had founded Tomorrow's Business Leaders. He was on the soccer team and played in a recreational basketball league. He captained the shooting team, although Inchoy—also on the team—was a better shot. Chet was interested in music and deejayed parties. He drove an Isuzu Gemini, a low-end sedan often used for taxis. He came from a big family and all of his siblings had fancier vehicles—BMWs, Audis, Mercedes—but he had wanted the Gemini because he was interested in engines and he could work on it himself. I would sit with him in his garage, baking in the heat, drinking kalamansi juice dosed with vodka, while he lay on his back beneath the car. My job was to hand him tools. He also took it upon himself to teach me how to drive, and this Chet did in a new subdivision that was being developed just to the west of where he lived. Even though most of the lots had yet to be sold, all the roads had been laid, and I spent many hours in this great concrete network with no traffic and no people, grinding through the gears as the car stuttered and stalled, until I was able drive at a dangerous speed. At seventeen, death and even injury seemed impossible. Despite my lack of ability and unearned confidence, Chet was never concerned. He would duck beneath the dash to light his cigarette then peer up to see us careening dangerously toward the edge of the elevated concrete roadway and show no fear. Occasionally he would even laugh.

None of my girlfriends had any interest in learning to drive. They were expected to procure husbands who would procure drivers. I wondered how they lived their lives without losing their minds, although the scheduling of hair and manicure appointments, trips to the dressmaker, shopping at the Greenhills Mall, and manifesting the sum of all that activity into an appearance acceptable for the required attendance at parties and bars and discos did consume a lot of hours.

Chet and I would frequently split up. He was too busy and I was too stubborn. When this happened, I would accept the invitations of other guys. I would insist that these boys let me drive their cars, although I had no license and was usually drunk.

But Chet and I would always get back together.

Inchoy never understood why. He thought that despite my performative shallowness, I had the makings of a good radical. Before Chet and I became involved, under Inchoy's tutelage I had attended anti-Batac meetings and gone to anti-Batac rallies. At one rally I had been shot at by the police. As I ran to get away, I'd lost one of a favorite pair of shoes.

We pulled up to Tita Rosa's house and Chet blared the horn. The guard swung the gates open and we drove in at an alarming speed, stopping just short of my aunt's car. Top Gun got out and opened the door for me.

"We'll go to a movie on Wednesday," said Chet. "I'll pick you up around seven."

"A movie?" A movie seemed like a date. "When was the last time you went to a movie?"

"I don't know. A while ago." He kept his eyes focused on my aunt's car. "It was something with a kid and balloons and a talking dog."

"Won't C. G. and the kids want you around on the weekend?"

"They're going to Hong Kong."

"Without you?"

"Jesus Christ, Ting. What do you want me to say? That we have problems? Because we don't. This is just how we are."

I got out of the car and Top Gun got into the passenger seat. The instant the door shut, Chet began reversing. He sped toward the gates and was gone before I had a chance to process that he was back in my life.

VI

The Philippines is a nation of seven thousand islands and 182 non–mutually intelligible languages. There is a big island to the north—Luzon—where all the real things happen, mostly in Manila. The national language is "Filipino," which is actually Tagalog, Manila's primary language and the language of my family. President Batac was from the northern part of Luzon, Ilocos, but Ilocanos are generally (and particularly) inferior to Tagalogs, a fact that they counteract somewhat with their work ethic. In the mountain provinces, you have the Igorots, who were headhunters and aren't anymore but are still known for it. In the southern part of Luzon is Bicol, where people smile all the time and there are lots of coconuts. There is also the province of Pampanga, famous because it is the only province where people actually say "f" as in "ffff," which is ironic because there is no "f" sound in Filipino (which is really "Pilipino") and also because Pampangans can't say Pampanga. They say "Famfanga." Women from Pampanga are supposed to be fierce and beautiful. They tell you this, even when they are ugly.

In the middle of the Philippines there is a large group of islands called the Visayas. All the islands are different. Cebu is famous for its mangos and beef. Leyte is famous for being the home of Imelda. Siquijor is where all the witches come from. Bohol is famous for the "chocolate hills," which must look like some kind of chocolate, but it's one I've never seen. Negros is where the sugar plantations are and also old world colonials, the kind who cut the hands off workers who displease them. There are a lot of these islands and a lot of boats going to these islands that often sink and sometimes a really big typhoon comes along (think Yolanda) and the islands sink too. In the far south is another big island, Mindanao. Mindanao is where you get stinky durian and crazy Muslims. Tourists go there to get kidnapped. Missionaries go there and bring the Bible as reading material. Also Conrad. Most Filipinos have never been there, and by Filipinos, I really mean Tagalogs, because who else are you going to be talking to?

I was spending the afternoon with Inchoy, who was working through another deluge of grading. We sat side by side at an air-conditioned coffee shop on Morato, me with my laptop and him scribbling his comments in red ink. I had written these ridiculous paragraphs in response to a challenge from Ann, who had suggested that orienting people to Philippine culture might be one way of opening the book. But I was again stymied. The identity of the Philippines was deeply subjective, and although what I had written was offensive and unfair, would anger non-Tagalogs, and ran counter to my personal opinions, it did clearly illustrate the prejudices of my circle. I wondered if I were capable of writing something less inane.

Ann had offered other suggestions. Filipino overseas workers sometimes made their way into the news, and Timicheg was, after all, an overseas worker who had met a tragic end. Or, since

Gumboc's extrajudicial killings, or EJKs, had put the Philippines back on the map, I might tie the plight of Timicheg to what was happening in the present-day Philippines. These were objectively good ideas, but I found it intrusive that Ann would want to guide me in this way, although I knew I had to make the book timely.

Gumboc was a member of a powerful Cebuano family. His father had been in Batac's cabinet, but Gumboc presented himself as a tough guy from the wilds of Mindanao. Gumboc's faltering English made this inaccurate portrayal stick. In the foreign press you seldom heard about his training as a lawyer, yet it was Gumboc's knowledge of the legal process that made him such an effective manipulator. I would have to think about how to address the president, because writing about Gumboc made me nervous. And Timicheg had never known Gumboc, which seemed yet another reason to leave him out of the narrative.

Inchoy had plowed through a bushel of papers in the last hour. I had watched his industry with a mild jealousy, amazed that he could maintain this level of academic engagement without losing his mind. But Inchoy loved his job. Many of his students were first-generation college attendees, the children of overseas workers who had slaved and saved and were now able to pay for the tuition, uniforms, books, and housing that might pull them out of poverty. A generation ago, this would have been impossible.

Inchoy had one student who he thought had the makings of a first-rate philosopher or even a politician—the kind the country really needed. This student's mother was a nurse in Israel. His father minded their family of five—cooking, cleaning, and supplementing their income as a Grab driver. All around me, I saw the working poor toiling in merciless conditions for little compensation. I was proud of Inchoy's work. I felt his hope.

"Done," he said. He began tidying the papers, arranging them to fit back into his bag.

"The work of the just in the face of the adversary is never done," I replied.

"How about you? Anything you'd like to share?"

I looked at my introduction. "Absolutely not."

I took a taxi back to my aunt's house. Inchoy and I were going to meet at Café Adriatico that night, a get-together for our friend Zackito, a novelist and journalist who was back from Honolulu.

When I entered the foyer, I could hear Tita Rosa's voice bubbling musically from the dining room. She was entertaining someone but whoever it was remained hidden in the corner. I was not in the mood to smile at one of my aunt's Konyo friends, women who often addressed me in Spanish, which I looked like I should be able to speak and could not, but my aunt was speaking English.

"Ting!" she said. "I'm so glad you're back! Come meet Laird."

Laird Bontotot presented himself, coming to stand beside my aunt. Dark skinned and tall, he was wearing a short-sleeve, collared white shirt and immaculate jeans. His shoulders were thrown back as if he'd been in the military, and he raised his somber, black eyes to me in a dignified way.

"Ting," he said, nodding carefully.

"Hello, Laird," I responded. "Nice to meet you." I looked over at my aunt, eyebrows raised.

"I was telling Laird how good it is that he has dropped by today as you are going to your dinner with all the journalists and writers." My aunt seemed genuinely happy at the accident. "And that of course he will join you. You young people who are interested in writing and books have so much to talk about. And he must be so bored listening to us old folks."

Tita Rosa was old, but she was never boring. Still, I watched the slow wash of relief work its way over her as she felt herself being unburdened of Laird. I excused myself to freshen up and change. What annoyance I had at Tita Rosa's ambush resolved itself quickly: this was Manila and duty presented itself in clear, direct ways. Resignation was the backbone of survival here. Resistance only created anxiety. And at least Laird wasn't in shorts or wearing some ridiculous T-shirt. He seemed quite presentable, which I had not anticipated.

When I emerged from the house, he was waiting at the bottom of the steps, standing perfectly still. Mannie brought the car around and got out, giving Laird an appraising look no less intense than my own. I introduced them, and there was no fist bump, just a polite hello. Laird was matching my froideur with his own extreme reserve. We sat together in the middle seat of the van as we pulled into the street.

"Is it cool enough for you?" I asked. "I can ask Mannie to turn up the air-conditioning."

"Thank you, Ting, but I am fine. I prefer it on the warm side."

Laird seemed to take this as a point of pride.

After a brief barreling down to the corner of Twelfth Street, we were soon stalled, and found ourselves inching through the traffic on E. Rodriguez.

"I read your article in *Vice*," he said, finally. "One can learn something of the current political environment in it but little of your views."

"That's journalism," I replied.

He nodded but seemed unconvinced. The conversation—brief as it was—already seemed in danger of dying.

"So," I said, "I hear you're getting married. Congratulations are in order."

"Yes." Laird shifted in his seat and cracked his neck. His poise struck me as studied. "Cheryl's great. Have you met her?"

"Not yet." I tried to sound regretful about it, but it rang as false at it was. "But I'm sure Tita Remi will bring us together sometime soon. How did you two meet?"

"I was speaking at a protest and she introduced herself afterward."

"A protest?"

"Against Gumboc. At Berkeley."

"I didn't know you were at Berkeley." It was the wrong thing to say, as my surprise was undeniably snobbish, and I caught his weary smile.

Laird said, "I was getting my master's in political science."

"What's your area of interest?" I asked mildly.

"My thesis was on the relationship between the United States and the Philippines during the Batac era with a focus on martial law." Laird let this sink in, then turned his heavy gaze on me. "Thank you for bringing me to this dinner. I need to meet people. It's next to impossible to do anything in this town without an introduction."

We fell into another silence.

"I was talking to a taxi driver," he said finally. "And I asked him what he thought the major problem was in this country. I had assumed he would say corruption, but do you know what he said? Traffic."

"I could see why a taxi driver would say that, or anyone, for that matter," I replied stupidly. I felt that I was delivering someone else's lines but couldn't seem to stop. "Do you speak some Filipino?"

"You mean Tagalog."

I had, of course.

"No. Well, just a few words." He halted and adjusted himself on the seat. "The taxi driver spoke some English." Laird checked his phone, which might have been a tic, but he seemed to be composing himself, thinking too deeply. "Traffic affects all the workers in the city. Hours that could be productively spent they waste like this." He gestured out the window. We were now crawling along España. In front of a Jollibee, a giant bee mascot was waving and handing out fliers. "What the Filipinos need," he continued, "is better infrastructure, work on the Light Rail Transit, expansion into the neighboring areas surrounding Manila. With this workforce and our labor a major international economic presence, there's no need to be struggling like this." He nodded, affirming his statement and, apparently, waiting for a response.

"All that is fairly obvious," I said. "Who doesn't want better infrastructure?"

Laird was suddenly alert. "Yet you're anti Gumboc?"

"Absolutely. I know that overseas workers overwhelmingly support him," I said. "And his ideas for expanding Metro Manila largely reflect yours, but he hasn't solved anything. Of course I'm anti Gumboc."

"But you are in the minority," Laird said. "It was your article in *Vice* that taught me that and all the reasons for his popularity. People have made peace with his presidency."

"His supporters, maybe, but not me, and I am not alone." I set my eyes on Laird. "Even if Gumboc did manage to fix the Light Rail Transit and traffic, I wouldn't support him. He's a thug and a murderer."

"You think ontologically rather than consequentially."

"What, I put morals over results?" I shook my head. "You are intentionally misunderstanding me." I wondered what the stakes of this conversation were. "The results of Gumboc's presidency are that the poor live in fear for their lives and with reason. Gumboc's army of assassins operates in a price per head economy and there is no due process. These people are murdered for money as part of a government-sanctioned program. No amount of public transportation is going to offset that."

Laird was unperturbed by my outburst. He calmly nodded, as if I had delivered a lecture in a classroom, as if my points were a few of many that should be considered. "Who did you support in the last election?" he asked.

"Me? Gig Lijé."

"So the Loyalist Party." Laird was not surprised. Lijé had been the status quo candidate of the educated upper class. "Would Lijé have solved the corruption in government? Would it not have been business as usual, with his cronies getting kickbacks and the poor living in much the same state as before?"

"Laird, if you spend enough time in this country, you come to believe that the problems are largely unsolvable." I was as unhappy with my response as he was, although I was speaking the truth. "Gig Lijé was the only viable candidate, the least corrupt of the choices," I said.

"And you were willing to vote for him?"

"We have to assume that all men are bad," I said, quoting something badly.

Laird processed this and offered a cold smile. "Of course. Machiavelli," he said. "The ends justify the means in that universe."

I was getting visibly annoyed. "Are you turning my words against me to make an argument for Gumboc?"

"No," he said. "I am simply pointing out that your candidate and Gumboc both suffer by being flawed." He inhaled, flaring his nostrils, summoning some personal conviction, and turned to me, pronouncing: "The future of the Philippines is being conducted on the world stage, and the extrajudicial killings are wrong and should be stopped."

"You are committed to that?" I asked. Something about Laird unnerved me.

"I understand there has been a positive result with drug usage and crime dropping," he said, his face gelling to an impenetrable mask. "But the EJKs need to be stopped. Yes. I am committed to that."

When we finally arrived at Café Adriatico, the group was largely assembled. There were close to twenty people there, mostly journalists and academics but also a painter who I recognized but had never met. I hadn't seen Zackito in a year, but he looked much the same, handsome, well dressed, the kind of person who never looks disheveled no matter the heat. He was standing with José Martin, a reporter incarcerated during Batac's martial law. José Martin was short and thin and looked like an old man, even though he was only a decade older than me. Although I didn't know the particulars, he had suffered greatly during his imprisonment but was undeterred from the pursuit of the truth in its wake. He spoke several Filipino languages and had written op-eds for the *New York Times*. I was walking across the room to join him and Zackito when I registered with some annoyance that Laird was following me. Of course he was. Had I thought I could abandon him at the door?

"Zackito," I said, kissing his cheek. "So good to see you. And this is Laird, unless you've met. He's a writer who lives in the

States." I knew they hadn't met but was unsure how else to make the introduction. "And José Martin. Good to see you're still alive."

"Call it what you will," he said.

I retreated by Zackito's shoulder, letting him make Laird's introduction to José Martin. José Martin was undeniably a journalist and as Laird had wanted to meet journalists, I felt absolved of further responsibility. And José Martin was interesting, active, real. He had been covering the Muslim insurgents—Abu Sayyaf—in Marawi but had come back for some sort of powwow with his editors as they worked out their next moves. As José Martin related all this, Laird had his large eyes trained on him with such focus that it seemed he was trying to levitate him.

José Martin was amused by the attention. "Do you want to meet some of my colleagues?" he asked.

"Yes," said Laird. "I would greatly appreciate that."

Laird and José Martin were now sucked back into the larger group, but I was happy at the fringe with Zackito. Inchoy came to join us. He was drinking a whiskey on the rocks and he rattled the cubes with drama as he watched Laird, a parody of seriousness, shaking hands and looking directly into the face of whoever happened to be attached to the handshake, as if he'd learned this approach from an online seminar.

"What does your cousin do?" Zackito asked quietly.

"He's more of an in-law," I explained. "And as for what he does, I'm not sure. Right now he's trying to figure out the Philippines, possibly with the aim of solving all our problems."

Zackito laughed. He waved the waiter over and ordered beers for me and for himself, and then as an afterthought, one for Laird. "Poor bastard's going to need it," he said.

* * *

I was mostly quiet that evening, standing on the edges of others' conversations, laughing at the right time. I waited for someone to ask about my husband, as gossip like this crossed the Pacific speedily, a relief from the horror of Gumboc. My horror was a small, reasonable thing. Zackito chatted away, letting me know that I was frequently mentioned but no one knew the details of my separation, as I refused to provide any. He said, "Some people were surprised, but I wasn't." I found Zackito's saying so strangely comforting. At around eleven, Zackito left with Inchoy, who was going back to Bibo's. Although the party was just getting going, I decided it was a good time to leave. I crossed the room to let Laird know that I was heading home, but Laird had somehow insinuated himself into a political debate with the journalist clique and said that he would find his own way.

As I left, I could hear Laird interrogating the others, asking why martial law in Marawi would not spread throughout the country, wanting to know Gumboc's reasons for removing a Supreme Court justice, which had been blowing up into a major scandal. I heard him pose question after question in the same uninflected American English, and the answers flew back, blossoming into arguments. But if anyone had a question for him, no one posed it, perhaps flattered that he had accepted their superiority in their own country, which was not a given when it came to Americans, Filipino background or not. Or perhaps because they thought that Laird had nothing of his own worth knowing.

I arrived home close to midnight, exhausted and a little tipsy. My reflection in the hall mirror revealed that my hair, sleek earlier, had started fanning out around my head in the humidity.

"Ting," called Tita Rosa from the library. "Something came DHL."

In the library, my aunt was seated at her desk before an ancient adding machine, working on her accounts. She punched some final numbers into a board and then turned the handle, creating a computational magic that had probably been devised in 1900.

"So how was your evening?" she asked.

"All in all, a success, I'd say. Laird made some friends."

"He doesn't smile," she said.

"True," I said. "He doesn't let his guard down."

My aunt nodded then picked up the DHL envelope that was resting on a stack of files and handed it to me. I took it from her and let it dangle by my side. "I'm exhausted, Tita. I'm going to bed."

"Aren't you going to open it?"

"That's what tomorrow is for," I said. "Or the day after." I was not going to open it then because I knew what it was. Or at least who it was from. Even my aunt's scolding eyes could not budge me.

I entered my room, feeling the exhaustion in every inch of my being, tempted to crash in my clothes. I left the envelope on top of the dresser, next to a framed picture of Tita Rosa's grandchildren, taken in the eighties, people who all had kids of their own. I knew that the envelope had been sent by my husband, that I likely had something to sign, which I would send back to America. Then I would be free to start my new life. This should have been appealing, but I felt as intimidated by that prospect as I did by staying suspended in my separation. In the bathroom, the bucket of cold water awaited me, and although the thought of being clean was inviting, I hesitated to take the plunge.

VII

It was Wednesday and I had been tasked with retrieving Tito Ben from the Jesuit retirement home. I stood by the reception counter, sobered by the strange quiet, which seemed unnatural in Manila. The building was new, the walls all painted white, and there was little decoration: a predictable print of the kneeling Saint Ignatius offering his sword, a statue of some tonsured, robe-wearing Spaniard, his neck garlanded in sampaguita. At the end of the hallway, a disturbingly lifelike cutout of the pope raised his hand in benediction, as if advertising the salvation that was soon to come to the aging priests. I heard the elevator doors slide open and Tito Ben appeared, leaning on a surprisingly tall male nurse, having descended to this level from his room on the fourth floor. He had recently been moved there from the third floor, although his first room had been on the second. It was if as if he were slowly inching his way to heaven.

"Ting," he said, "You look more and more like your mother, only not so angry."

* * *

My aunts and my tito Ben were the survivors of what had once been a group of seven siblings. One boy had not survived the war, another, cancer. The eldest had died of something appropriate for a person his age, and perhaps my mother had too: Parkinson's in one's eighties seemed more of a category of exit than an injustice.

We had done the usual, a trip to Christ the King for Mass, a meal at Tita Rosa's, and, dinner now over, we sat together at the dining table as Beng began to clear the plates. Tita Rosa was relating a ghost story that had happened during their childhood in the provincial home of Gapan, where my mother and most of her siblings had been sheltered during the war. Apparently, a man who had been murdered had come back from the dead and visited the judge in the case, letting him know who the real killer had been. The wrongfully convicted man, now deemed innocent, was, of course, set free. And the guilty man found and brought to justice.

"So let me get this straight," I said. "A ghost tells the judge who his killer is, and that's admissible in court?"

"Who better would know?" said Tita Dom. She raised her eyebrows a few times to acknowledge the mystery of this.

I said, "You know that's ridiculous, right?"

"Of course we know it's ridiculous," said Tita Rosa. "But I'm also living in a house with a dog that I don't want." She gestured down to her left, where Tito Iñigo was, as usual, parked. He sensed that Tita Rosa didn't like him and he was going to win her over. "The maids are too scared to clean the upstairs bedroom because they say that the ghost of your tito Iñigo likes to stand by the mirror.

But they also say he's reincarnated as a dog. I tell them, 'You can have one or the other. You don't clean the upstairs and the dog goes back outside, or you have your dog and you clean because he can't be behind the mirror and be the dog at the same time.'"

"Filipinos are very good at believing," said my tito Ben. "They are just a little indiscriminate."

There was then a knock at the door and Beng went to check. Standing in the entry, to the surprise of all, was Chet.

Chet seemed unprepared to see me sitting at the table. He walked across the sala into the dining room and took a seat next to Tita Dom. "Titas," he said, politely. "Father Klein," he said, acknowledging my uncle.

"You need a plate," said Tita Dom.

"No, thank you, I've eaten."

Everyone fell silent for a minute because no one knew why Chet was there, and all were too polite to ask.

Tita Rosa nodded to my uncle. "This is Chet Rey, son of Dinggoy Rey. Your father is Dinggoy Rey, right?"

"My father is Gabi Rey. Dinggoy's my cousin."

There was another moment's silence.

"Dinggoy Rey," said my uncle. "He was at the high school when I was principal, wasn't he?"

"He's an Atenista, so, very possible," said Chet. He gave me a look that demanded to know why he was having this conversation.

"I remember your cousin. He was a terrible student and not very nice, but I liked him."

"I feel the same way, Father."

"I really should have kicked him out. There were a lot of kids I should have expelled, but something about the bad kids made me want to keep them there. Good kids are good anywhere they go. Bad kids need you. If we truly wanted to do God's work, we really should have kicked out all the good kids."

There was another silence.

"Ting, if you're done eating, maybe we should get going," said Chet.

"Going where?"

"To the movies."

I had completely forgotten about the movie date and, now that I remembered, still didn't think it was anything I had agreed to. I felt settled in for the night and the idea of leaving seemed unfathomable. But as I sat there, full after too much of Tita Dom's famous-in-the-family chili con carne, I could think of no other way to get Chet out of the house.

Chet, for sentimental reasons, had first wanted to go to Ali Mall in Cubao. We had spent a lot of time there in college, but it was still rush hour, so we ended up at the much newer, much swankier Robinsons, which was only a mile from my aunt's house. Malls like this had sprung up in the years I had been away, cavernous, gleaming, and chilled. The doors slid open as if guided by some god of commerce and I found myself wondering who shopped here.

The cinema was on the third floor, reached after a series of escalators. The English-language offerings were mostly action or horror pictures, dinosaurs leering over large, red type, houses dripping blood, stern cops, and flamboyant drug lords. The Tagalog films were likely neither exclusively drama nor comedy but a hybrid: a film, for example, in which a character on roller skates careening down a busy street, encountering fruit vendors, plate glass, and chickens, all to comic effect, might suddenly encounter a bus. A jump cut would bring the audience to his funeral. People would laugh. And then cry. This was an actual set of scenes from a film I'd seen in high school. None of my friends had found the juxtaposition of action and tone remarkable in any way and they all had found my incredulousness at the narrative bizarre.

There were sparse other offerings: a costume drama and a not costume drama. Chet was looking at the poster for the not costume drama.

"Nothing romantic," I said.

"Why not?"

"Because I'm getting divorced and I don't believe in love."

"If you don't believe in love, why aren't you staying married?"

Chet must have intended this to be funny but had, accidentally, stated something wise. There was an awkward pause. I said, "Let's see *The Purge*."

The film had started a half hour earlier, but starting times of movies in Manila were more suggestions of when you might want to take your seat. You watched the film until the end and if it was inspiring enough to make the beginning seem worth your while, you stayed through the trailers and continued on. Sometimes you liked a film so much you stayed to watch it a second time. Once, Chet and I had sat for five and a half hours in the Ali Mall cinema watching *A View to a Kill*.

All of the *Purge* films had roughly the same story: people were given carte blanche to kill whomever they wanted for one night a year, which gave those in power the license to rid themselves of undesirables and to use any force or person to realize it. I sat in the theater watching as the body count rose. I could tell by the smell that somewhere close by someone was eating fried chicken, and in the row in front there was a shrieker, a person who managed to be surprised at each new knifing and the resulting volcanic eruptions of blood from the various violated arteries. The movie was awful, but I had to acknowledge that I was having fun. I entertained the idea of screaming in a moment of calm—at the shock of it, as in this moment, when the film's heroine was adjusting her blouse in the mirror. Finally, amid a communal relief as gratuitous as the previous violence, the film exhausted itself. As Chet and I shuffled out, I waited for him to make the easy joke, that every day was *The Purge* in Manila, that ten thousand dead and no convictions seemed a number that the world of *The Purge* could only aspire to. But the film had made Chet strangely pensive. I wanted to make the joke, but Chet gave his head one quick shake as if to warn me off.

"Let's go to Makati," he said.

"Why all the way to Makati?"

"I left my cigarettes in the new apartment."

"Buy some here."

Chet was texting on his phone, presumably to let Top Gun know to bring the car around. He sent the text and leveled a warning look in my direction. "We're going to Makati. You are seeing my new apartment. Why are you being so difficult?"

"I'm not being difficult," I said. "Does everyone in your life do everything you want, no questions asked?"

"Not everyone." Chet put his hand on the small of my back, guiding me toward the escalator. "I have been refurbishing an apartment in Makati. I bought it from someone who had to leave the country, and I got a good deal. I thought you might like to see it. It is something you would have liked to see before. And I want to talk to you." He drew his eyebrows together, regarding me with either respect or distaste. I did not know which, although I recognized the look. "Sometimes you say you won't do things just to let me know that you have a choice. But you aren't doing anything now. Don't say no just because you want me to know you can. I do know, Ting. How could I not?"

VIII

We were speeding down Edsa, with its animated billboards and spiraling exits. There was never a time in this city when everyone slept, and this was the night shift. There were street cleaners; there were call center workers heading to the office, people who worked on American time. Chet was silently looking at the road ahead, switching lanes with perverse determination. Driving was never a neutral activity to him but offered the opportunity to be a winner rather than a loser. In the back seat, Top Gun was looking out the window, his hand resting on his hip, where I knew he kept his gun.

"Top Gun," I said. "How many children do you have?"

He seemed startled to be asked. "I have four."

"And how old are they?"

"The oldest is fifteen, the youngest nine."

"Are they in school?"

"Ting!" said Chet. "Leave him alone. Can't you see he's working?"

I wondered what Top Gun could be looking for, but then I saw his eyes rest on a motorcycle two lanes over. There was a man driving and a woman on the back, but they seemed to be merely commuters heading home after a day spent elsewhere. I wondered if Chet really had reason to believe that he was a target for assassination. His family had been rich for generations, a line of Spanish mestizos who, through clever business and government appointments, had managed to weather the ups and downs of Philippine history. Chet's father, before his retirement, had been a Sandiganbayan presiding judge, in the position of weeding out graft and corruption, which often put him in opposition to powerful and dangerous individuals. While Chet was in high school, there had been a six-month period when his father had feared someone might be kidnapped—one of the children, his wife, or he himself. In the Philippines, kidnappings were no joke. Recently, there was the unfortunate Korean businessman, Jee Ick-Joo, and his golf clubs. And the slaying of two kidnapped Canadians in the south by the ISIS-affiliated Abu Sayyaf. Gumboc had pledged to stamp out Abu Sayyaf, but they were still active, still a news story, still a threat, although not in the city.

It was easy to forget that danger was real, not just news stories, not just calamitous events that happened as if a force of nature, and to other people. One could not be relentlessly vigilant, and that's why Chet paid people like Top Gun to be relentlessly vigilant for him. I raised my eyes to study Top Gun in the rearview mirror. He was both focused and restless, his head moving back and forth like a snake. His eyes flicked up to the mirror and he caught me watching him. I looked away at the traffic in the next lane, which was moving past us, although slowly. This was how people were assassinated: a motorcycle with a gunman sitting on the back moving alongside a stalled car. I should have been nervous but was more curious, watching the traffic move by, wondering if something might happen.

There was a chiming sound as Top Gun got a text. He exhaled in a controlled way and leaned forward to whisper in Chet's ear.

"Sige," said Chet. "We're passing by Rockwell," he added, for my benefit. "I'll just be a minute."

Rockwell was a neighborhood of Makati known for its upmarket businesses and at this time, close to eleven, was swarmed by Manila's well-heeled set. Chet pulled up in front of a restaurant with long glass windows, its plush seats and light-spattering chandeliers visible from the street. People were still eating, and drinks were still being served. Through the car's tinted window, I watched as Chet chatted quickly with the valet staff. He mouthed "five minutes" at me with his hand raised and fingers splayed, but I knew it would be longer.

I sat in silence for the first ten minutes. Top Gun was sitting silently too, in the way demanded of so many drivers. They must have been a contemplative set, used to silence, used to disregarding the passage of time as they had no control over how they spent it. Finally, I turned to face him. "Are you working?" I asked.

"Oo po," he responded. Yes.

I looked around to see if there was anything that would demand Top Gun's attention, but there was no one close by except for the valet staff, who didn't really valet but merely monitored the parking. "Do you like your job, working for Chet?"

"I do," he said. "I like Boss."

"Aren't you worried that it's dangerous?"

He composed his face and delivered a deliberate nod. "Yes. But working construction in Saudi is also dangerous. I could be in security at a bank, also dangerous, and it wouldn't pay as well. And—" Top Gun was censoring himself.

"And what?"

"And I agree with Boss."

"Agree with him? About what?"

Top Gun looked around the corners of the car and his eyes came to rest, somberly, on me. "About what is happening in Manila."

"You mean his politics?"

Top Gun considered this but he didn't know what I meant by politics, and when I considered, under the weight of his confident, direct gaze, I wasn't sure what politics meant either. He said, "He is a good man. Boss buys insurance for me and my family. No one else does that."

"Do you mean health insurance? Or life insurance?"

"He buys both. He is a good employer."

Top Gun clearly felt that he was putting me in my place, and maybe he was. I wondered who he had voted for the in the last election and was about to ask him when Chet reappeared at the front of the restaurant. He was chatting with a man in his sixties, balding and on the stout side, who was smiling with unbridled confidence. They were nodding in agreement over something. I then saw a third man, tall, standing with them. As Chet made his way to the car, this third man turned and I thought I recognized him. The light was dim and he was at an angle, but it could have been Laird.

Chet got into the car, his face apologetic, as if he wished he were more considerate, but he wasn't. "Sorry," he said. "Some things you have to do in person."

"What things?" I asked.

"Business things. At least with Rocco Basilang. He likes to look you in the eye." Chet waggled his eyebrows dramatically.

"Who is that other man?"

"That guy? Some American interested in what Rocco's doing with the highways and the Light Rail Transit. He seemed harmless."

"So it was Laird," I said.

"Laird?"

"He's a distant relative or will be when he marries a distant cousin. He'll be my distant in-law." Now I could see, as he was angled in our direction, that it was clearly Laird, radiating the same unearned conviction. His eyes came to rest on the car, and he might have been looking at me as Chet pulled away from the curb, but he could not have seen through the car's tinted windows. Rocco Basilang had been awarded major contracts by Gumboc and was one of Manila's most powerful citizens, but why would Laird be talking to him? "I think he's writing a story about Gumboc."

"Pro or anti?"

"I really couldn't say." I was confused about more than this. "Why would Rocco talk to Laird? I mean Rocco is Rocco and Laird, well, he's nobody. And it's not as if Laird knows anything about building, although he does seem to have a passion for infrastructure."

Chet laughed. "Listen to you! A *nobody*. Two months here and all your egalitarian American bullshit flies out the window."

"That's not what I meant." Although I had a bad feeling that it was what I meant.

"Until we are a somebody, Ting, we are all a nobody. Even in Manila."

The new apartment was in a building of polished marble vestibules and brass-trimmed elevators. It could have existed anywhere—New York, Shanghai, Brussels—but it was here, in Manila, and the people checking the mailboxes and heading to the basement gym (even at this late hour) in shorts with towels draped across their shoulders were all Filipinos, except for a bulky, sweating man, who was texting madly just inside the front door.

Chet's apartment was on the twentieth floor, down a brightly lit, silent corridor. It felt like the quietest place in the city and standing there with Chet, I realized that we were actually alone for the first time in two or possibly three decades. Chet's key was attached by a paper clip to a card that had a number written on it. He stepped inside the door and ushered me in with an even pressure on my shoulder. There was a moment of darkness before he began, with no small amount of drama, to punch on the lights. We had entered a living room of a dimension almost unknown to me, a mythical square footage of city apartment space. A wall of windows gave out to the sprawl of Manila, a dazzling sea of electric luminescence and life that stretched on and on, uninterrupted, expanding into sea of blackness.

"I bought it for the view," he said. "It's the tallest residential building right now and I don't think that's going to change anytime soon."

I walked over to the window and placed my hands on it, dizzied by the dive to the street below. "How do you know that?"

"This is Rocco's building," he said. "Everyone wants a place here."

"And you have one," I said.

Chet nodded. "It needs a little work. I just put the floor in. This is all reclaimed parquet I bought in Vigan. I found some old carpenteros in Pampanga and they worked on it for weeks." The floor was made of exquisitely composed Versailles panels of a rich mahogany color contrasted with brighter brandy-colored pieces.

It seemed to undulate in the light. "It's the old way, you know, Ting. People don't know how to do it anymore. They put in carpet. Carpet, can you imagine? The person next door has his place all done in white." Chet shook his head. "But this floor, this is the Philippines. Smooth as glass, not a splinter, not a nail, not a gap between the pieces."

"Very nice," I said.

"Nice?"

"A work of art," I added, and this seemed to satisfy him.

"I have more ideas for this place." He smiled as if we were conspirators and headed down the hallway. I followed at a distance. Inside the first room, one of three doors that opened beyond the kitchen, Chet hit the switch that illumined a bare bulb. "Haven't done anything in here but the walls were yellow, so I painted them white so I could make a decision. What color do you think will work here?" he asked.

"Me?"

"I know you know how things should look. You always did." He pulled up a sheet that had been covering something leaning against the wall. Paintings. There were four of them. "Don't be nice. Give me your opinion."

He took the paintings and arranged them one by one against the far wall. The first was a Rembrandt, which made me laugh, but then I saw a drip of bright yellow and a bullet in the canvas. I drew closer to get a better look.

"Doesn't matter if you don't like that one. That's Luke Alarcon and it's a good investment."

"But you want to know my opinion?"

"I want to know what you like."

"I like this one." I took a different canvas and set it apart against the wall, then stepped back to better assess its merits. The painting was of a wolf's head facing a dog's head, both done in exquisite realism against a wallpaper of explosive graffiti elements. A comic book "bang" obscured where the wolf's eye should be, while the eye itself was embedded in its neck.

"Ronald Ventura," said Chet. "Predictable."

"You knew I'd like this? I thought I was being risqué. It's very edgy."

"But you have a soft spot for dogs." Chet gave the painting a quick appraisal. "It is also a good investment."

The other two paintings were also oils: one an impressionistic landscape, the other a portrait of a woman in traditional Bulaceña dress that might have dated from the Spanish era.

I asked, "Is there a painting that you find beautiful that you would have bought if it weren't a good investment?"

He dipped his head to one side, looking at the Bulaceña, and smiled. "To be honest, I like the old stuff. I can be sentimental, as you know."

I asked, "Is that why you like me?"

"Because I'm sentimental?"

"Because I'm old."

I had intended it as a joke, but neither of us laughed. The mood suddenly turned serious.

Chet sighed. His eyes had a heavy-lidded look, which meant that he was struggling with something. "There's no reason for you to go back to the States. Your mother's dead and now you're home. You could stay. Write. You could put a desk there or in the living room, where the view is better."

I managed an impassive look, although something within me was recoiling. I had not been expecting such an offer. I struggled to find a response, something along the lines of "you can't be serious," but he was serious.

I said, "This is when I remind you that I am married and that you are married. And you are not leaving C. G."

"You don't want me to leave C. G.," Chet said. "I'm thinking you need a place to live and I have one."

"You want me to be your mistress?"

Chet hung his head, beleaguered. "Ting, why use that word? Even here, that is an antiquated term. You're stuck in the eighties." He turned his face to the wall and shifted his eyes back to me. He pointed right into my face. "Everything is so right or wrong for you, but life is not like that. There are ways of getting what you want if you're willing to think differently."

I said, "Chet, I don't need your money. I have a job, and even if I didn't, I have a place to live."

Chet's expression was somewhere between boredom and anger. "You can't live with your aunt forever."

"Why not?"

"For one thing, she's ninety years old."

"I would like to go home," I said. "Can you please text Top Gun and ask him to drive me?"

"Ting—" he said, but I was already heading to the door. He put his hand on my shoulder and I pushed him off. "Oh, have I offended you? Have I offended your dignity?" He gave a sarcastic laugh. "There is Ting on her high horse again. How small do I look to you from your super height?" He threw his hands in the air. "I asked you to marry me."

"I was eighteen."

"So what? I was twenty. But you had to go to the States and get your fancy degree, write your books, go sleeping with American guys, and then marry one. So you could sit in a bar getting drunk on beer and laughing, *ha, ha, ha,* with all those Americans with their big teeth."

"You are forgetting that my father is an American."

"Oh, I know that, Ting. I know everything there is to know about you. I know you were having an affair with your husband's best friend and that man is now back with his wife—"

"Where did you hear that?"

"—and you're here with your old titas because they don't care if you act like a child. They like it. But they're not going to live forever and you, Ting, probably have forty years left. What are you going to do?"

I went to stand by the door. I could feel the stiffness in my posture and I was glaring at him. "I don't expect you to understand," I said. "How could you? All you know is Manila. In the United States, I am an award-winning writer. I'm respected. I like my life in the States. I have friends."

"Your friends? Girls who look for men online, drinking vodka drinks with stupid names? Is that what you want?"

"Could you please text Top Gun and ask him to drive me home?"

"No one there really knows you."

"How would you know?"

"I know you," said Chet. "I know you, and no one else really does."

IX

I spent the next week nagged by Chet's insolence. He seemed to think that my separation had created a vacancy that needed to be filled, as if I were incapable of being alone. As if a single woman were something to be fixed. He had made an insane assumption, bypassing any notions of romantic feeling and moving straight to his acquisition of me—as if I were a horse or a piece of furniture. And I wanted to know how he had learned about the affair, when I hadn't mentioned it to anyone he knew, not even Inchoy.

I walked into the kitchen, got a glass of water, drank it down rapidly, set the glass by the sink, and began pacing around the area by the front door. Tita Rosa was watching from her perch in the study, where she was entering figures in an enormous, clothbound ledger.

"Ting," she said. "What is wrong with you? You've been walking around in circles and muttering under your breath and I keep losing track of the numbers."

"I'm sorry," I said. "I'll stop."

"Why don't you go to the Santo Tomas? Miggie's French class was canceled and Mannie's just sitting there in the driveway. Or gambling with the security guard, which should be stopped before he loses all his money."

"You want me to go now?"

"Yes, now. Just be back by six."

I sat in the back of the minivan with my book bag and my sunglasses, sure that Tita Rosa was right to get me out of the house. The Santo Tomas library was always a safe place—a quiet retreat where everyone was rooted to their own studies and indifferent to my presence. At the circulation desk, the librarian would stamp the dates on the inside covers of the books, hand them back with respectful silence, and ask no questions. But I wasn't in the mood for silence or books, particularly not my book.

Mannie peered at me questioningly in the rearview mirror. "Saan po?" he asked. "Santo Tomas?"

"Not today. Let's go to Greenhills," I said.

Greenhills was home to Tianggé, and Tianggé was home to the pearl dealers, and buying pearls required some concentration but not much. I made my pilgrimage to the pearl dealers every time I was in Manila, despite rarely being in the mood to shop. The market was a warren of stalls, counters spilling over with strands and earrings, bangles and rings. Loose pearls were available, displayed in cases beneath the glass countertops. The music of tawad marked the proceedings as women bargained, grimacing, calculating, moving little piles of loot in with other little piles of loot as new deals were struck. Women in head wraps waved to me, calling out that they were the cheapest, the best. The pearl dealers were all Muslim, and the pearls from the exotic shores of Mindanao. I had my own suki, so I just smiled politely at those determined to entice me with their ropes of iridescent jewels and seductive prices and moved on. My dealer met my appearance with a frank nod. She knew what I liked and started to place merchandise on the counter.

Mannie had insisted on accompanying me, as Greenhills actually had a parking lot and he didn't need to stay with the car. He said I needed him to carry the bags, but I suspected he was just bored. He followed closely, listening to me barter in my flamboyant and often incorrect Tagalog, occasionally making suggestions as to what I might want to purchase. Finally, I made my way to the woodworking section of the market and acquired some heavy cutting boards, in order to give him something to cart around. Most of these purchases were pasalubong for when I returned to the States. In the past, I'd made a habit of stockpiling various gorgeous things when I traveled to Manila and, on birthdays and other special occasions, would present these to my friends. But I knew I was likely just shopping to reaffirm that I was indeed returning to the States. I had already been in the Philippines for over two months, longer than I'd intended, and Chet's offer—appalling as it was—revealed that others too could see my hesitancy to leave.

When I entered the house, Beng was there to take the loot from Mannie. She was peeking into the bags, curious to know what I had been up to.

I opened a couple of small, iridescent bags to show the long, looping strands of pearls. I had bought three for about twenty dollars apiece. I intended to wear them all at once, as if I were Anna Karenina. I had also purchased a number of small studs, ridiculously cheap, in different colors—yellow, green, pink, white, and black. I picked out a pair of pink studs. "Ito ang kulay mo," I said and folded them into Beng's hand.

"Ting!" came Tita Rosa's voice. She was calling from her desk.

I left my bags by the door and stepped into the library. "Tita?" I said, questioning.

Tita Rosa was looking very formidable, impressive as she was dwarfed by the size of her desk. "When you were a baby, you were crawling under the dining table, so cute, and you kissed my leg. I remember that, although I'm sure you don't."

"I don't remember it, but you retell it often, as did my mother." My mother had used this story to remind me that my love for Tita Rosa was illogical and also potentially disloyal.

"And once, when you were crawling around, at a similar age, you stuck your finger into the socket and nearly electrocuted yourself. The lights all dimmed."

This was another apocryphal tale and I had heard it many times, having luckily survived to do so. I had always wondered how I'd managed to fit my finger into the socket and had spent much of my childhood looking at sockets and then looking at my finger. "Yes."

In response to this, Tita Rosa raised the DHL package that had been gathering dust on top of the bureau in my room for the last week. The envelope had been opened and I knew she had read it.

"This is unacceptable," she said. "You must fight it."

At this point my American self was weakly signaling me that my privacy had been violated, while my Filipina self was reminding me that privacy was not a value understood or privileged in the current circumstance.

"Why?"

"You are relinquishing all your rights to his retirement? Your husband is a wealthy man. Why would you do this?"

I inhaled, exhaled, and sighed. "He doesn't want to end the marriage."

"So what does that have to do with anything? So you're not a good wife now, weren't you a good wife for twenty years? I cannot let you sign this. You're not signing this."

Although this was annoying, I felt strangely comforted.

"You kissed my leg and you stuck your finger in the socket."

"What does that have to do with anything?"

"You love me and you do stupid things, but even your tita Dom thinks it would be stupid if you agree to this."

I felt bothered on two counts, first that Tita Rosa had shared the envelope's contents with Tita Dom and second that the "even" meant that she was, again, denigrating my beloved tita Dom. Rhetorically, I was not sure how to proceed.

"Don't say anything," Tita Rosa said. "I'll take care of it."

"How can you take care of it?" I asked. "It's American law with American lawyers. We're out of range."

"Every morning I wake up and I ask, 'Lord, why am I still alive? Shouldn't I be dead?' And then I read something like this and I know why I'm still here. Jim will know what to do." All-powerful Cousin Jim was often appealed to by my aunt to solve a range of problems, even if they had nothing to do with him.

"Jim? You're showing that to Jim?"

"No, of course I'm not showing it to Jim. Jim is very busy. But he has an American lawyer based here who is getting back"—she checked some notes that she had written on the back of an envelope —"in four days . . . or maybe five."

"I think, Tita, this is when I remind you that I'm nearly fifty."

"And I'm ninety. So what?" She rattled a pillowcase that was resting on the desk beside her. It was a floral pillowcase, faded, filled with some mystery thing, and I, who had been wondering why the pillowcase was there, was now wondering how rattling its contents helped my aunt to make her point.

"Tita," I asked, "what's in the pillowcase?"

Tita Rosa looked over at the pillowcase and composed her face in a look of extreme serenity. "That is your lola," she said.

"Lola?"

"Yes. We had her disinterred because now that Jim has had the chapel built, he is transporting all of his ancestors to be buried in the family crypt."

"Why do you have Lola's bones on your desk?"

"To keep her close," said my aunt.

The pillowcase easily contained what was left of my grandmother, who I remembered as a full being—a woman who I had prayed the rosary with, whose legs I'd massaged when she was in pain. My lola's soap opera was *Flordeluna* and we had watched it together, eating chicharon, drinking Coke. That there was a connection between the pillowcase and the woman seemed impossible. And surely there was a better place to keep the bones than in this pillowcase and on this desk, but before I could question my aunt further, we were distracted by the ringing of the telephone.

Beng's slippers flapped across the parquet as she rushed to answer it. "Hello," she said in her deepened phone voice. She then turned to me, holding out the phone. "Ate Ting," she said. "It's for you."

I exited the study. "Babae o lalaki?" I mouthed at Beng. Woman or man? Tito Iñigo was sitting there, head cocked and ears up, awaiting the response. I had been avoiding Chet's calls for over a week.

Beng gave me a bewildered look and shrugged.

I took the phone from her.

"Ting?" came the voice. It was Bibo.

Bibo wanted to get together and so the following day, I got a GrabCar and headed to Tondo. To occupy myself during the two-hour ride, I brought a book on Truman Hunt, a medical doctor who had gone over to the Philippines in 1898 and, in the way of colonial occupiers, become the completely unqualified lieutenant governor of the Bontoc province. I'd checked the book out of the Santa Tomas library, hoping that it would mention Schneidewind, but even if it didn't, I would learn more about the Bontocs' relationship with the United States, which was necessary to undergird whatever narrative would one day need undergirding. I slid into the back of the car, a tiny Toyota with itchy fabric upholstery, and started reading.

Timicheg and his tribe were not the first group of Igorots to make it to the United States. In 1904, a trial outing was funded by the US government to the tune of 1.5 million dollars and brought thirteen hundred Igorots to be displayed at the Saint Louis Exposition. It was a huge success. One and a half million sounds like a lot of money, but when one considered what was at stake, this was chicken feed. The annexation of the Philippines had not won universal approval and it was in the best interests of those who supported the venture to demonstrate the Filipinos' inability to govern themselves.

When, after a stint in Saint Louis, Hunt returned to Bontoc in 1905, he brought an enticing offer: he would pay any willing Bontoc fifteen dollars a month in wages to travel to the United States and perform their most barbaric selves for a hungry American public. Though of course that could not have been how he sold the venture to them. Maybe he proposed that they would perform their dances, play their music, and present their culture to those lost in the ignorance of American isolation, with the hope that the Americans would thrill to see the practices of the Bontoc, as they had never seen anything like it. Maybe in the conjuring of their drums and graceful, frightening dance, they could transport the American public to the vine-choked gullies and miraculous rice terraces, to the softly chilled mountain air, to the sun striking rays over the ridge of mountains at dawn, to the rustle of a doe in the long grass and the *shink* of an arrow that brought her to her knees, and to the gory red of sunset that threw the warriors in silhouette as they came marching back from a successful outing against their foes.

And the Bontoc had seen nothing like America and had never earned a wage. Why not go?

There's a photograph of Truman Hunt's tribe at Coney Island five years before Schneidewind's Bontoc arrived. They are penned off like cattle, mostly naked, wearing loincloths fashioned from handwoven, richly colored native cloth. Most are huddled around a fire. We see their backs. It must be cold, because the white observers, lounging on the railing, are all in jackets and hats. One woman around the fire is bundling herself into a blanket. But the kicker in the photo is the Bontoc man who is pointing at the camera. He has singled out the photographer as his target, humorously, and seems to be saying: "Your head next." Seated by the fire is his laughing compatriot, holding a weapon, also angled toward the photographer. They are making fun of the situation, the absurdity of it.

They are getting paid and, they think, will soon be heading home.

The journey to Tondo took a hundred pages, which was as useful a gauge as any for judging the traffic. I made the steps to the apartment in the semidarkness, hearing the chatter that drifted through the other doorways, the slamming of pans on stovetops, the mild admonishing of children. Bibo greeted me at the door to her apartment with a glass of chilled water. The air conditioner was off and the room had reached a temperature that seemed capable of poaching my organs. Air-conditioning was seen as an exorbitant waste of electricity. Bibo probably didn't use the air conditioner except when Inchoy was visiting, but that did not explain why the windows were all closed and the curtains drawn.

Bibo was wearing an immaculate white T-shirt and jeans and pink Converse low tops, shoes that I had brought back from the States—a special request made through Inchoy—a year earlier. Despite the heat, her glossy, straight hair was down around her shoulders.

"I was going to suggest getting our nails done," I said. I lifted Bibo's hand and looked at it, at the long, pointed nails that were a dark and shiny purple. "But yours are perfect." I let her hand go. "And you are perfect and look absolutely beautiful."

"It's because I'm in love," Bibo replied. She picked up her handbag, a knockoff Louis Vuitton, and we stepped back into the hallway, which was an equally unbearable temperature. "Come," she said. "I've set up a reading with Aling Ligaya."

Fortune-tellers were a dime a dozen, but Aling Ligaya was of a different caliber. She was a bona fide seer who had an earned reputation for her accurate readings and incorruptibility. Aling Ligaya could have held her own in Delphi, but she lived in Tondo just a few blocks from Bibo's house and was a regular fixture in Bibo's weekly routine. Chok-Chok was manning the store and we stopped for a quick chat. I tried to buy some cough drops, which were, of course, gifted. I didn't really want cough drops but I knew that I had to try to purchase something just to allow Bibo to refuse my money.

Across the street a construction project had resulted in the assembling of a rickety scaffold made from lashed bamboo and planks. A ladder of equally fragile design leaned up against it and men in rubber sandals were scaling and descending the structure, weighted with flat baskets filled with rubble and chunks of concrete. It looked like a scene out of *Ben-Hur*.

Bibo and I crossed the street, weaving through the stalled cars and jeepneys. The shopfronts offered an assortment of appliances in Chinese boxes and racks of loud clothing. The rattle of a sewing machine emanated from some dark corner of a tailor shop.

Aling Ligaya's house fronted the street, sandwiched between a sari sari store much like Bibo's and another business that sold a variety of discarded things: old tires, dusty TVs, a coiled chain, a child-size bicycle. Presumably, as a resulting perk of her profession, Aling Ligaya had nothing to fear and her door was wide open. Tied by its leg to a chair by the door was a small dog that, when it realized we were coming to visit, greeted us by first thumping its tail enthusiastically and then growling. Bibo called into the darkened hallway.

"Halika, halika," came Aling Ligaya's voice. We entered, our eyes adjusting to the dark, aware of some throbbing light that outlined boxes and stacks of newspaper and broken chairs. The source of the light was a statue of Jesus resting atop a derelict refrigerator, his Sacred Heart exposed and electrified. Jesus held his hand delicately beneath his blinking heart, his face composed in awe-inspiring calm and generosity.

At the end of the hallway, the space brightened and we entered the kitchen, which also functioned—as evidenced by a neatly made up bed—as whatever else was required. The entire right side of the room was filled with stacks of old magazines. One tower supported a buzzing electric fan, another a cage with finches, which were hopping about and grunting musically.

Aling Ligaya was seated at the end of a table in the small space that was left clear, cutting up a chicken. She raised her keen eyes to us, tiny and wizened, wielding the knife. "Umupo kayo," she said. I wasn't sure where she wanted us to sit as the two chairs available were occupied—one by a stack of clean laundry, the other by an angelic little boy in an undershirt and shorts. He looked up at me with his enormous eyes and vacated the seat. Bibo set the clean laundry on the bed. Aling Ligaya pushed the cut-up chicken down the table and pulled herself to standing to wash her hands in the sink. This done, shaking her hands of water, she sat back down and picked up a linen napkin, folded into quarters on the table. She dried her hands in a manner so deliberate that I wondered if it had a particular significance.

"Ikaw," said Aling Ligaya, indicating me. She took a deck of cards that she must have had hidden in the pocket of her dress, a floral dress much like the one I wore at my tita Rosa's. These were not tarot cards but merely playing cards, softened with use and humidity. I knew the drill. I would shuffle and pick six. How she intuited any meaning from these was a mystery, as it was intended to be, as was my desire to spend my time searching for meaning in this way. Aling Ligaya held the cards, closing her eyes and then opening them. She leveled a look at me, not ready to release the deck.

"Magkano?" I whispered to Bibo.

"Limang daan," she replied.

I took out my wallet and placed five hundred-peso bills on the table. Aling Ligaya handed over the cards and I shuffled them, trying to empty my head of all useless thoughts, although, once those were cleared, there wasn't much left. I selected my six and she slowly began to turn them over. The child, who had been leaning against me, crawled into my lap. He smelled of Lifebuoy soap and must have just had a bath because his skin was still cool, his hair slightly sticky with damp.

Aling Ligaya hummed over the cards, which I recognized from long-ago readings: the ten of diamonds, which was money; the jack of spades, a young man of questionable integrity; the king of spades, an older man of equally questionable integrity; and then a heart, but just the deuce, so not worth much. I couldn't remember what clubs stood for, but I had both a six and an ace. I was happy I wasn't playing poker. But I also knew that Aling Ligaya didn't read in the traditional way, that the usual narratives spun out of suits were irrelevant to her. She took the little finger and ring finger of her left hand and began tapping the cards. "Eh-to! Eh-to!" she said each time she tapped a card. She did this at a moderate speed and then faster and then sat back in her chair, eyes closed, in a trance.

We waited patiently. The child shifted in my lap, his seat bones pressing into me. The finches hopped about their cage. Outside, a hawker called, "balut," his voice growing louder as he came up the street. Finally, Aling Ligaya opened her eyes. "It's all lies," she said. "All of it. There is no truth. But you"—she pointed at me with a finger bent with arthritis—"you are tough." The word she used was "matapang," which made me seem almost thuggish. "You always survive. But don't trust anyone." Her face relaxed into a smile. "Anyone, except for me."

I waited, but that seemed to be all she had to say. "Anything else?"

"He loves you."

"Great," I looked over to Bibo, who was stifling a giggle. "I wanted to ask about my book. I write books, you know."

"I know," said Aling Ligaya. She was done.

"Am I next?" asked Bibo.

Aling Ligaya looked steadily at Bibo and then waved her hand dismissively. "Not today."

"Next week?"

"We'll see."

Ejected, on the sidewalk, I tried to process what Aling Ligaya had said. I didn't believe her pronouncements but at the same time did not completely discount them. "You know, Bibo, last time I went in there she told me I was spending too much money and that I should grow the nail on the little finger of my left hand. Also not to eat chocolate for a month."

Bibo shrugged. "Last time I was in there, she told me not to worry about saving my money, that I should spend it on pretty things."

"Weird," I said. "Let's go to Max's for lunch. My treat."

Max's Fried Chicken was emptying out as it was now past the lunch hour, but it was still busy with the mostly uniformed middle class and students who could afford to eat there. At times the entire nation, with a few exceptions, seemed to be in uniform. Uniformed people looked as if they had a sense of purpose, which was so often missing in the fervor of fatalism that dogged the culture. Maybe their presence helped to balance out the general disorder. Regardless, it was a kindness, because it simplified the demands of dressing for those who likely could not afford an extensive wardrobe. I ordered fried chicken, rice, and chop suey. Bibo ordered the same thing and we sat there sipping our Cokes, waiting for the food to arrive.

"I wanted to ask you," said Bibo, suddenly serious, "what I should get Inchoy for his birthday."

"His birthday? That's not for another two months."

Bibo shook her head gracefully and folded her narrow, long hands, one upon the other. "It is a special birthday. I want to do something special."

Inchoy was turning fifty. He and I had become suddenly old. "You make every day of that man's life a birthday," I said.

"Thank you. But I don't know what to get him. I have been saving. Maybe a watch?" Bibo threw up her hands in genuine despair. "It's so hard. He's a socialist."

Bibo was right. Inchoy was not an easy person to buy for. Sometimes I'd bring him cheese from the States, which he liked, but he would also remind me that many Filipinos had full, vibrant lives without American cheese.

"I know," I said. "Why don't you take a trip?"

"A trip?"

"Why not? Go to Baguio for a few days. You can go visit the Kalinga villages and maybe you can buy Inchoy some artwork. He can pick it out."

"Ay, Ting," said Bibo, her face alight. "That is perfect." She was already planning, shifting her head from side to side, working out the details. "To make it really special, you should join too."

"Me? Don't you want a romantic getaway?"

"Every day in my life with Inchoy," said Bibo, suddenly somber, "is a romantic getaway."

"All right," I said. "Sounds like fun."

Bibo took my hands in hers and held them. "I will book rooms at the convent." She and Inchoy always stayed at the convent. "Inchoy will really like that gift."

Our food had now arrived. I looked at the fried chicken and the chop suey. As usual, hiding in the bokchoy and carrot and sauce was a small, gray chicken liver. I wasn't sure if this was actually a thing elsewhere. I stabbed it with my fork. "Bibo," I said. "Do you want my liver?"

When I arrived home, my aunts and my uncle were just finishing dinner. I had forgotten that it was Wednesday as my routine was organized into roughly indistinguishable days. Even the typical weekly punctuation of Sunday Mass had been reduced as a result of my family's enthusiastic attendance. As I took my seat at the table, I could tell from their smiling and general solicitude that they had been talking about me.

"Where were you, Ting?" asked Tito Ben.

"I went to Tondo and met with Aling Ligaya."

"And?" asked Tita Dom.

I considered. "I got the ten of diamonds."

"Good," said Tito Ben. "Because you cannot afford to sign away your retirement."

I looked first at Tita Rosa and then at Tita Dom, who were innocently remorseless. "How are you, Tito Ben? How are things?"

"With me?" Tito Ben put his spoon down on the plate with a dramatic clang. "The church is at war with Gumboc and he with the church. That's what's up with me. Of course we are sheltering those unjustly accused of crimes. Of course we are getting involved."

A few churches, including the iconic Baclaran, had actually started creating schedules among their parishioners to make sure those seeking sanctuary and now living in the church were fed.

"You need to be careful, Ben," said Tita Rosa. "Remember, you got in trouble with the Jesuits over that Batac thing."

"That Batac thing" was the Edsa Revolution. Batac would never have been toppled if the church hadn't wanted it. My uncle had been a real picture-in-the-papers force, and the role of the church in politics questioned; Rome, at least on paper, was opposed to clerics taking sides. "Rosa," he protested, "I can't go marching anymore. I can't even go to the bathroom without assistance. But, yes, I support the church opening its doors to those in need. Sanctuary is a centuries-old tradition, one of the few—and we have many in this country—that actually helps people."

I thought to remark that allowing people to hide wasn't exactly help, but my uncle really wanted the church to improve the lives of his people. He knew that his religion was the opium of many but would rather it had been the food bank. I kept my thoughts to myself because Tito Ben had given his life for this, for a church that would shelter the downtrodden, and sanctuary, at least literally, accomplished that.

X

The following Saturday, Inchoy and I were seated in Tita Rosa's garden at a tiny table on tiny chairs, this a result of Cousin Carmi's granddaughter's birthday party. Miggie was turning seven. The theme of her party, because children's birthday parties in our circle needed themes, was "Old Manila," and to this end a kalesa had been acquired, which had been taking children on rides around the neighborhood. As it was now time for lunch, the driver was sitting in the cart, parked on the nearby driveway, eating his food off a plastic plate with his hands. The horse, in a festive harness, seemed unimpressed, his head bowed low, one back hoof cocked in a defeated way. He too was eating lunch, some sort of grain that he chewed dispassionately as a great of amount of gritty drool accumulated at the edges of his mouth. Around the other tiny tables were little children in uncomfortable clothing, napkins tucked into their collars, being attended by their uniformed yayas, who coaxed food into their wards' mouths. One boy, hands idle at his sides, opened his mouth for a spoonful of lasagna, then chewed despondently, much like the horse. I wondered if the act of feeding himself would have dispelled some of his boredom, made him a little more animated, although less immaculate in his attire.

Inchoy was taking in the spectacle with his usual disdainful acceptance. All the expense for this party could no doubt have been put to better use, but if Inchoy had only stayed friends with those of acceptable moral standing, he would have been a very lonely man.

"I know what you're thinking," I said.

Inchoy laughed wryly. "Your family puts on a good show."

"That they do, but this is when I remind you that although they are family, and I love them, I come from a different world. This is their thing, their people. I'm just a well-liked family member who is allowed to hang out. And gets to eat for free." I picked up a chicken drummer and waved it at him.

Inchoy pursed his lips and wrinkled his brow, delivering a disbelieving look.

"Inchoy," I said. "I am not a Konyo."

"Why, because you're not Castilla?"

"Exactly. I'm American. This Old World society thing, I don't belong to it."

"You're not off the hook, Ting. You American mestizos are complicated."

"In what way?"

"Well, for one thing, you come in many different varieties, but people try to put you all in the same category, which causes confusion. But *you* are the result of the Spanish-American War. You are an Old American mestiza."

It was true. Great-grandfather Benjamin Klein had come over in 1898. In an odd circumstance, my name too was Klein, as I'd regained it through marriage after spending the majority of my life, courtesy of my father, as "Christina Johnson." I now wondered if this had been part of my husband's appeal.

"The Old American mestizos," Inchoy continued, "slid into the same category as the Konyos."

"Well, the Konyos wouldn't say that. Some of these people trace their roots back to the fifteen hundreds."

"True, but to look at you"—he indicated me with a head-to-toe gesture—"you could be one of them. The origins of white privilege become less important over time." Inchoy considered and went on. "Because of the American thing, you get conflated with the Fil-Ams, but much of the time Fil-Ams aren't mestizo at all. They are simply the children of Filipino workers and sailors seeking to improve their lot in a less arcane culture. They're raised as Americans."

"Americans who are raised by Filipinos. Laird, for example." Laird had, of course, been invited to the party. He was now standing by the kalesa driver, chatting with him, and the kalesa driver, in broken English, was trying to chat back, intrigued by the attention. "He might not be plugged in to the culture, but I don't think he'd be very happy that you're calling him an American."

"I don't know about Laird," said Inchoy.

Together we regarded him.

Inchoy said, "We should ask him."

"Oh, God, please don't call him over."

"Why not?" asked Inchoy.

"He makes me uncomfortable. I always say things that I can't believe I've said, things that aren't so much what I meant to say but what I think he thinks I'll say. He brings it out in me."

"Why is he still here?" asked Inchoy.

"I don't know." I had also been wondering about this. "He's supposed to be getting married in the States."

"When's the wedding?"

"I can't remember." I watched as Laird patted the horse, listening to the fascinating kalesa driver. "I saw him talking to Rocco Basilang when I was with Chet in Rockwell. Apparently, Laird's really into improving the roads. And the LRT."

"You say that as if it's a bad thing," said Inchoy.

Right then a car entered the drive. The gates had been left open, ostensibly to facilitate the circling of the kalesa. The car moved quickly, braking just short of the horse, who didn't seem to mind, as if he'd accepted the possible collision as just another reminder of his general defeatedness. I knew this car. It was Chet's.

"What the hell is Chet doing here?" I asked. I waited for Inchoy to make some equally outraged statement, but Inchoy was silent. "Did you invite him?"

"I didn't exactly invite him, but I did tell him where I'd be when he asked."

"Why?"

"Why would I lie?"

Chet got out of the driver's seat and Top Gun followed, walking around to the rear of the car, where he proceeded to wrestle something out of the trunk. I could see various family members alert to his arrival, as well as their guests. At that moment, the yard was filled with groups of well-dressed adults finishing up their lunches, awaiting the next diversion. This, I could tell, was Chet, who walked up to us with his usual swagger. Top Gun struggled behind him carrying, as I saw when he drew closer, a Hello Kitty car with a big red bow taped to the hood. The thing must have weighed 150 pounds. Chet, looking at the miniature car, then at my knitted eyebrows, seemed very pleased with himself.

"Where's the birthday girl?" he asked.

She was on her way over followed by a number of children, many of whom still had napkins tucked into their collars. Miggie had no idea who Chet was, but she did understand the gift, and her eyes were round with desire.

"Happy Birthday, Maggie," he said.

"It's Miggie," I dryly corrected.

Chet was unfazed. "I'm your tito Chet."

Top Gun set the car down and Miggie looked at it, then at me, then at Carmi, who had made her way over accompanied by her own group, which included Tita Rosa, who leaned heavily on Beng's arm.

"Chet!" said Carmi. "What a beautiful gift." She looked over at Miggie.

"Thank you, Tito Chet," Miggie said. "I love it."

She got into the car and turned the wheel. She made a car noise.

"You have to charge it first," said Chet. "But then you can drive it all over the place."

"With yaya watching," added Carmi.

"This is too extravagant a gift," I said. Miggie looked over at me, momentarily alarmed.

"Nonsense," said Chet. "The girl needs wheels. Look at her. She's the sporty type."

Incredulous, I mouthed "sporty type" at Inchoy.

"How's your father?" asked Carmi. "We were in Punta Fuego together last summer and he absolutely killed me at mahjong."

"Well, he's in good health and still ruthless," said Chet.

There was a moment's silence.

"Have you eaten?" asked Tita Rosa. "The chicken lollipops are very good. And we have lasagna. If you prefer something sweet, we have Brazo de Mercedes."

"Sure. I just ate, but that sounds wonderful, Tita."

Tita Rosa transferred her leaning from Beng to Chet and together they began to make their way to the food.

I watched them journey through the tables and balloons, past the clown, who put out his cigarette and resumed juggling. "This is a disaster," I said to Inchoy. "People will talk."

"People are already talking," said Inchoy. "It's your fault."

"My fault?" Just past the fountain, the agaw bitin was being set up. Beng and I had spent some time that morning decorating the bamboo frame with streamers, attaching little toys and bags of candy to it. This apparatus was then tied to a rope that would be thrown over a branch and someone would lower it and pull it up as kids tried to grab the treats. I saw the rope thrown over the branch and noted with some alarm that Chet had volunteered to operate it.

"I need to talk to Chet," I said.

"Yes, you do," said Inchoy. "But that involves having something to say." Inchoy raised his eyes to me with a grave kindness. "I have to ask. Why didn't you go with that other guy? The guy you had the affair with?"

"Oh, so now Chet's telling everyone," I said.

"I am not everyone," said Inchoy. "And Chet, shithead that he is, would never do anything to harm you, so relax."

"Really?"

"He did ask you to move into his apartment and that was inappropriate."

"Yes it was." I felt myself stiffen. "Strangely, even given Chet's buying power, I am not for sale."

"Ting, chill out. Maybe Chet's being opportunistic, yes, but he's doing it because he loves you. He's always loved you."

I didn't believe this. But Inchoy wouldn't have said it if he didn't think it true. "The feeling is not mutual. And how did Chet know about—" I didn't want to say it out loud. "You know."

"He probably hired an investigator. When you have money like Chet, no one has any secrets. But you still haven't answered my question. What happened to that other guy?"

I watched Chet pulling at the rope and the children leaping to grab the prizes. He was laughing and making jokes. He caught me looking and delivered a dazzling smile.

"I didn't want another man," I said. "I just wanted out." This was the first time I'd articulated this, even to myself. "I had forgotten who I was and I wanted to remember."

XI

A few days had passed since Miggie's party. My laptop was sitting in silent accusation on the nightstand, but I thought I should bathe first. When I was done, I stepped into the bedroom, surprised to find Beng standing there. I stood, dripping in my towel, as Beng fumbled with a small package wrapped in metallic blue paper.

"Tita Ting," she said. "There's a gift for you." Beng handed me the package and waited. I really ought to have gotten dressed before I opened it, but I knew that Beng was hanging around to see what it was—although, from the size and weight of it, I was sure it was a book and that it would disappoint.

"Who brought it?"

"Si Kuya Top Gun po."

So Chet had bought me a book. That was, if nothing else, a first. I tore off the paper and held the book for Beng to see. On the cover in big letters was written: *Mutuality: Anthropology's Changing Terms of Engagement*. Beng was, indeed, disappointed but shrugged it off and left me to my privacy. I sat on the bed, wrapped in the towel, and opened the book's cover. This book was a library copy and looked to have been borrowed from Ateneo, the university where Chet and I had first met. There was the paper slip taped in the front with various dates stamped in it, but on the bottom of these was written, in Chet's handwriting: *Today to Ting, with Love, Forever.* He must have been punning on checkout dates and due-back dates. I dropped the book onto the bed just as my phone started to ring. The caller was, of course, Chet.

"Do you like my gift?"

"Chet, did you steal it?"

"Only three people have checked it out in the last five years. It's about Schneidewind and Timicheg. You can use it for your book."

Schneidewind? Timicheg? Chet must have been talking to Inchoy. "You should bring it back."

"I can't. I already wrote in it."

I turned the first page and there, beneath the title, was written, *To Ting, who doesnt understand forever and will have to learn with me. Love Always, Chet.* I would find out what he meant by this later. "Chet, I don't know what I find more amazing, that you stole the book or that you went to the library."

"I was going to buy it," said Chet. "But when I tried to get it on Amazon, it was going to take two months." There was a pause. "It's a good book, about your thing."

"My thing?"

"Your work in progress," said Chet somberly, catching himself. "But it's the right book. Inchoy said you were reading all about this other guy and there was stuff online, but this has an essay that you need."

"I should have known Inchoy was involved."

"Ting, I needed his help." There was another pause. "Sometimes you think that I don't respect your work, and the truth is I don't understand it. I don't. But I understand you and that is what's important."

I wasn't sure what to say.

"Aren't you going to thank me?" asked Chet. Now he was teasing me.

"It's stolen."

"I'll make a donation to the library."

I flipped to the table of contents and saw that a chapter was focused on Igorot villages and expositions. The essay was, indeed, all about Schneidewind's background, something that I had been unable to dig up elsewhere.

"Are you still mad at me?" asked Chet. "Don't answer that." He yelled something, and I heard him assent to the car being brought around to the front of some building. "You're not going to stay mad, Ting. That's the thing with you. You're really hotheaded but can never stay angry for long." Then he hung up.

Chet was determined to make things right, the book an apology. I held it in my hands. In reality, I wasn't angry with him. I was in battle with myself. I'd imagined my retreat to Tita Rosa's as a way of fleeing from society, as if my aunt's house were some sort of medieval nunnery and I a woman revoking all to be there. I didn't want another man in my life. But I also knew that if Chet were to disappear, I would miss him. I was dogged by the memory that my mother had adored Chet, had loved him, his astonishing confidence and his manners. When Chet saw my mother, he would throw his hands in the air—even at twenty years old—in appreciation of her beauty. And she would acknowledge this recognition with a wry smile and a nod to me. He seemed to be saying to her, then, that if I was nearly that beautiful at her age, he would be the happiest man alive. And now I had reached that number of years and a few more. He had predicted that I would age well and now felt affirmed, and even though a part of me was weakly signaling that I was more than this, it felt good, at almost fifty, to be so desired.

I went to the sala with the book and a glass of Coke and sat on a low velvet chair. Once, my uncle's life-size portrait had hung on the wall opposite and the outline of where it had been was visible on the faded wallpaper. A standing fan rattled energetically a few feet away. I took a swig from my glass, set it on the side table, and opened the book. So what if I accepted Chet's gift? What did it matter? It was research, my research, and I had a right to it.

Schneidewind was not actually a doctor but a nurse. He had first traveled to the Philippines in 1898, having enlisted in the army and been assigned to the field hospital corps. He arrived in the Philippines ill with typhoid. On his recovery, he left the army and found a job in the Philippine postal service. Around this time, he also married a local woman, Gabina Dionicio Gabriel, who gave birth to a son, Richard, and promptly died. Schneidewind continued his work in the postal service until it was discovered that he was running an export business on the side, using his official position to grease the deals. Labeled a smuggler, Schneidewind returned to the States, leaving his son in the care of maternal relatives. But there was something exploitable back in Asia and he was going to benefit from it, although he was not sure how.

The following year, he found himself working a cigar concession stand at the Saint Louis World's Fair. It was here that he met Truman Hunt and, more importantly, his troop of traveling Igorots.

The show was a huge success and the Americans were enthralled by the ways of these primitive Filipinos. Unbeknownst to Hunt, the Igorots were also enthralled, but by the ways of the litigious Americans, and had been assembling materials to sue Hunt for mistreatment and withholding pay. The case was filed in Tennessee and, surprisingly, given the racial attitudes of the time, was successful. Hunt was imprisoned and the Igorots, presumably because of Schneidewind's familiarity with the Philippines, were placed in Schneidewind's care.

Schneidewind had found his calling.

Shortly after, he returned to the Philippines to assemble another troop of Igorots. The returning tribespeople, despite the lawsuit, must have had something positive to say about their experience, as another group did sign up, persuaded by the cash and trinkets if not by what the job actually entailed.

On this trip, Schneidewind was also reunited with his son, who he brought back with him to the United States, placing him in the care of American relatives in Detroit. Richard "Dick" Schneidewind was a very good student. He did his work, showing a particular aptitude in science. While his father traveled the world with his second wife and their children, Dick Schneidewind lived with his German-speaking relatives. He graduated from high school in 1917 and went on to study at the University of Michigan, where he earned first a master's and then a PhD in engineering research. He became a professor in the College of Engineering and generated numerous publications and patents relating to such things as chromium plating and iron casting. When still a young man, he became engaged, but the relationship ended when the fiancée's parents learned of his dark skin. Professor Schneidewind married late in life, but only under the condition that the union produce no children. Apparently, the role of American mestizo, which was downgraded in the United States to the less desirable "half-breed," had been traumatic enough that he would never wish it on another.

I wondered if Dick Schneidewind would have been better off if his father had just left him with the relatives in the Philippines, where he would have enjoyed not only acceptance but also status. It would have been a life without patents, but maybe he would have been happier. As in some regards I was happier in the Philippines, where I wasn't needled with questions from strangers who, on learning I was Filipino, wanted to know how my parents had met, if my father had been a soldier, questions really posed to determine whether my mother had been a bar girl or worse. They were wishing for something salacious and were always disappointed by the truth.

That evening, my phone lit up with a call from my husband. I watched it ring and let it go, knowing that he would not leave a message and would soon call back. It was seven in the evening here, seven in the morning there, which meant that calling me was the first thing on his list for the day and he would not quit until I picked up. The phone went quiet and then resumed its assault. I let it ring twice and answered.

"Hello," I said.

"Christina, we need to talk."

I considered. "I'm not sure that we do."

"Well, then, I need to talk and you owe me that. You have engaged a lawyer and things are getting serious."

It occurred to me that I had indeed engaged a lawyer, or at least Tita Rosa had, although this was the first time the reality had really sunk in.

"You can't expect me to take these demands seriously," he said.

My heart was pounding and I was holding the phone so tightly that my fingers had started to ache.

"You haven't read it, have you?"

I said, "Read what?"

I heard him groan on the other end. "What your lawyer has in mind. I have given you what you wanted, which was space. But enough is enough."

"We agreed to get a divorce before I left."

"No, Christina, you agreed to get a divorce. And then you packed a suitcase and ran off."

"You sent me that package DHL."

There was silence as he came to understand that I hadn't read that either. "Christina," he said. "You have to read the documents. If we do go through with this, you will be in a bad position. You should know that." He had never intended for me to sign anything. He had only meant to scare me by showing me some figures. "Whatever you make from your teaching and your articles doesn't even cover your clothing budget."

"I don't want to have this conversation," I said.

"Well, you're not prepared for it." This was the familiar condescension. "And if you haven't noticed, you didn't leave me and achieve a life of independence. You're mooching off your aunt. You can't do it, Christina. And we don't have to fight about this, because you are coming back. I know it, and you know it."

I knew no such thing but couldn't manage a response.

"You need to grow up," he said, and then—with his usual lack of ceremony—he rang off.

I threw the phone onto the bed like it was toxic, then headed to the kitchen to see if there was any beer in the house. Maybe I did need to grow up, but the prospect did not appeal. My husband and I were pursuing different lines of action. I wanted the divorce; he wanted the marriage. We again diverged on the narratives of what had caused our relationship to falter. He thought he'd been neglectful, egomaniacal, and likely that I had found out about an earlier affair with a coworker named Blaire, which I had, but that had nothing to do with my wanting to leave. My husband's fault, in the end, had been to mistakenly think he knew me when he didn't, a delusion that made him unwilling to try for more. In one of our final arguments, he'd said to me: *Don't you know what marriage is? What it means?* He'd meant it ironically, but sitting at the kitchen table in my bathrobe, rolling a now-empty wineglass between the palms of my hands, I realized that I didn't.

There was no beer in the house, but on the fridge, lurking behind an ancient owl-shaped cookie jar, was a bottle of Kahlúa, still sporting a green ribbon from some long-ago Christmas. It had never been opened, but I took care of that, and then—sticking with the holiday theme—poured a good portion into a green plastic tumbler. I didn't know how I was going to handle the storm ahead, but as I dropped ice cubes into the creamy liquid, I knew at least my weapon of choice.

XII

The following Friday the family headed to Batangas for the reinterment of my grandmother in Jim's chapel. The family—cousins, their children, their grandchildren, and a stunning array of uniformed servants—was assembled outside Tita Rosa's house, as well as a fleet of vehicles to transport us all. Tita Rosa stood at the head of the stairs shouting orders, her hair neatly pinned and lipstick applied. Shipping the family out to Cousin Jim's holiday house felt akin to preparations for the Battle of Normandy. Jim, along with the cars, had sent the family minibus, and it pulled into the driveway followed by a battered yellow taxi. I watched the taxi warily and saw Laird step out and pay the driver. Tita Dom arrived at my side.

"Ting, where's your bag?" she asked.

"Already loaded."

A gaggle of children and their uniformed yayas were already piling into the minibus. Tita Rosa descended the stairs, propped on Carmi's arm. Beng followed, carrying the floral pillowcase, her face composed in a nervous horror.

"Ting," said Tita Rosa, "you're in the Camry. You too, Dom."

"Why?" I said. "I want to be in the bus with the kids."

"No room," she said.

Resigned, I opened the car door and noticed, with some alarm, that Laird was entering on the other side. The front passenger seat was already taken by Miggie's yaya, Nini, sitting with a cauldron of food on her lap. The driver, one of Jim's, adjusted his sunglasses in the rearview mirror. I moved into the middle and Tita Dom, noting Laird's presence with concern, followed inside. At the last minute Miggie was deposited on her lap. The door swung shut with a clunk.

"Hello Laird," said Tita Dom. I smiled politely.

"It is very kind of you to include me," he said, sounding stiff and rehearsed.

"Of course," said Tita Dom. "You're family." She looked at me, indicating that I should now say something. I wanted to respond that he wasn't really family but held my tongue.

"Jim's house is amazing," I said. "We always have a good time there." I felt Laird's thought echoing in my head: *Do you people ever not have a good time?*

The ride was probably going to be two hours long and I began planning for civil, subject-based conversation, naps, and general contented smiling out the window. We were barely down the drive when I became aware of Miggie's intense scrutiny of the right side of my face.

"Tita Ting," she said. "Is Tito Chet your boyfriend?"

"No. Tito Chet is not my boyfriend. I'm married to your uncle Bob."

"Where is he?"

"Your uncle Bob is in the States."

"Why? What's he doing?"

Miggie didn't know her "Uncle Bob" but had probably heard a lot about him in the last few weeks, although none of it from me. "Well, it's ten thirty here, and with the time difference, I think he's probably going to bed." Just talking about my husband was giving me a wave of panic, this inflamed by our recent conversation.

Tita Dom began scrambling through her purse and produced her phone. She quickly pulled up *Candy Crush* and handed the phone to Miggie. Miggie gave me a look of unmistakable dissatisfaction but was, thankfully, unable to resist the phone.

"So, Laird," I asked, "what have you been up to?" What I really wanted to know was when we would be relieved of his presence in Manila but thought I should save that for later in the journey.

He sat with the question for several seconds before finally answering, "Not much. Seeing the sights."

"Oh," said Tita Dom, grabbing the soft lob for her own, "what sights?"

"I went to Fort Santiago," he said. "I had never been to Intramuros."

"I haven't been there in a while," said Tita Dom. And then to me: "Ting, we should go." She adjusted Miggie in her lap. "You know, that's where the family lived. All my brothers and sisters, before the war."

"And you?" asked Laird.

"Well, I was born there, but I don't remember. My siblings were sent to the provinces, where it was safer, but I was just a baby, so I stayed with my parents. And one brother also stayed, in the city."

The story was about to get very dark and I thought—selfishly—that at least this would create, after its telling, a situation conducive to silence.

"You actually lived in the Walled City, in Manila? I thought you were . . ." Here he struggled to find a word. I heard attempts flicker through his head: *farmers*, *plantation owners*, *feudal lords*. "People who ran farms," he finally said.

"Yes," said Tita Dom. "But we lived in the city. My father was a doctor, but he really didn't have a calling to it. He became a doctor because his mother wanted him to. He worked for Parke-Davis, as a representative. We had a nice house. But then the Japanese invaded, and things in Intramuros got very dicey."

I imagined that Laird was again filing through the facts in his mind, thinking about the history of the Philippines, of the Second World War, of how old people would have been at certain times: trying to put the human factor into his roster of events. "You are lucky you survived," he said.

"Lucky? I don't know about that. My mother was, I don't know, what's the word, Ting? Idiosyncratic. In her own way, resilient."

I nodded to both.

"She didn't want to leave her home. Then the Japanese commandeered the house, and she was on the street. At one point she was sleeping in the church, with me. She would go to Santo Tomas, which is where the Americans were interned, and her father-in-law would pass her food through the bars. The American POWs were hungry, but the Filipinos were starving." She had a long, inward look. "It is right that we're talking about her," said Tita Dom, answering some unvoiced question. "Aren't we burying her today, after all?"

I felt it might be valid to point out that this was the second time we'd done so. But it was also unnecessary.

"And what about your father?"

"What about him?" asked Tita Dom.

"Why isn't he being interred along with your mother?"

"Because he is at Fort Santiago. His bones were never recovered. But he is with his son, my brother, so they are not alone."

Tita Dom had succumbed to a nap with Miggie napping in her lap. Both their mouths had slackened into Os and it sort of looked as if they were singing. The reaches of Edsa were ending in a final act of extreme concrete. You could see Manila in the process of consuming the countryside. Laird flicked his eyes sideways, gauging my attention. I met his glance.

He said, whispering, "I don't mean to pry, but what happened to your grandfather and your uncle?"

I adjusted myself in my seat to face him. "They stuck it out in Manila and made it to the end of the war, but when the Americans were at the gates of Intramuros, the Japanese rounded up what was left of the Filipino men—including boys of thirteen, that was my uncle—and imprisoned them in a dungeon in Fort Santiago. The Pasig, at that point, was tidal, and the dungeon set in such a way as to make use of the rising water, old Spanish ingenuity. Quite a few people drowned. My grandfather and uncle were in that number."

Laird's eyes became alert. "I read the plaque," he said.

"Yes," I said. "You read the plaque."

Batangas, a coastal province to the south of Manila, was not our home province. That was Nueva Ecija, to the northwest of Manila, a place marked out in rice paddies and small, dusty towns. The rainy season would quickly turn the roads to rivers of silty mud.

Carabaos still plowed the fields and people still used the woven salakot to keep the sun off their heads as they bowed to the mud to plant the rice. Nueva Ecija was all industry. The music of it was the flat drilling sound of motorcycle engines as the tricycle taxis circuited the concrete buildings and shopfronts, the storehouses, the mostly abandoned ancestral homes. These houses were now occupied by ancient doñas unwilling to leave the only life they knew and by the maids to whom they were most likely, although distanced by legitimacy and social standing, related. Although we still collected the seasonal tribute from the kasamas, our percentage was small and what the workers were left was such a sliver of profit as to make life survival at best. The wealthy in my family had moved on to business, real estate, technology, infrastructure.

My cousin Jim had bought the acreage in Batangas thirty years earlier and embarked on a building project somewhere between Versailles and the pyramids. Batangas had all the advantages of the coast—views, beaches, waving palms—but also got hit with the brunt of typhoons and was ever threatened by that most awesome specter of the Philippine psyche: the tidal wave. When Jim had first shown up, there was already an impressive house in place, complete with swimming pool, but this structure was soon downgraded to the status of guesthouse and another house built on such a scale that the terrace was the same size as a luxury hotel, something you might find on Waikiki. His most recent project had been a tower, equipped with an elevator, which had glass panels that gave a 360-degree view of the property. Guest rooms were tucked into the various floors below the viewing area. From the outside, the structure looked like an air traffic control tower. From the top floor you could see everything: the island that Jim had constructed because he wanted to see an island; the lake he'd carved out to raise his own sturgeon and lobster, although the climate was not cooperative; the family museum; the chapel; the playground; the helipad; the horses that had once been corralled in a stable and ridden with varying degrees of success by his children and me but that had been set free and now roamed: a mix of Arabian, quarter horse, and thoroughbred, skittish and imposing, nibbling at the grass, galloping away when we tore through the fields on our ATVs.

We gathered on the terrace as lunch was being served. I poured myself a glass of kalamansi juice from a sweating jug. Jim's kids were all there with their children, and Jim's sister, Cousin Carmi, with her kids and their kids. Tita Dom's children would be showing up sometime soon with their kids, and so on. And after we had gained critical mass and eaten, we would all go to the chapel to watch my grandmother's bones be slid into the wall with the others, who had all been removed from their first final resting place to be put to rest again.

I had finished my kalamansi juice and was about to ask a servant to find me a beer when a group of maids rushed out of the kitchen with net covers and began hurriedly placing them over the food. Tita Rosa's face crumpled in a frown. "Why?" she asked. I heard the sound of chopper blades as my cousin Jim's helicopter swung to the front of the house. Bits of grass and dust began to churn in the air. She shouted, "Why have a helipad if you're going to land your helicopter right beside the house?"

I shrugged and shouted back: "You know Jim isn't a big fan of walking."

"But he could get someone to drive him from the helipad." This was true, even though the helipad was only a hundred meters away.

The helicopter touched down and my cousin Jim and his wife, Cha Cha, disembarked, along with their eldest granddaughter. No sooner had they exited than the helicopter immediately ascended again, heading off to the left, where it disappeared back over the roof of the house. Jim came straight to me and we kissed, his cheek smooth and cool and smelling of some expensive thing. He was as light skinned as I and had the same watery green eyes, the hallmark of mestizos. "How are books?" he said.

"Books are good," I responded.

"I heard you were thin."

"Was I fat before?"

"No, but now you're really thin."

Satisfied with our exchange, he began making the rounds of his grandchildren. Cha Cha was now pinching my elbow hard. "Ting, so good you're here. We always see you and that's good."

"Why do I leave?" I asked.

"Yeah, we all wonder. Don't go this time. I hear you have some sort of scandal with your husband, but we're family and we don't care."

"Thanks," I said. The gratitude sounded ironic and had originally been delivered as such, but was now, on reflection, sincere. My family was deeply loyal to me, as I was to them, a love that never faltered no matter what you did or how deserving you were of approbation, so long as your victims remained outside the clan.

Cha Cha was now sighting across the lawn, where Laird was wandering alone, his expression inscrutable as he took in the view to the sea. "Is that him?" she asked.

"Yeah, that is him," I said.

"Well, he's better looking than I thought he'd be but so dark." She laughed. "And he's the one who's in the sun."

Just then a group of men showed up in white shirts and black pants. They had lanyards around their necks that dangled official-looking ID. Several of them had cameras. I looked over at Jim, who was talking to a member of his security team. Jim set his gaze in our direction. "Press," he mouthed.

"Press?" echoed Cha Cha.

Jim walked slowly back across the lawn, his brow creased. He came to stand beside us, looking at the photographers with skepticism. "They say it's some sort of society spread, but why didn't they call us in advance?"

"Society spread?" asked Cha Cha, unimpressed. "Do we let them stay?"

Jim considered. "Why not?" His head of security had also joined us, standing at a respectful distance. Jim's eyes drifted over to him. "Tell them they can stay but only for a few minutes. And no pictures at the chapel during the Mass or interment." The head of security promptly lifted his radio, barked a few words, and then strode purposefully away.

Jim looked suspicious. "They should be following Gumboc."

"Gumboc is in Israel," I said.

"Israel," said Jim. "First Korea, then China, now Israel. You would think there was nothing here to do." He considered. "Maybe there isn't."

The press men were now walking across the lawn in Laird's direction. Laird turned, looking surprisingly composed, and they snapped his picture.

"Oh my God, Ting, go! Go!" said Cha Cha.

"I don't want my picture in the papers," I said. "Why don't you go?"

"I have to change my shoes. Ting, hurry!"

"Why?" I said.

"They're all going to think we look like Lord."

"Laird," I corrected her, resigned and already heading for the cameras. "His name," now over my shoulder, "is Laird."

Later, I would understand the true purpose of those photos, but at the time I wondered what Manila society would make of the shots of me, Laird, and the group of twelve children who were hamming it up for the camera with an inventive array of cheesy grins and jutting hips. Most of the family had retreated, plates in hand, more interested in the food than the photos. Cha Cha appeared at some point in a pair of easily identified Chanel spectator flats and smiled attractively a few times for the camera, and then, with an imperious wave of her hand she dismissed the journalists.

For society-page journalists, they looked a little rough. They were thugs in black rayon pants and short-sleeve white shirts, no oily manners, no attention to fashion that one associated with columnists devoted to showcasing the lifestyles of the rich. Is this my memory now playing tricks on me? Was the one wearing dark sunglasses really scoping out the place? Or were they just journalists, bored with Gumboc away, and needing to fill the pages with something: the ambitious architecture of my cousin's house or perhaps the excesses of the upper classes, people who could afford not only one burial for their departed loved ones but as many as they felt like, while the poor of Manila's crisis of grief was quickly followed by another: the problem of how to pay for the funeral of their gunned-down dead.

XIII

I had moved a chair up to the second floor of my aunt's house and set it on the balcony because here I could catch a breeze and smoke—and also get my texts. It was the most peaceful place in the house. The ghost of my tito Iñigo kept the servants away, and even his namesake would not cross the room to the balcony but rather would stand on the threshold, quivering from his nose to the tip of his tail before retreating down the stairs. I was fine with my uncle's company, though, because even if he was lurking by the mirror, he had little to say. From my perch above New Manila, I could track the endless stream of shouting vendors that sold fresh tofu, ice cream, balut, and pan de sal. The rag dealers had their own call, as did those looking for old bottles and newspapers. It all seemed part of one big song, occasionally joined by a crowing rooster or a backfiring tricycle or the grind and clang of my aunt's gate being opened and shut. From here, I could see it all.

I was leafing through Carl William Seidenadel's seminal work, *The First Grammar of the Language Spoken by the Bontoc Igorot*. The book was a record of Bontoc speakers telling stories, with a literal transcript that was awkward but captured the voice of the long-ago storyteller. This account was of the Battle of Caloocan and covered how the largely Tagalog-speaking insurrectos had tricked the Bontoc into joining the fight, telling them that they were to perform as dancers in Manila. But the charade was soon exposed, the Bontoc unarmed, underfed, and in the line of fire.

At the Battle of Caloocan, the Americans had held steady, knowing that if they waited, the Filipinos would summon all the troops they could from wherever they might find them, including Bontoc. After that, conveniently assembled, the Filipinos would be decisively crushed in one swift maneuver.

Later, one of the Bontoc, Januario Galut, would side with the Americans and act as guide, showing them a secret path to the Tirad Pass, where a band of insurrectos would find themselves suddenly surrounded by the enemy. When Schneidewind showed up in the region six years later, these battles would have still been fresh in the minds of the Bontoc, and some of them would have been veterans. And at that time, my great-grandfather Benjamin Klein would make the decision to stay in this country, that after shooting these people, he was now going to marry one. And make me a person who had stakes on both sides of the battle.

My phone began to ring. Chet was calling. A quick glance down at the street revealed Chet's car pulling up to my aunt's gate.

I answered the call, and before I could say anything, Chet started to speak.

"Can I pick you up?" he said.

I found the invitation acceptably vague, as I wasn't sure what exactly I was agreeing to and could at least pretend to myself that my only commitment was to riding in a car. I could have said no, but I couldn't bring myself to do it. Maddening as Chet was, he'd gotten to me.

"All right," I said. "Wait in the driveway. I need to get changed."

Chet was in a good mood but trying to hide it as he knew it would provoke me. He knew me so well. Too much smiling and I would have felt the need to knock him down, tell him he'd accomplished nothing with me, that I was not allowing myself to enter into anything with him, and once I'd said that, I would stick to it, as my dignity (he would call it my stubbornness) would demand it.

We were stalled, already, on E. Rodriguez, barely a mile from my aunt's house. In the back seat, Top Gun was snapping his gum. I would not tell Chet about the phone call with my husband. It was none of his business. Instead, I chatted about the trip to Jim's holiday house, about Laird's being there, and how the press had shown up.

"They didn't look like society photographers," I said.

"What do they look like?"

"Oh, you know. Usually they're wearing knockoff Prada. And they're sycophants, always saying how amazing everything is and how amazing you look. They're into lifestyle."

"But Jim didn't let them stay for long. Maybe if he hadn't kicked them out, they would have asked you about your shoes or something." Chet was momentarily distracted. "Gumboc's in Israel. Maybe they were real journalists looking for something to do."

"That's what Jim said."

Chet nodded, the problem now solved.

I asked, "Why would Gumboc go to Israel?"

"It's a smart move," said Chet. "Do you know how many Filipinos are working in Israel right now? Over thirty thousand."

"He went to visit the overseas workers?" I produced a wan smile. "How nice of him."

"Ting, the Jews understand us."

"They do?"

"Yeah. They're all over the place and we're all over the place."

"You should go into foreign policy," I said.

"Thank you, Ting. I hear the sarcasm. But remember, you asked me why Gumboc is in Israel. And why did you do that?"

"Because I'm bored." I said it in a mild way. I realized that I was flirting and saw Chet register this.

The official word on Gumboc's visit was that the Israeli government was thanking the Philippines for taking in Jewish refugees during World War II. This little-known moment in history was now significant enough to get Gumboc an invitation to inaugurate a Holocaust museum in Jerusalem, despite the fact that Gumboc was on record as having compared himself, with pride, to Hitler, his war on drugs as merciless as the Führer's own inhuman projects. But Gumboc had recanted, said that he hadn't really meant it, scratching his head, throwing up his hands: just a guileless joker who occasionally spoke without thinking. Of course there were the usual rumors that Gumboc had been visiting arms factories, which might be passed off as a hobby, but it was hard to watch a man like Gumboc do this without wondering who exactly was destined to be on the receiving end of the weapons. Regardless, the Filipinos had aided the Jews in the Second World War, President Quezon, like Schindler, disguising the rescue as simple recruitment of labor and saving the lives of twelve hundred people. If this reason for a visit to Israel was simply a cover for Gumboc's actual goals, it functioned well.

I looked over at Chet, who was lost in thought, the act of driving, his brand of meditation. We were now in the heart of Makati, its gleaming glass and skyscrapers, a stretch of city with smooth roads and an even, sunlit glow that evidenced no poverty, a kind of Disneyland where one could pretend that the Philippines was a first-world nation.

"Where are we having lunch?" I asked.

"That's a surprise."

"I don't like surprises."

"Yes you do."

"I do?"

"Yes. If you haven't had time to analyze and make a decision, you think you're off the hook. You don't like to decide things. You like things to happen and then pretend that it had nothing to do with you."

I was still processing this when Chet pulled up in front of his apartment building and got out of the car. Top Gun opened my door and then went around to take the driver's seat. I had nothing to say and stayed quiet, wondering if I was just letting things happen in order to distance myself from them. Chet swung open the glass door and steered me down the hall with his hand on the small of my back. He liked to do this, as if he thought I might wander off otherwise. We entered the elevator and I watched him texting furiously, although seemingly bored by the exchange. He dropped his phone back into his shirt pocket and smiled at me as the elevator doors slid open.

The apartment was now furnished. There was a sprawl of dining table and a pair of butaca chairs and a rattan-backed rocker. In the corner were some boxes and a rolled-up rug. A chandelier was lying on its side on a sheet. Across from this was an antique couch and a chest inlaid with shell, which had been set up as a coffee table.

"Nice," I said. "All Filipino?"

"The chandelier is from Spain," he said. "But that's very Filipino."

The Ronald Ventura dog/wolf painting was prominently displayed in the center of the right side wall, but leaning on the floor beneath it I noticed the Rembrandt reproduction with the bullet hole.

I looked up at the Ronald Ventura then down at the Luke Alarcon. "You prefer the Alarcon," I said.

Chet shrugged.

A maid then exited the kitchen with two glasses of water and handed one to Chet and one to me.

"You've hired help?" I was stating the obvious, when I should have been asking who the help were supposed to be serving as the apartment was supposedly vacant. Chet's phone rang and, checking the number with a grimace, he answered. He began listening and nodding intently and gestured to me that I should explore the rest of the apartment.

The bedroom was also fully furnished and painted in a soft rose. I wasn't sure what I was supposed to look at, so I looked at the bed, which was some fancy antique no doubt, and the coverlet, likely hand embroidered at great loss of sight. One wall of the room was a built-in closet with mirrored doors and I had the unsettling experience of watching myself wander around, which made me feel more like an observer than an actor. I opened one closet door, and it was empty. I opened another closet door and was surprised to see it full of Chet's clothes. I closed it and then reopened it, as if expecting a different result. No, there were Chet's clothes, and not just fancy barongs and seldom-worn suits but a solid yard of the plain white sport shirts that he wore every day. I pulled open a drawer and was confronted with Chet's underwear. Would the next drawer have Chet's socks? It did. On the bedside table there was a photograph of Chet's children, somehow taken without C. G. in it.

I wandered back into the living room as Chet was ending his call. The maid was setting lunch, two places at the far end of the table.

"Well?" he said.

"You moved out?"

"I moved in."

"You're crazy."

Chet shrugged. "We can get married."

"No we can't."

"I'm taking care of it."

"What are you taking care of?"

"The annulment."

"You're having your marriage annulled?" The maid passed by with a plate of fried fish and set it carefully on the table. "You can't do that to C. G."

"I'm doing it."

"On what grounds?"

"I'm crazy. I was crazy when we got married. That's all you need for the annulment."

"But you're not crazy."

"You just said I was." He was looking at my face intently, nodding almost imperceptibly. I watched, unable to move, as Chet's face relaxed into a smile.

"What?" I asked.

"We should eat," he said.

I served myself some fish, but my appetite had deserted me. "I *am* going back to New York," I said.

Chet shrugged. He didn't believe me, and why would he? I was still there, eating his food, making the rounds with my family, as Gumboc's drug killings mounted and offshore a typhoon was threatening. I was still taking notes for a book that might never get written. I was still there. "Why would you go back?" He looked at his empty plate.

I was under assault but also unsure of what I was working so hard to defend. "Why are you doing this?"

"I don't know," said Chet. "Sometimes I wish I'd never met you." He raised an eyebrow and smiled. "You, Ting, are a bad investment."

XIV

Preparing for an outing to Dad's World Buffet, like preparing for a colonoscopy, entailed a certain amount of fasting. Tuesday was the day to go (as it was less crowded). Tita Dom, who was turning seventy-five the following weekend, was an expert on how to maximize the experience. She would start with sashimi, move on to tempura (here I substituted the Filipino pork bar, preferring the lechon, crispy pata, and bagnet), only include vegetables if they looked exceptional, and leave room for the halo-halo. She had a Happy Diner card that she dug out of her bag as we hit the top of the stairs. You could eat as much as you wanted at Dad's, but if you left any food on your plate, you had to pay double.

"Okay, Ting," she said, handing me a plate at the buffet. "What did you have for breakfast?"

"Water," I replied.

Each of the counters held a shocking excess of mostly meat dishes, glistening in the bright light, arranged according to country. There was Korean barbecue, Japanese fish, Filipino fiesta food decorated with the head of a lechon pig, blind to the proceedings, its crispy eyelids having been forever sealed upon the spit. My tita Dom heaped a decent amount of raw tuna on her plate and then on mine. She looked at me, her face lit with anticipation. At the pork bar, she argued with the attendant that the crispy pata didn't look that crisp, and he quickly provided a new batch fresh from the fryer. I looked at the mound of food on my plate, carefully engineered into the shape of a volcano.

"Do you have enough?" Tita Dom asked.

I shrugged. "There's always seconds."

A waiter led us to a table by the window and we ordered mango shakes. I didn't really want a mango shake, but it was tradition to get one.

I took a bite of the bagnet and closed my eyes in reverence. It was crunchy, salty, and oily. It was the taste of heaven.

"Really, Ting," said Tita Dom. "How can you live in the States without bagnet?"

"I don't come here for the bagnet," I said. "I come for the family."

"Come for the bagnet. Stay for the love."

Tita Dom had for a while run a radio station, for which she had written the ad copy for a range of products. She had also been a pizza czar, an accountant for Jim, and a number of other odd and disconnected professions, all successful, but she was happiest in her retirement doing nothing after a life of work. "What do you know about Laird?"

"Laird? Why?"

"Rikki was asking." Rikki was her son, who worked at the bank. "He said there was something strange about him. Also, why does Laird keep hanging around? He's supposed to be learning about his in-laws. That's not us. That's Remi and her brother and all those Santiagos."

"I've been wondering about that too," I said. So far Laird had managed to show up at my cousin's daughter's baptism, a family outing to Magnolia for ice cream, and even Wednesday Mass. But despite Laird's showing up at everything, I didn't feel that I knew him any better than the first time we'd met. "Why was he at the blessing of Carmi's new restaurant?" I asked. "I wasn't even sure why I was there." Tita Dom laughed. "I got stuck in this weird conversation with him about morality versus truth and the shaping of public opinion."

"That sounds interesting."

"Well, it wasn't. We couldn't agree on what 'public' was. I could have come up with something, but I just wanted him to stop talking to me, so I played stupid. And then he went on and on about the state of the LRT and how traffic affects the poor."

"Traffic affects everyone," said Tita Dom.

"Tita Rosa needs to stop inviting him to everything." My tita Dom nodded in agreement. What else did I know about Laird? "Did you know he studied martial law under Batac?"

"Yes," she said. "I googled him. That's in his bio."

"Find anything interesting?"

"Not really. There's a paper of his online, all about the October Revolution."

"The Russian October Revolution?"

"Is there another?"

I shrugged. "Well, that explains a lot."

"It does?"

"It might. He's studying Manila society. Maybe he wants to write about us, you know, because we're relics of a feudal society, like the Romanovs."

"He thinks we're the Romanovs?" she said. She had moved on from the sashimi and was now eyeing the tempura, deciding whether it was friend or foe. "So Jim is Nicholas and Cha Cha is Alexandra?"

"And Tito Ben is Rasputin."

"No," said my aunt. "Rosa is Rasputin. We should all say no to her, and we can't. And you, Ting, are Anastasia."

"Why Anastasia?"

"Because you show up all over the place, surprising people."

"When I should really be dead."

"Well, I don't know about that," she said, spearing shrimp and waving it at me sagely. "But you could take better care of yourself."

"What did Rikki have to say about Laird?"

"Just that he asked a lot of questions. He was asking Rikki about Marawi, if he knew anyone down there."

"Marawi? What does Rikki know about Marawi?"

"Just what everyone knows. The city was destroyed. And there are Muslims and they kidnap tourists and we don't go down there. It was a short conversation." She took a bite of the shrimp and chewed thoughtfully. "What is going on with you and Chet Rey?"

"Nothing." I had moved on from the bagnet to the crispy pata: the second pork course. "He moved out on C. G. and is living in this apartment in Makati."

"I know."

"How do you know?"

"Cha Cha told me. No. It was Carmi. Carmi heard from someone."

"Regardless, it has nothing to do with me."

"Doesn't it?" She was studying my face, which I was trying to compose into a look of blankness. "Ting, why would you involve yourself with another man? Isn't one husband enough?"

"More than enough." My aunt, a widow, had never remarried.

She continued to watch me, growing suspicious. "If you're sick of staying with Rosa, come live with me. There's a room."

On the far side of the restaurant, the musicians, who had been orbiting the tables, had launched into a rendition of the theme song from *Titanic*. I looked down at Morato, where the traffic inched along, like pork in an alimentary canal. Across the street were business offices, the headquarters of the *Philippine Telegraph*, and in between a honking, walking, vending mess of humanity, but my aunt was following the singers, who were circling closer.

"Do you think they know 'Send In the Clowns'?" she asked.

"Do you really want them here singing 'Send In The Clowns'?" I responded.

She was laughing at this when I saw him get out of the car. He stood briefly on the sidewalk in his pastel sport shirt and jeans, looking around as if he were worried he was being watched. "Tita!" I said. "Look. It's Laird."

"Oh, Ting. You're right. What's he doing?"

He swung open the door to the *Philippine Telegraph* and entered.

"Why's he there?" she asked.

"I don't know. Maybe he's writing something for the paper? But why him?"

"Is that suspicious? Because you're making it seem like it's suspicious." She laughed. "Wow, Laird is so exciting! I wonder what he's up to."

We waited for him to come out, but it must have been a long meeting, because we were done with our meal and on our way home before he reemerged.

There *was* something suspicious about it. Whatever Laird's credentials as a writer, there were dozens of people more capable of writing on Philippine issues than he. Gumboc was now back from Israel and I wondered if Laird had managed to get an American outlet to commission an article. I wondered if some of my antipathy toward him was actually jealousy. If I hadn't been so at sea with my own project, I might have been friendlier, more curious about Laird's activities, and less derisive. If we had encountered each other in the States as writers or people with an interest in Philippine history, it would also have been different. Laird would have met me on even ground, not as we connected here, me with my clan, he a fringe relation who had nothing to offer, who was at the edge of every gathering, saying little and always watching.

That evening, I decided to take stock of what I had for *The Human Zoo*. I wanted to have something to show for my few months here, if not for my editor, then for myself. That conversation with my husband had struck a nerve. He was wrong about my requiring a robust clothing budget, but I did need to feed myself. If, miraculously, the book did well, it would buy me my freedom or at least more time to figure things out. I flipped through my notebook, which was filled with little outlines, names and dates, clipped bits of Philippine history. I had also jotted in some random pseudophilosophical musings including: *What is it to be other? If one is other, what is the thing that is not? Check Achebe on* Heart of Darkness. The inspiration for all of this, Timicheg, was just a historical figure, not yet even a character. And he certainly did not justify the three-hundred-odd pages of writing necessary for the book. I still didn't know how I would organize the material, but there were a few models I admired. I'd been looking over *King Leopold's Ghost*, by Adam Hochschild. Hochschild brought the characters to life and that's what I needed to do. But I kept circling back to a central problem, which was how to make the book necessary to an American reading public. At this point, had I been back in the States, I would have called Ann and asked her to take me to lunch. We would have had a meal of branzino and wilted spinach, washed it down with a glass of Sancerre, and this would have reminded me that I was actually a writer, because writers were people who had lunch with editors, and thus fortified, I would have plowed on. Instead, I had summoned Ann's voice, imagining what she might say to me. I was reminded of that Pico Iyer book, *The Man Within My Head*, in which the writer had claimed to be in constant dialogue with Graham Greene. Initially, I had tried to summon Greene, but he was very cynical. And had nothing much to say to me. The voice of my editor, however, once conjured, had several opinions.

Christina, what is the book about?

Well, you know that. It's about Timicheg.

But you've written almost nothing about him. I can't see him. What is he like?

There isn't a whole lot of information on Timicheg. He lived and then he died and then the Belgians named a tunnel after him.

That's a very short book. What is it really about?

I suppose it's about what killed him.

Pneumonia?

No. I think America killed him, that the Americans sold him this idea of advancement and then abandoned him.

Good. Because readers will want to hear about the bad deeds of their forebears in order to think they're better. Write it in a way that will make forward-thinking Americans feel good about themselves.

Of course my editor hadn't actually said that and wouldn't have. But I had used her to give voice to my deep insecurities about writing anything set in the Philippines for an American audience. I had known people who, when they learned of my Filipino background, launched into ad hoc speeches about the tragedy of human trafficking, or declared that they were really hoping to get a Filipino housemaid, or commented on how lucky I was that my mother had married an American. It was as if the United States still needed the Philippines to be recognizable but savage in the same way that *Heart of Darkness* needed Africa to make Europe seem enlightened. It was as if the human zoos had accomplished their purpose and Schneidewind had won.

Maybe you can make this a love story, said my editor, sounding more like herself. *Give it a happy ending.*

And then Graham Greene chimed in and said, *Love guarantees a complicated ending because the element of the personal and irrational balanced against the machine of history is what makes a book worth reading. Morality is the spine of fiction, even if it is most often twisted and deformed.*

Morality? Love? I kept compiling notes.

XV

It was a Friday and Tita Dom's daughter, Ali, had arranged tickets for us to go see a play. Her sorority was sponsoring it and all the family members who were willing to go see things—an anemic percentage—were in the minivan headed to Malate. As the writer in the family, I was an obvious participant, as were Tonio, Tita Dom's youngest son, his wife, Meli, and their son, Luke, who lived next door to Tita Dom and were assumed to show up at anything she sponsored. Ali would be there with a few friends from work as her husband and kids were not people willing to go see things. A late-season typhoon had made landfall to the north and Manila was being pounded with rain. Tita Dom asked Mannie if he thought that the streets would be flooded. I thought it pretty likely that they would be. As we left the Scout area, the water was accumulating, and that area was at a higher elevation than most of Manila.

"I have to tell you," said Tita Dom, breaking into a giggle, "that I've invited your best friend."

"My best friend?" I sighed. "Laird?"

She nodded.

"Why?"

"I had an extra ticket. Ali bought one for your tita Rosa, and you know she hates plays."

"Everyone knows Tita Rosa hates plays. Why did Ali buy her a ticket?"

"Because your tita Rosa would have been offended if she hadn't."

That was true.

"Tita Dom, you are as bad as Tita Rosa. I could have brought Inchoy."

"Remi called me this morning and asked me what I was doing, and then she was saying that Laird would like to go to a play, and you know, one thing led to another." She gave me a guilty look. "What could I say? Laird is staying in Malate. Besides, they'll be singing and dancing around, so you won't have to talk to him."

"Singing? Is this a musical?"

Tonio and Meli started giggling and Tita Dom joined in. They were all guilty.

"Oh, for pity's sake," I said. "Fine."

Luke looked confused. He was only ten and didn't know about my musical aversion. "Can we go to Jollibee?" he asked.

"Sure," said Tita Dom, "but just the drive-through. I don't think we have time to stop and eat." We had allotted the usual two hours, but with the reliable traffic and the exceptional rain, we could be cutting it close. A Jollibee was soon located and after the standard order, which I yelled into the speaker in the shelter of a concrete overhang, we returned to the pounding rain of the street and the ceaseless splashing made by the tires as they pulled through the inches-deep water. My aunt, paper bag in hand, tendered the burgers.

The play, now revealed to be a musical, was *Obra ni Juan*, about the artist Juan Luna, who, in addition to painting and fomenting revolution, was also known for having murdered his wife. Juan Luna's most famous painting was *Spoliarium*, a work that had won him the gold medal in the Madrid Exposiciones in 1884. Another painting, *Peuple et Rois*, was posthumously entered in the Saint Louis Exposition, where it earned a gold medal, while around the corner, the Bontoc were eating dog—at regular hours—for tourists. I wondered how the play—no, musical—was going to handle the fact that Juan Luna was both a national hero and a murderer. I wondered if it would be a comedy.

Mannie pulled the minivan into the covered drive in front of the auditorium and we spilled out like soldiers from a helicopter. The rain was so heavy that you couldn't make out the drops, and its pounding on the roof and exercising of the gutters was deafening. "Ay naku!" exclaimed my aunt. We pressed into the crowded lobby, which was slowly emptying into the auditorium.

"Do you see Laird?" asked Tita Dom.

"No. Let's leave a ticket for him at the desk?" I said. "We'll say to give it to the tall, joyless Fil-Am."

"Okay," said Meli. She took a ticket from my tita Dom and headed to a table, where two polished college girls sat looking excited and poised and wholly without purpose.

"I guess we should find our seats," said Tita Dom.

Before the show could begin, a number of preliminary actions had to be dispensed with. First, we had to stand to sing the national anthem. I knew all the words and sang loudly, much to the amusement of Tonio, who was in the seat beside mine. Next, we had to pray, which I did solemnly. Next, we had to see who of merit was in attendance: a cabinet member, a judge, and the minister of education, who stood as their names were called, waving around with pageant-queen smiles.

"Laird should really be here," said Tonio, "to meet the minister of education."

"Why would Laird meet the minister of education?" I asked.

"Isn't he the type who likes to meet people?"

I supposed that this was true. Finally, the lights went down and with a swelling of music, the actors made their way onto the stage. My Tagalog was not really up to the task of following all the action. I spent the first act wondering who that guy always onstage with Juan Luna was supposed to be, then figured out—through some miracle of osmotic comprehension—that he was also Juan Luna: there was good Juan, the one who painted and loved art, and bad Juan, the one who killed people. My tita Dom, flanked on one side by Ali and her friends, made it to the start of the second act and then, despite the volume of the singing, fell asleep. Beside her was the empty seat, saved for Laird, who had failed to make an appearance. When the lights came back up and she startled awake, her first action was to check that empty space.

On the way home, the cars plowed along, tires half submerged in the road that was now a river. Tita Dom kept apologizing to Mannie, who kept saying it was okay, but we were all nervous that the engine would quit and we would get stranded.

All around us, people were trying to find their way home. A tricycle driver in a garbage bag poncho pushed his vehicle up the street. Women under disintegrating umbrellas took delicate steps through the ankle-deep water. The light was fractured and then smeared into streaks on the windshield: with each beat of the wipers, there was a moment of clarity that was quickly obscured by rain.

Tita Dom dug around in her purse and found a bag of Choc Nut, which she opened and passed to Luke. "I wonder why Laird didn't show up."

"Did he say he was definitely coming?" I asked.

"Remi said he would join us for sure," she said. "She said he was on a trip somewhere, but he was getting back around noon. She thought there was plenty of time for him to get to the play."

"Maybe the typhoon made it hard to travel," said Tonio, which seemed like a good explanation.

I spent that night at Tita Dom's house because any more driving, even if it was not that far, seemed unwise. She rifled through the guest room closet and produced a floral shift. There must have been a hundred of these dresses, laundered and folded, waiting in closets all around Manila for me to show up and wear them. I was exhausted, but my adrenaline was high after the ride, and I had a hard time falling asleep. I switched on the light. On a shelf packed with notebooks, accounting ledgers, folders, and papers, there was an old copy of *Jonathan Livingston Seagull* and a paperback of *Love Story*, the cover a photograph of Ali MacGraw and Ryan O'Neal. Crammed alongside were eight books by the motivational writer Og Mandino, who must have motivated, at some point, some member of my family. A leatherette-bound copy of *War and Peace* kept strange company with the other books. I took it off the shelf and opened it. The onionskin pages fluttered open, revealing the tiniest of print and a fresh smell at odds with the general dampness that had worked its way into the other volumes. I decided on *Jonathan Livingston Seagull*, which I'd already read—this exact same copy—some thirty-five years earlier, and after the first few pages of Jonathan's dissatisfaction with the seagull life, I fell into a restless sleep.

XVI

I'd breakfasted with my tita Dom, pan de sal and lansones, and by the time I made it back to my tita Rosa's house, it was almost time for lunch. The weather had cleared and the air seemed washed, the storm of the previous night more in the realm of nightmares than weather.

"Do you know who missed you last night?" said Tita Rosa, walking out of the kitchen. To answer her own question she gestured dramatically down at her side. Tito Iñigo was wagging his tail with such energy that his whole rear end was wagging too. He ran over and I reached down to pat him. "I can't take this dog in the house anymore. It's over. You know, he urinated on your tito Ben's leg."

"What did Tito Ben say?"

"He was taking a nap. I thought it better not to wake him." She thought for a minute. "And then I forgot to tell him." Tita Rosa got a stern look on her face. "Enjoy him while you can. I'm giving him to my chicken suki in the market. She needs a dog to keep away the rats."

"You can't do that," I said. "She'll feed him chicken bones and it'll kill him."

"He's a Filipino dog, Ting. That is their life."

"But he's already ruined. We've been feeding him hamburger and he sleeps on a blanket."

"And he urinates on the blanket. And on people."

"I'm going to train him," I said. I picked him up. He looked nervous, understanding that his life was in the balance.

"You can't train him."

"Why not?"

"He's a Filipino dog. You can't train Filipino dogs."

"Give me three weeks." I said. I set the dog back on the floor. "Five hundred pesos says I can train him." What I was really saying was that Tito Iñigo wasn't doomed, that given the advantages of an American dog, Tito Iñigo would perform equally. On some level, my aunt understood this. She knew I was frustrated by her habit of sorting all dilemmas into *how things just were* and *how they would never be*. But she also knew that this was the correct way to think.

"Fine, three weeks, no accidents," she said. "But it's easy money for me." Tita Rosa grabbed my elbow and started steering me into the kitchen, leaning heavily against me. "Oh, I am forgetting," she said, stopping. "Have you heard from Laird?"

"No. Why would I hear from Laird?"

"Remi telephoned me. Laird hasn't come home and there's still no word from him."

"He wasn't at the play. It must be the weather. Tita Dom said he was out of town."

"He was. His plane was delayed, but it landed this morning. He didn't show up for the flight."

"Where was the flight from?"

"Zamboanga," said my aunt. I helped her settle into a wicker chair. "What would he be doing in Mindanao?"

"I don't know. Tita Dom and I saw him going into the *Philippine Telegraph* offices last week. Maybe they know something."

"Why didn't you ask him what he was doing?"

"We saw him from the window at Dad's." An element of the ominous had entered this narrative. Something was off—or was this just me being suspicious of Laird? I wasn't sure. "Tell Tita Remi to call the offices of the *Philippine Telegraph*. Maybe Laird was on assignment."

"I'll give Remi's number to you and you can fill her in."

I really did not want to get involved, but I also knew that refusing the request of a woman in her tenth decade was unacceptable. "Let me ask some people, Tita, but I can't promise you I'll learn anything."

Tito Iñigo, like most dogs, was happy outside. He enthusiastically urinated on a plant and on the tire of my aunt's car and then began trotting down the drive to find more places to empty himself, intrigued by the praise each time he lifted his leg. I followed, lit cigarette in hand. Laird must have been writing something for someone, but why would the *Philippine Telegraph* send him to Zamboanga when they had a slew of seasoned journalists who spoke English, Tagalog, and the difficult-to-master Chavacano—a Spanish creole wrestled into its own language through the mangle of Cebuano—as well as Cebuano itself? Zamboanga was the largest city in the Muslim-dominated part of Mindanao, but Davao was the largest city on the island. Zamboanga had a branch of the Jesuit university, Ateneo, and for a time—roughly five years—my tito Ben had lived there. Famously, no one in my family had visited him. Because people did not travel to that area.

The wealthy Muslims and Catholics in the Bangsamoro had learned to get along but were now plagued by terrorist groups. The ISIS-affiliated Abu Sayyaf was the most violent of these. Their recent attempt to establish a califate in the city of Marawi had resulted in the five-month siege that eventually routed the attempt but also ground the city into rubble. All of Mindanao was now under martial law.

Over twenty journalists, Filipino and foreign, as well as a slew of missionaries, bird-watchers, tourists, and one unfortunate Malaysian gecko trader had been kidnapped by Abu Sayyaf in the past two decades. When Abu Sayyaf's demands for ransom were not met—and on occasion when they were—they beheaded people.

Laird must have known all this and more. What had happened to him? He was not my responsibility, but as I cast an eye to the top of the stairs where my tita Rosa was standing, looking out across her domain—the driveway, the fountain, the stand of orchids, and then me, I knew it was my American self that had stated that: in the Philippines, everyone was responsible for everyone else.

I started with Inchoy, but he did not pick up, so I sent him a text. Next, I tried Zackito, who was at that moment shopping for a debut gift for his niece at the Robinsons in Padre Faura. "I don't know anyone at the *Telegraph*," said Zackito. "But I remember at that party at Adriatico, your cousin was talking to José Martin, and even if he doesn't know where your cousin is now, he's the man to find out, especially in Mindanao." Zackito had his number handy and sent it to me.

I left a message for José Martin and headed back up the stairs with Tito Iñigo in tow. Tita Rosa was back at her desk, looking despondently into the air before her.

"Well?" she said.

"I called a couple of people. Let's see if they know."

Tita Rosa nodded grimly.

"Did you check with Jim?" I asked.

"Carmi's calling him." Tita Rosa's face crumpled in confusion. "This is why Filipinos should not go to America. It deranges them. Why would Laird go to Mindanao?"

I took the seat on the opposite side of the desk. "Right now, you have to stop worrying and do what you're good at."

"What can I do, at this age?" She held my gaze with her eyes, which were wise but, I now noticed, were growing milky with cataracts.

"This," I said. I took the rosary beads from the corner of the tabletop and poured them into her hands. "It's Friday. Sorrowful Mysteries."

She looked at the beads but did not move. She was really worried. I took the rosary back from her. "All right, Tita, I'll start. Agony in the Garden." And I launched into the first Our Father.

Wednesday evening came and there was still no word on Laird. We were gathered at my tita Rosa's with Tito Ben and Tita Dom for our traditional post-Mass meal, and despite the fact that my aunt's cook had made kare kare, a family favorite, the mood was subdued.

"I knew something was wrong when Laird didn't show up for the play," said Tita Dom. "I knew it."

We were mostly quiet through dinner. Tito Ben was wearing shorts, which I found unusual, and when I questioned him about it, he said something cryptic about getting old and going to the bathroom being difficult in pants. Tito Iñigo was sitting by his leg, looking a touch guilty.

I asked, "What did Remi say Laird was doing in Mindanao?"

"I don't know. Visiting some new friends. Seeing the Philippines. Laird is not one for sharing." My tita Rosa shook her head. "Remi said he was so reserved, always reading in his room or insisting on taking a taxi and not the driver. She didn't know what he was doing all the time, and he made it hard to ask." She pushed her plate, half the food uneaten, to the center of table. "He was like an American. She couldn't ask him things."

Late that evening, as I was getting ready for bed, I got a call. It was José Martin. I'd been wondering when he was going to get back to me.

"Ting," he said. "I don't have anything for you. I don't know anyone at the *Telegraph*. You know that's Gumboc's paper."

"It was worth a shot." I sighed. "Look, can you keep an eye out? I'm not close to Laird Bontotot, but he is a relative, and my tita's worried. This feels like it could be developing into a news story."

"Yeah, well, that is definitely a possibility."

"Can you let me know?"

"You scratch my back . . ."

This surprised me. "What could I possibly have that you might want?"

"Aren't you in thick with Chet Rey?"

"I know him."

"Yeah, that's sort of what I heard, but not really." He laughed.

Now I was curious. "Why would Chet be of interest to you?"

"Okay, Ting. Something called Eagle's Nest keeps coming up in connection with Rocco Basilang. It's in his emails."

"Rocco's emails?" I wondered who had managed to hack into Rocco's account. "It's got to be some construction deal. Why is that suspicious?"

"Only because no details are there. Nothing. Just references to Eagle's Nest that circulate with some powerful players, Chet included."

"How do you know he's not investing in gambling or brothels? Ten years ago, Chet had all those deals going down in Macao. Maybe it's drugs?"

"It's not drugs, Ting."

"How can you be so sure?"

"Because in one of the emails, it goes straight to Gumboc." Gumboc passionately hated drugs and would never have involved himself in a drug-related venture. "I'm sure it was sent accidentally through the wrong account, so it's just good luck that I found out that Gumboc's connected. If I knew Chet's involvement—"

"José Martin, I don't spy on people. I find it bizarre that you would ask me to."

He chuckled to himself. "So you don't want to speak against your own. I get it. But you could do some good. Don't you want to be more than the aging beauty queen who comes back to Manila and then has Chet Rey following her around like a puppy dog?" He was teasing me.

"I'm actually fine with that," I said. "I understand you're chasing a story, so I'll forgive your asking, because I'm sure there's nothing there. When Eagle's Nest reveals itself to be the hotel or nightclub or elite gambling circle that it most definitely is, I will let you know, so that you don't lose sleep."

José Martin hadn't given up but knew now was not the time to press me. "Sige," he said. "So your cousin . . ."

"Sort-of cousin," I corrected him, "Laird Bontotot. Do you think I should be concerned?"

"What do you think? One minute he's here; the next he's gone. And last thing we know, he was headed for Marawi."

"That's news to me," I said.

"I have to verify it," said José Martin. "But that's the rumor."

And then I remembered. "I saw Laird talking to Rocco a few weeks ago. It was outside a bar in Rockwell. Do you think there's a connection?"

José Martin was quiet for a moment. "Why was he meeting Rocco?"

"I think he wanted to write a story about infrastructure and the poor."

"Which would be good for foreign investment in Basilang's projects. He's always trying to get coverage for his shit."

This was true.

"Look, Ting, I have to go. I know your number and you know mine." And then he rang off.

Eagle's Nest sounded familiar, but it was probably nothing. Even the bit about Rocco's emails could have been made up. José Martin was just digging, which is what journalists did, and was being opportunistic because I'd asked him a favor. I had heard Chet mention Eagle's Nest on the phone, one of the calls that he took on the way out from whichever room I had happened to be standing in. But Chet didn't tell me anything about his business dealings, which could have been all legal or all illegal but were likely some combination. And to be honest, I wasn't sure I wanted to know.

A few days passed, but there was no news. Laird's absence was becoming just another factor in our daily lives, another topic of conversation that we polished like a stone without effecting any change. I understood that Tita Remi was doing what she could, but the talk in my family centered on the absence of Laird's family. Why were these people leaving the task of finding their son to his future in-laws? We concluded that Laird's family probably didn't have the money to buy plane tickets to the Philippines, which were close to two thousand dollars when purchased near time of travel. And maybe he had a pattern of disappearing. Maybe there was no reason to worry.

My phone rang then, and I hoped it was José Martin calling back, but it was Chet.

"I'm in the neighborhood," he said.

"Are you outside the front door?"

"No," said Chet. I heard the front door swing open. "You know what I want to eat?" he said.

I walked into the hallway, still carrying my phone, and rang off. Chet smiled. I was, for once, actually dressed in a decent pair of pants and a nice shirt. I was showered. "What?" I asked.

"I want steak."

"Are you inviting me to lunch? Or are you just stating a fact?"

"Sure. Where should we go?"

"Do we have to go somewhere? Why don't we just send Beng to the market to buy steaks? My aunt's cook is good."

Chet checked his watch. It was almost 11:00 a.m. "Too late for good steak at Kamuning. It will all be sold. I have an idea. We should go to Rockwell and convince my friend Tati to give me a tomahawk."

Chet's friend Tati owned one of the newly hip restaurants in Makati, and it was famed for its tomahawk steaks, which were pricey but also fed four people.

"So who's going to cook it?"

"I am," said Chet.

There was no one at the apartment. The maid and cook, who had been there the previous time I'd visited, had been called back to Chet's house in Dasmariñas.

Chet said, "C. G. has something going on with her batch mates and asked to borrow them for the afternoon." He set a cast-iron pan on the stove and the gas flared to life beneath it. His head cocked to one side and then the other. The steak rested in its paper on the countertop, a hefty chunk of glistening meat anchored to a plank of bone. He poured some corn oil into the pan and then olive oil. He watched as the oil heated.

"Aren't you going to put the steak in?"

"Not yet." Chet seemed amused. "Ting, don't you know how to cook?"

"No."

"How is that possible when you've been living in the States all this time?"

"I live in New York. And my husband can cook."

Chet salted the steak heavily, flipped it, and then salted the other side.

"Chet?" I asked.

"What?"

"Are you involved in anything crazy?"

"Yeah. You."

"That's not what I mean."

He gave me a questioning look.

"It's just, a journalist friend of mine was asking about you, some business deal . . . with Gumboc?"

Chet sighed, shaking his head. "Ting, I'm involved in all kinds of stuff. And you don't need to know about it. And you know who really doesn't need to know about it? Your journalist friend. But just so you know, I don't have a business deal with Gumboc. But I make a point of keeping my dealings private. I never discuss my business, not with anyone, not even C. G. And we'll never talk about this sort of thing, not because I like to keep things from you, but I have a reputation for keeping my business to myself and you know why?"

I knew the answer. "Because it keeps the people close to you safe."

"That's right. You don't know, and that makes you useless to people who want to know."

There was some wisdom in this.

Chet's phone began ringing. He picked up immediately. "Yeah," he said. "Yeah, yeah. Hold on—" He leveled a look at me and meeting it, bored, resigned, I left the kitchen. I heard him say, "I can't go to Baguio until Tuesday." And: "I don't care who's asking. If I can't go, I can't go. There's stuff going on."

In the living room, Chet had replaced the Ventura painting with the Alarcon, his choice.

From the kitchen I could hear the steak sizzling in the pan. The smell of frying meat, almost dizzying as it reminded me of my hunger, would better accompany the Ventura.

I placed a chair by the wall and took off my shoes. The painting was not heavy and once I'd managed to unhook the wire from which it hung, I could easily put it on the floor. I had replaced the Alarcon with the Ventura and was just about to step off the chair when I heard Chet, who must have abandoned the steak, clearing his throat dramatically. I looked at him from the chair.

"I was just—"

"I know what you're doing," he said.

"You can put the Alarcon back."

"Why would I do that?" He walked over and extended his hand to help me, and I stepped down from the chair. His hand was shaking, an obvious tremor.

"Why are you shaking?"

"Why are your shoes off?"

"I didn't want to get dirt on the chair."

I thought to ask after the steak but couldn't bring myself to. Chet was still holding my hand. He breathed deeply in his throat but didn't move. I was losing track of time and wasn't sure how to bring the moment to a close. I remembered what it was like to kiss him but then immediately doubted the memory. It was so very long ago and so many kisses had interrupted whatever had been shared between us. I wanted to say something funny, to call attention to the fact that all the blood was draining from my hand, that my shoulder was growing stiff. I thought I could draw his attention to the paintings, to talk about colonialism and brushstrokes and patricide. But I couldn't speak. I wondered what emotional dependence on Chet had been developing inside of me, this inconvenient love that I had been refusing to acknowledge as anything but the sentimental crush of a bored woman. And then I felt as if I'd stepped beside myself. I witnessed my hand released from his, moving to his face, my other hand rising to mirror it, and then I was kissing Chet, not passionately, but with such excruciatingly slow determination that the gesture seemed to be a seal of Shakespearian proportion. I pulled back and finally, finding my voice, said, "The steak."

XVII

Was it Chet? Or did I just not want to go back to the States? Some lawyer was hammering out a divorce agreement, and although I knew intellectually that this was something that needed to be done, a part of me felt all the legal stuff was overkill, somehow irrelevant. Although I'd only been gone a few months, my American life seemed unreal, a world of meeting women for cocktails, and habits, like going to the gym for yoga, rituals I no longer had. When I tried to picture New York, I thought of people swearing loudly on the street as if scripted by Scorsese and then wondered if I was actually remembering a Scorsese film.

I had just packed a couple of books and was winding up my laptop charger when Tita Rosa appeared at my door, waving some bills in my direction. "Take it," she said.

I took the money and counted. "It's five hundred pesos. What's this for?"

"Your dog. Three weeks without an accident. I keep my promises."

"That was a joke," I said. "You can keep your money, so long as you remember that sometimes I am right."

"So it was a joke?" She laughed wryly. "Buy something funny. You have to keep the money. It's already in my accounting." Tita Rosa looked at my bag and gave me a once-over, noting I was dressed to go out. "Where are you going?"

"I'm going to Chet's."

She shook her head.

"I thought you liked Chet."

"Who doesn't like Chet?"

"I'm working on my book and the apartment has really good internet," I said.

"What's wrong with the internet at Santa Tomas?"

"The aircon in the library is weak," I lied. I picked up my bag. "Besides, Chet isn't even there."

My aunt raised an eyebrow, unconvinced. "Well, as long as you know what you're doing." Which she knew for a fact I did not. "Have you asked Chet about Laird?"

"I have asked everyone about Laird, including Chet, and no one knows what happened to him. What did the American embassy say?"

There had been some meeting between Tita Remi and her family and an agent the day before.

"They said that all American citizens had been warned not to go to Mindanao."

"Remember, Tita," I said. "We know hardly anything about Laird. What if he joined the New People's Army or some other fringe group? People do that sort of thing." I actually didn't know if people did or even what fringe groups were operating in the region other than Abu Sayyaf, but it was worth considering.

She said, "But he's engaged to be married."

"Then why was he here?"

Chet's apartment at this time of day was very quiet. I had my books sprawled across the dining table and an espresso, made with the brand-new Italian machine that had appeared in the kitchen. Perhaps I could spend more time on headhunting. Without this and the human zoo, the Bontoc were just an ordinary tribe of brown people in loincloths, planting rice and hunting deer. Headhunting, a practice both religious and social, was basically a system of revenge. A Bontoc tribe would go on a mission to a Kalinga tribe to collect heads as restitution for an earlier assault that had resulted in the loss of heads, and this "settling" would go on and on. Given the practice, it was surprising that the males in these tribes hadn't evolved into a shorter gender that terminated in a set of shoulders. But headhunting wasn't always simple retribution. There was liget, an emotion that existed only among the headhunting tribes. Liget was a form of grief that laid one bare, that could be unburdened only through fearsome violence. Liget was an energized sorrow that led one to take a head.

My laptop was open to an intimidating, blank document—an accusation of smooth, pixelated white—that even the curious practice of headhunting seemed incapable of marring.

Having given up on my work for the day, I was currently using the good Wi-Fi to stream the latest season of *Poldark* as I flipped through a thick compendium of fabric samples. I could hear the cook and the maid chattering quietly as a soap opera played in the kitchen. Chet had wanted drapes in shades of beige, which he said would look natural, but the apartment, with its proscribed layout and expanse of glass, already inclined to the office-like. Curtains could warm the place up, although I did wonder why he needed curtains at all. The apartment was up in the clouds and thus, gloriously isolated.

When the phone rang, I thought it had to be Chet telling me that he wasn't going to be back in time for dinner. But it was Zackito.

"Zacky, what are you up to?"

"Ting," he said. "Where are you?"

"I'm at Chet's. Why? What's wrong?"

"Turn on the TV now. Channel Four."

"Give me a minute." The remote bristled with mysterious buttons, but I managed to navigate to Channel 4. The rapid-fire news story was difficult for me to follow. The police had discovered a body, another EJK. The body was lying on its back, a tall, thin person but hard to identify because the head had been wrapped entirely in yellow tape. Someone had taken the time to wrap that person's head so neatly that it looked more like a hive than a head. I listened hard, listening also to Zackito's breathing on the other end of the line—but all I could understand was the much repeated "droga," drugs, and then a name, Sebastiano Pagangpang.

"Zack," I said. "Who is Sebastiano Pagangpang?"

Then I saw the hand lying beside the body—the long fingers curled up and nails lacquered perfectly in a dark, rich shade of purple.

"Oh my God," I said. "Where are you?"

"I'm in Malate."

"Does Inchoy know?"

"I don't know. I was hoping you were at your tita's and could get to him."

"Shit." I wasn't crying. I was shaking. "What do we do?"

"Call Chet."

"Right. Right. I'll call him. Are you going to Inchoy's?"

"I have a Grab booked but it's another twenty minutes. I won't be there for at least an hour and a half. I don't know how you'll get a car in Makati."

Bibo. Bibo. Bibo. What have they done to you? I was fumbling with my phone but finally managed to enter Tita Rosa's number. First I got Beng, and after what seemed like a century but was probably only a few seconds, I got Tita Rosa on the line. "Tita, where's Mannie?"

"Mannie? He's taking your tita Dom for her checkup. Why?"

"I need a ride. I'm in Makati."

"Oh. You're in Makati. Call Carmi. She's there dropping Miggie at her French lesson. If you call now, you might catch her."

"Okay. I'll do that."

"Ting, what's wrong?"

"I'm fine. I just need to get to Inchoy."

"Why?"

"Long story."

Although it was a short story.

As we drove the two hours to get to Scout Castor, I wondered if I would survive the air-conditioning purring from the vents of Carmi's car, dropping the temperature to a Kelvin stillness. I'd been concerned that I wouldn't be able to manage small talk, but Carmi was fielding a business deal that was spiraling into a complete disaster. She punched angry texts into her phone and then placed a call to yell about a building permit that had been approved weeks earlier, now mysteriously withdrawn by some ignorant peon. Carmi took a deep breath, looking out the window as a cigarette vendor on the sidewalk, and on foot, overtook us. "Sorry, Ting. I should be spending more time with you. I'm going to my costuera tomorrow. Do you want to join? I have a really nice piece of silk that I don't know what to do with. It's a good color for you. You could have a dress made."

"Not tomorrow, but maybe later on."

"Ting," she said. "Are you all right? You look kind of sick."

"I'm just tired," I said. "I didn't sleep well last night." I didn't want to tell her because I didn't want to hear myself telling someone about Bibo. I was barely holding it together as it was and knew that Inchoy needed me, that to fall apart would be callous and irresponsible.

"Okay," she said. "You should try to nap." Carmi most likely assumed I was having Chet-related problems that I didn't want to share. Another text pinged in, and this one seemed less contentious, although—by her expression—disappointing. "Do you know how to play mahjong?" she asked. "We need another person for Saturday."

Later she asked me if I was hungry, if I wanted to pass by Jollibee.

When we finally pulled up in front of Inchoy's house, I realized that despite my hurry to get there, I was now filled with dread. A small yellow Toyota pulled up and I was relieved to see Zackito get out. He took a handkerchief and wiped his forehead, turning to look up the street just to delay the inevitable but saw me there instead. As I stepped out of the car, I realized I'd forgotten to change my shoes and was still wearing my slippers.

"Did you call Chet?" he asked.

"He's coming."

We stood by Inchoy's gate, the flat steel expanse of it, the curled spikes at the top. On the other side a dog had started barking and in response a neighbor's rooster, impervious to time of day, began to crow. Zackito raised his hand, hesitated, and then knocked.

The maid was soon pulling the bolt and then Zackito and I were standing in Inchoy's entryway beside the Santo Niño, an extravagant Infant of Prague in rich robes and long Restoration hair, its gentle fingers raised in benediction, all contained in a glass dome. The statue was old and valuable, but I knew that Inchoy detested it, that his mother talked to it as if this child Jesus were her confidant, the one who agreed with all of her decisions. Inchoy would have preferred to have standing at his door one of those ferocious Ifugao guardians, carved from ancient wood, someone to protect him and his loved ones, someone who would do better than this ridiculous doll.

Inchoy was wearing shorts and a T-shirt that had a smiling old woman's face on it above "Happy Birthday Mommy!" It wasn't his mommy but probably a cousin's, the T-shirt a remnant party favor.

"Oh," he said when he saw us. "Did we have a plan?"

"No," said Zackito.

A moment passed.

"Do you want a Coke?" Inchoy looked over to the table and we were moving slowly in that direction when the door banged open, startling us all. It was Chet. He saw our solemn faces and without saying anything went straight to Inchoy and grabbed him in a fierce hug.

"Paré," he said. "I am so sorry."

I knew where Inchoy's thoughts were going. Chet was not a hugger and our somber demeanor attested to the fact that Inchoy was about to face intolerable grief. He could read the signs, and the problem with having an intellect as sharp and sensitive and quick as Inchoy's was that he could not shelter from the truth for long.

Inchoy was ungodly still. Finally he said, "There is a mistake," his voice muffled by Chet's embrace.

"It's on Channel Four," said Zackito. "She's been identified."

"There is a mistake," Inchoy repeated, but this repetition told me that he at least knew the situation. How could he not? Inchoy had been worried for over a year. Inchoy, of course, had tried to reach Bibo, but the phone had not been answered. Inchoy had then called Bibo's mother, but when she had picked up the phone, her voice uncharacteristically strangled with pain, Inchoy had hung up on her.

I think maybe an hour passed while Inchoy asked short questions, and we responded. The news had identified Sebastiano Pagangpang. We didn't think anyone had been arrested. Together, we watched the story repeated on the news cycle, the closeup of Bibo's hand. I was struggling with my own grief but knew that Inchoy's was greater. Inchoy's mother stood looking from the kitchen door, wondering what had occasioned such a joyless assembly.

The tears and wailing came later. Inchoy's mother kept asking what was wrong, but all we could do was say that a friend had died and try to eat the very expensive sliced ham that she offered us, sweet and succulent, a ham that I knew was good, but in my mouth at that moment, as I chewed it into pulp, was almost inedible.

XVIII

I spent the next few days in a stupor. I would wake in the middle of the night and wonder why I was no longer asleep and then remember. Not one for tears, I didn't have that release. Rather I stayed in bed with my mind racing, trying to fix the past, wondering what we could have done differently—which would occupy the minutes but accomplish nothing else. My tita Rosa had noticed my drop in appetite, the general malaise, but I was not forthcoming and there was much on her mind. She knew a friend had died, which was all I told her. Bibo's identity was still a secret.

Ten days had passed since Laird had gone missing and Tita Remi was getting desperate. How could he vanish without a trace? Tito Ben contacted people he knew at Ateneo de Zamboanga, but what would they know? They were just priests teaching Lacan in English to the Chavacano-speaking, uniformed youth of the south. Unless Laird had presented himself in the rectory or tried to eat at the cafeteria or shown up for Mass, how would they have seen him?

If Abu Sayyaf had kidnapped him, why hadn't they asked for a ransom? Laird had made the news and the photograph of him taken at Jim and Cha Cha's house was being circulated, one of many stories being broadcast across the airwaves. I wondered when the foreign press would pick it up and if that would pressure someone to do something. Would this reach the top? Would the United States become involved, or would this just be another strange disappearance, a Filipino *Picnic at Hanging Rock* with Laird slowly stepping across a stream and into oblivion.

Tita Rosa was arranging her papers to make one of her frequent trips to the bank. She sifted through the stacks on her desk, assembling the files. "Ting, can you see the rubber bands? I think they're on the shelf."

I handed her the nest of bands and sat on the rocker. I picked up Tito Iñigo and seated him on my lap. Tita Rosa started to bundle pesos, dropping them in a woven straw shopping bag. "You know his parents are coming."

"Whose parents?"

"Ay dios mio. Whose parents? Laird's."

"Do you think he's dead?"

"What use is thinking like that? He's in the hands of God somewhere. Maybe he was hiking and fell. Isn't that what crazy Americans do? Go walking all over the place by themselves where there isn't a path, falling into ravines, breaking their legs?"

"That is what they do." I patted Tito Iñigo's head.

She looked at me with some impatience. "Why are you so depressed? Who was this friend of Inchoy's?"

"No one important. Just someone I liked." My aunt didn't know that Inchoy was gay, and I was hesitant to talk about Bibo to someone so skilled at reading between the lines.

"And how did he die?"

"Accident."

"Accident? Why so mysterious? Did he kill himself?"

"They're still figuring it out," I said, which was both true and untrue. "I don't have any black and I have to go to the wake today."

"Get a dress from Carmi. If you go right now you can catch her before she leaves for Punta Fuego."

The car ride to the wake in Tondo was going to take the requisite two hours. The Grab driver was playing a soap opera on the radio, which offered its usual diet of despair and hope. I listened to how Mario was missing his wife, who had gone to Dubai and hadn't written him in three weeks. Their child was sick and people were trying to figure out how to reach her. A neighborhood girl had been discovered while selling flowers on the street and was now going to be an actress. That much I could understand.

I texted Chet, first on his main phone line and then, when he didn't get back to me, on the private number, which was used only by me and C. G.

Ask your people about Laird.

I already did.

Ask again.

A policeman was standing in the middle of the traffic, blowing his whistle and waving. I remembered my tita Dom telling me that when the pope had visited the year before, the police were out in full force and had been instructed to wear diapers because they were not allowed to leave their posts for any reason. She had told me how you could see their pants were a bit too snug and how they had all looked humiliated, as if they knew that everyone knew, because everyone did.

The phone buzzed. It was another text from Chet. He was, of course, running late.

When we reached our destination, the driver of the Grab asked me if I was sure this was where I had to be. We were bordering a slum. A skinny cat with a kinked tail was slinking around a pile of trash. In my black silk dress and heavy pearls, I imagined I looked photoshopped in. I knew that I would be a spectacle attired like this but also that Bibo would have wanted me to dress up, to show respect for her and her family.

The wake was set up in a small room, down three crumbling concrete steps flanked on each side by caged roosters. Mariah Carey, Bibo's favorite singer, was playing. Relatives were crowded on plastic chairs. The room opened into a small garden where a table was set with food. Two women stood to serve, waving laconically to keep the flies off the vats of adobo and kare kare. A square table had been set inside and at this table were cards and money and men gambling with focus. They were playing pusoy. The family would take a portion of the proceeds to pay for the funeral, which was one way the poor raised money to bury their dead. At the back of the room was the coffin, white and open, by which Inchoy sat, collapsed, his hands folded in his lap, his eyes puffed and unfocused. He was not facing the coffin but rather seated beside it, as if Bibo were napping or ill in bed and Inchoy keeping watch. Beside him was a woman with gray hair fanned around her shoulders, her lips pursed. This must have been Bibo's mother. A young girl sat by the woman's feet fanning herself with a woven paypay, occasionally fanning Bibo's mother in a futile effort to take the weight from the humid air.

"Hi, Inchoy," I said. Inchoy raised his head and then shook it. Chok-Chok from the sari sari store rushed over with a plastic chair for me. I thanked him and carefully went to stand by the head of the coffin. It was open and Bibo's face was heavily made up with foundation, fuchsia lipstick, and thick lashes, her hair sleek over her shoulders. She was in her favored attire, an immaculate white T-shirt, jeans, and her pink Converse. I could still see black gummy traces by her hairline and ears, residue from the tape that her head had been wrapped in. I wondered how they had managed to make her hair look so presentable, what efforts of combing and cutting the family had made to remove the impact of Bibo's violent end.

I took my seat with Inchoy, reached for his hand, and held it in mine in my lap. He watched the gambling with a resigned despair. A girl came to me with a glass of electric-green juice. I had no idea what it was but knew it would be very sweet. I thanked the little girl and asked her how old she was. Did she like school? The girl responded politely that she did, then returned to the other children, who were quietly watching something on a cell phone.

A half hour later Zackito appeared in an aura of citrus cologne. After checking in with me and Inchoy, he began making the rounds of the room, chatting politely, asking questions. There was a shout from the gambling, "Pusoy!" Someone would win double. Zackito, out of politeness, asked if he could join the game. People like us didn't have fundraising tables at our funerals and I'm sure he didn't want Bibo's family to feel self-conscious. I found myself wondering if Zackito was any good at cards.

I had told myself that I would stay at the wake for a couple of hours and then see if I could pry Inchoy away, take him for dinner, give him an opportunity to talk. I wondered what his plans were for the sari sari store. I knew that it had been operating at a subsistence level, that the space was rented, and even once the stock was sold, it would not cover the costs of the funeral. Whatever Inchoy had from his salary went to his own expenses and the rental on the apartment. Inchoy lived from paycheck to paycheck. How long before Bibo could be buried? Even if the family managed to raise the money, the wait at the funeral homes was long. Sometimes it took months to bury people, as the EJK murders had added thousands of dead. The burial places in the poorer areas were packed to capacity, even though the spaces were most often concrete mausoleums, endless corridors that had been more than adequate for burials in the years before Gumboc.

I stepped out to have a cigarette, even though everyone was smoking inside. I needed a break. A pair of men who were grooming a fighting cock across the way eyed me unapologetically. I took long, slow drags, aware of the attention but beyond caring. A tricycle pulled up a couple of doors down and discharged a familiar figure, dressed in a white short-sleeve shirt and jeans. It was José Martin. He registered my presence with surprise and then appreciation.

"So what brings you here?" I said.

"Me? I'm a journalist covering the EJKs. I'm at all the funerals. Or as many as I can cover."

I offered him a cigarette and he took one and then another, which he stuck behind his ear for later. I handed him the lighter.

"Better question is: 'Why is Ting Klein here?'" He looked into the room. "And Zack Palanca. What brings the gods of New Manila down from their Valhalla?"

"I knew her," I said.

"Is that all?" José Martin took another look into the room and I saw him register Inchoy and his grief. He gave me a questioning look.

"The deceased was very close to Inchoy. Let's leave him in peace." José Martin too was gay, and he would respect Inchoy's privacy.

José Martin took another drag and brought the lit end of his cigarette around so he could see the slow burn of the good tobacco. "Any news for me?"

This was not the time. I gave him the look I thought he deserved.

He whistled in response. "Wow. You mestizas. Shit, Ting. I expect more from you."

"More from me?"

"A little less form, a little more substance. I'm following a lead and you could help. Gumboc has to go. You take out the head, and the body crumbles. For all you know, your little bit of information could put an end to all of this."

"What more do we need to condemn Gumboc? Everyone knows he's a murderer. Everyone. The United Nations, Amnesty International, every world leader. Gumboc's not going anywhere. And my friend is dead—"

"And you're wondering what more could happen? If this is as bad as it gets?"

"Why would I wonder?" I gave him a withering look. "Things are always lovely in Valhalla."

"You're upset. And you think I'm a fly at the corpse. But this is not the time for sentimentality. Gumboc just extended martial law in Mindanao, and why? Ever since the siege ended in Marawi, Abu Sayyaf has been in disarray, unable to organize, on the run."

"You're scared that martial law will be declared nationwide? We are already living without due process," I said. "Isn't that what martial law is?"

"No, Ting. Do your research. Aren't you a journalist?"

"I have to go."

"Let me leave you with this. Every day of my life I deal with my coworkers and my friends, my kabarkada, telling me how ballsy I am. 'Paré, you're small,' they say. 'But the size of your balls? Grabe!' They say that because I'm fearless. But Ting, I only have one testicle, courtesy of martial law. That's ironic, isn't it? Because what keeps me at it is not what I know I have but what I know can be taken."

I knew I was getting hotheaded, but my anger was what was holding me together. "Is that a joke?" I asked.

"It is a Filipino joke," he said.

"Any news on Laird Bontotot?"

"Do you really care?"

I threw down my cigarette, which died in a greasy puddle. "People I care about care." I turned, preparing to head in. "Honestly, I think Eagle's Nest is a hotel. I heard Chet mention Baguio. It must be a resort of some kind."

"I think you're wrong there," said José Martin.

"How can you be so sure?"

José Martin composed himself. "The way they talk, it's like some kind of club. Or a new political party. They talk about traffic and highways, overseas workers, but you know what they don't talk about? Building. No plans. No permits. And Chet's in it, that's irrefutable."

I had nothing to share, no *little bit of information*, and on some level, José Martin knew that, but something was up. Chet had been traveling back and forth to Baguio. Once, when Top Gun and I had collected Chet on a corner somewhere off España, I'd seen Rocco

Basilang getting into a car on the opposite side of the street. When I'd asked, "Isn't that Rocco?" Chet had denied it. I'd let it drop because Chet was signaling that it was one of those things that I did not need to know.

"Chet doesn't tell me about his business and I don't ask," I said.

José Martin shook his head and raised his eyes to me, direct and unblinking. "Your friend is not the last person who's going to die," he said. "And that attitude"—he pointed at me with his cigarette—"is as deadly as any bullet."

José Martin questioned the relatives and Chok-Chok, but no one knew who had killed Bibo. She had been shot in the chest at short range, her head then wrapped in tape, maybe to delay identification or maybe as a dehumanizing gesture. The actual shooting had not been witnessed. All that was known was that Bibo had gone to her nephew's birthday party at her sister's house, then headed to the corner to flag a tricycle to go home. Chok-Chok had called the sister when Bibo was not at the sari sari store for lunch, as was her habit, and in the hour following, Bibo's body had been found. There was speculation about who might have done it but no way of knowing. Someone had supplied Bibo's name, knowing her long-ago history with drugs, and someone had killed her for the seven thousand pesos. It was a narrative that persisted like a disease, a set of circumstances with a constant supply of new players.

A group of women had gathered and I saw the beads come out. I had remembered to bring my own and, picking up my chair and going to them, asked if I could join. Just as we were about to start in on the first Joyful Mystery, the women raised their heads, distracted, and I turned to the door to see Chet standing there, his arms weighted with lilies. Behind him was Top Gun carrying boxes from Aristocrat Bakeshop. He saw me in my black with my beads.

"You look like someone I know," he said in English.

"Don't start, Chet," I responded.

He gave the bouquet to a woman, who began arranging them in a plastic bucket. Bibo's mother watched as the woman then placed the arrangement on a chair by the head of the coffin. The lilies released a powerful perfume into the air, a gorgeous death scent, a reminder that we were easing Bibo into a painless afterlife.

Chet went to Bibo's mother. He took her hand and brought it to his forehead, then, crouching on the ground before her, began speaking earnestly. He produced an envelope—cash—and placed it in her hands. She looked at the envelope with an immense sorrow, knowing that she should produce gratitude but unsure of how to muster it. Chet looked over at Zackito, who was holding a hand of cards. "Game's over, paré."

"Really?" said Zackito. "I had a full house. Queens."

"Of course you did," said Chet.

Zackito threw his hand down, chatting with the other men, who laughed among themselves and then patiently, reluctantly, began to pack up their cards. No doubt there would soon be another game for them. Top Gun was now handing out bottles of whiskey and cigarettes. Inchoy had started shaking again, crying, but trying to hide it. My group had abandoned the rosary as the ensaymada from Aristocrat was now being distributed. The children were opening the rolls wrapped in crinkly paper. I started crying then, big fat tears that I knew were leaving trails of mascara down my face. I couldn't make myself wipe them away or pat beneath my eyes with the back of my hand, which is what crying women did.

"Ting," said Chet. "Ting, later."

"I can't—"

"What?"

"It's just that Bibo—" I paused. "It's just that Bibo was so happy."

II

I

The call demanding ransom came four days after Bibo's funeral. Abu Sayyaf wanted 30 million pesos and they wanted it in two weeks or Laird would be executed. Laird's parents, Richard and Crystal, had arrived in Manila along with my tita Remi's granddaughter, the girl Laird was marrying. I didn't want to meet the parents. I reminded myself that I was in no way responsible for Laird, that I hardly knew him. But this in itself produced an element of shame. He had admired my writing and I should at least have appreciated that. He had been serious in his desire to improve things, although the particulars of this desire remained unknown. I had been successful in protecting myself from him and now he was just a mystery sealed in silence.

José Martin had also been caught by surprise by the abduction. He thought that Laird didn't fit the profile. Abu Sayyaf kidnapped a lot of people and at the current moment were thought to have twenty hostages, but the ones who made the headlines were the white guys: the two Canadians, John Ridsdel and Robert Hall, who had their boats moored at a resort, easy prey with access to dollars.

The Canadian government did not do business with terrorists and first Robert Hall had been executed, the matter of his final moments unflinchingly recorded. Ridsdel's family had desperately attempted to collect the funds for his release, but while they were still counting the dollars as they trickled in, he too had been killed. I remember following the story, after watching the fate of Jürgen Kantner, the German who had been snatched from his boat, his wife shot as he looked on. These three had all been beheaded. John Ridsdel's head had been left on the streets of Jolo township in a plastic bag. Townsfolk had seen two men on a motorcycle deposit the bag and then track quickly out of town. Then they were absorbed back into the jungle, improbably disappearing without a trace.

I had been called to the dining room to report any knowledge I had to the Bontotots. My family presented me as a person with connections to other journalists, someone who might know something, but I was as in the dark as a person could be. We had all considered that Laird might have been kidnapped by Abu Sayyaf, but the truth is none of us had believed it.

The Bontotots were at my aunt's house because they were underfoot in Tita Remi's house. My aunt had volunteered to help any way she could and this was the responsibility that had fallen to her: to keep the Bontotots distracted so that Tita Remi's family could focus on the investigation. Was it a kindness that Laird's mother turned out to be dead? That his father, Richard, seemed as emotionally ill-equipped as I was? Crystal, his second wife, was a weepy blonde who seemed tailored for disaster, and I wondered if her marriage to Laird's father was a dress rehearsal for future sorrow.

I suspected from his clothes and manners that Richard was a laborer of some sort, but he knew—confronted with our houses and servants and general ease greased with privilege—to keep this to himself. He was a "businessman" who lived in Los Angeles, as joyless as Laird, narrow eyed, and mean looking. Crystal was oblivious to Manila's Byzantine class structure and code of behavior. She staved off waves of tears with sweets, mostly biko, which we kept in steady supply at my tita Rosa's, and whatever else was available to eat. We did keep offering the food, but she really ought to have occasionally refused, as it was considered proper to do so. I didn't disdain this response to stress, although I felt bad for the woman because other members of my family were less understanding. Or maybe my aunts and cousins were just desperate for something funny, and this woman's impressive eating provided that. Life went on behind the scenes, and that was real, if everything else seemed less so.

My tita Rosa was the only member of our family skilled in small talk, and this she was deploying in an expert way, the result of close to a century of practice. Weather exhausted, Richard and I looked on as the conversation turned to Tito Iñigo. Crystal was wondering what sort of dog he was, to which my aunt replied that he was a native dog, even though he was clearly mostly Chihuahua. I sat in silence, unable to think of what might engage Laird's father, who was inhaling and exhaling in a regular, loud, and performative way. The ancient fan made its transit hitting each spot with a beam of focused cool, rustling the flowers on the table, blowing my hair across my eyes.

"Richard," I said. "Do you smoke? Would you like to join me outside for a cigarette?"

He nodded and stood from the table.

* * *

On the porch, he sat down on the cracked tile of the topmost step and rested his head in his hands. I hadn't sat on these steps since I was a child, but I seated myself at a comfortable distance beside him. I offered him a cigarette and he took one. I lit it for him and then lit one for myself.

"I'm sorry I'm not more help to you," I said.

"What are you supposed to do? What am I supposed to do?" He shrugged. "You know, I have a hard time believing it's really happening. I read the newspaper and I say, 'This is what's real.' But a part of me can't make myself believe it." He looked at me and his expression softened from the hard look to one of complete bewilderment. "What can I do? I don't have the money and the State Department knows the situation."

No one in the Philippines would help to pay the ransom for the same reason that governments hesitated to get involved. Raising the money supported the system of kidnapping. It made targets of your family members. What we hoped is that Laird could be located and a raid made on the camp. But Abu Sayyaf moved quickly, their headquarters always changing.

"Is there anything you can tell me about Laird, what he might have been up to in Mindanao? I don't know if it will help, but sometimes a little information like that adds up to something when you put the facts together."

"What do I know about Laird?" He had addressed the question to himself. "I'd never met his in-laws until this week. I'd never even met his fiancée."

I studied the man's face—lined, dark. Laird had gotten his cheekbones from his father, but Bontotot pére was a more horizontal being, broad shoulders, thick legs.

"Richard," I said. "When was the last time you saw Laird?"

He grimaced. "They said you were the smart one."

In my family there could be only one smart one, one pretty one, or one nice one.

"I haven't seen Laird in four years. He wanted little to do with me after I left his mother, and after she died, well . . . He never cared for Crystal. I think I embarrassed him." He looked out across the lawn and I tracked his gaze. A houseboy was dragging a bucket of water along a flowerbed, watering the plants with a repurposed can. "I have a hard time believing that this is happening to Laird because he isn't a person that things happen to. He's a person who makes things happen. He's always in charge. He controlled all his friends, his mother. He was always at the top of his class. Even when he was little, he was very organized. He'd lay out his clothes each night before school. And we didn't have a lot of money to get nice things, but he managed. He never looked untidy. He's not the kind of guy to do something stupid like get kidnapped." Mr. Bontotot's eyes were open with disbelief. "He has a master's in political science from Berkeley."

The security guard had emerged from the guardhouse, his shirt hiked up, and he stood in the sun scratching his belly, yawning.

"So who did Laird get his brains from?"

"His brains? That's me. His mother was a good person, but she was all hard work and prayers. Me, I like to read." He turned to look at me, as if I might challenge him. But I saw no reason to.

When we reentered the house, my tita Rosa was showing Crystal a photo album, pictures of the siblings in the fifties, black-and-white relics of my titas and titos leaning on swanky cars or picnicking together. She must have been getting desperate for ways of entertaining her guests. I was relieved by my phone's pinging with a text from Chet, who had been threatening to make an appearance for hours, something that I'd hoped would not happen because we didn't need another person in the mix, but that I now recognized as my escape. I texted back that I would meet him outside.

"You have to excuse me," I said. My aunt looked up from the album with a disapproving frown. "I have to meet a friend."

I sat next to Chet as he backed down the drive at high speed, looking past Top Gun, who, as usual, was sitting in the center of the back seat. "I thought you didn't want to come to Makati today. You said you had to be with your family."

"I changed my mind. There's only so much of this stuff you can take. There's nothing happening, which is anxiety provoking, but it's hard to think of news that would make it better."

"Laird is—" Chet stopped himself and shook his head.

"What?" I waited for Chet to respond.

"I feel bad for his parents," he said.

By the time we reached Makati the sky had begun to grow dark and the wind was picking up. Trees were nodding and on the sidewalk newspapers were spiraling up in an ominous way. When we got out of the car, I could hear dogs barking, although where we were, in a landscape of concrete and glass, I could not see the dogs that were responsible.

"Is there a storm coming in?" I asked.

"Yeah, but it's not supposed to be so bad. Just stay for dinner. The cook's making bagnet."

"She's always making bagnet."

"That's because you're always eating it."

By the time we had finished dinner, the rain was blowing against the windows in sheets. I rested my face against the cool glass, seeing people—tiny from this distance—running along the sidewalks to take shelter.

"I have to head home," I said. "It's not looking very good out there."

Chet checked his phone, scrolling through, I assumed, to follow up on the weather, when the phone began to ring. He picked up and after an initial angry response, he began to deliver directions on how to secure a construction site that must have been one of his projects. He was being very specific at making sure that they stored all the corrugated iron safely as that had a tendency to blow around in storms and had been known to kill people. He reassured whoever was on the other end of the line and said to call him when all the actions had been completed.

"Ting," he said. "You're not going anywhere. Power lines are coming down. It's not safe."

I thought about the implications of this statement. "And here, is it safe?"

Chet rolled his eyes. "I just want to hold your hand." He took my hand and began to bend back the fingers one at a time. Then he flipped my hand over as if he were reading my palm.

I left my hand in his. I wanted both to take it back and to leave it there, but my mind had left my body and seemed to be hovering over the proceedings as if I had no say in what was happening. I said, "It'll be my hand and next thing you'll want my elbow."

Chet nodded, his hand now on my elbow. He closed his fingers, which now touched, encircling it. "Yes, and then your shoulder."

"It's like being eaten by a snake," I said. Whatever was about to happen seemed inevitable. I could have pushed him off, stepped away, but I was curious and, also, strangely sad.

Chet laughed. "There you are, thinking and thinking."

"I don't want to be inside the snake," I said.

"Ting," Chet replied, putting his arms around me, pulling me to him. "Inside the snake is the safest place to be."

II

Tita Rosa had finally put her foot down about the Bontotots, claiming that she could no longer play the host because of her high blood pressure. She had returned to her desk and her endless task of accounting, the ancient adding machine cranking through its gears in regular intervals, this sound the heartbeat of the house. She registered her disapproval about Chet by not asking me where I had spent the night. Maybe she was making peace with it, but by steering clear of the subject she was avoiding complicity in an inarguably immoral situation. It was the correct thing to do.

Originally, I had planned to have the car to myself all day and was going to Bibo's apartment to help clear it out. But in the morning, one of Carmi's restaurants had lost power, and she asked if I would bring Miggie to a birthday party in Magallanes.

Miggie sat next to me with her wrapped gift, playing a game on her iPad. Her yaya, Nini, sat on the rearmost seat, quiet, her perfect features set in an inscrutable expression. Nini was very pretty and her prettiness was remarked on, as was her ability to sit through any number of situations without uttering a word. Her stillness seemed to me a form of protest, as if her good looks should have earned her some better station in life, but there she was in her striped yaya uniform, looking out at an uncaring world, waiting to wipe Miggie's nose or be ordered to do some other thing that other beautiful people were not subjected to. Miggie set the iPad down and fixed me with a penetrating look. "Tita Ting, why are you going to Tondo?"

"I'm doing a favor for a friend," I said.

"In Tondo?"

"Yes." I returned her look. "Someone died and I'm packing up their apartment."

"Why you?"

"Because there's no one else."

"Why is there no one else?"

Thankfully my phone started to ring. It was Chet. "Where are you?" he said.

"Just entering Magallanes. Why?"

"I arranged for Cherry to help you." Cherry was Chet's maid.

"I don't need Cherry. I'll be fine. I have Mannie to help."

"He'll carry the boxes for you, but you need someone packing. I've already arranged it."

Cherry was legendarily efficient. "Okay. I'll come by the apartment."

"No. Cherry's at the house in Dasmariñas."

"She's back in Dasma?" Understandably, I was wary of anything that brought me into C. G.'s orbit.

"Just for the morning. She's waiting. And she has boxes."

"Chet, I'm really fine."

"Don't be stupid, Ting."

He was right. I was being stupid. Dasmariñas was not far from Magallanes and at this point, what was the difference? Cherry was one of those Ilocanos who justified the "industrious" stereotype. I didn't want to be alone in Bibo's apartment with all her things, and we had to get it done today. The lease was up on the apartment on Monday, and Inchoy had left the task of packing up her belongings to the last minute and then proven incapable of taking part. Originally, we had planned to settle Bibo's apartment together, but that just seemed a recipe for disaster. Inchoy would be shuttling along just fine and then—as if a fog were descending—he would freeze, seized by grief. Tears would follow. But he was still keeping up with his teaching. The work was saving him from complete disintegration.

Miggie's mother, Leonora, was already at the party, waiting—in response to my text—as we made our way up the circular drive.

"Oh, sige, Miggie, there's your mom. Have fun." She leaned over presenting her cheek, her mouth pursed in the polite kissing gesture perfected by the family's children. "Leonora," I said, shouting in the second before Mannie slid the door shut. "Let's get together soon."

Chet's house in Dasmariñas looked much like the house where I had just left Miggie. One entered through the towering gates and angled up the drive. Masses of tended greenery seemed to revel in nature and deny its riot simultaneously. Like a Mayan temple, the colossal house emerged from behind the palms, an edifice of adobe brick. It was a palace humming with Freon and money. You could feel the coldness of the polished marble floors just by looking at it, an exponential chill mirrored in the reflecting surfaces of windows. There were two cars parked in the drive, an Audi and a Mercedes, and the latter of these was being buffed to excess by a uniformed driver making careful circles on its surface with a damp chamois. I texted Chet to text Cherry that I'd arrived and was checking my phone when the car door slid open and, to my surprise, C. G. entered and sat next to me.

C. G. sat in an aggressive cloud of what I identified as Prada Candy. She inhaled, seemingly bored, and angled her gorgeous head in my direction. She was a Chinese mestiza, all cheekbones and lozenge eyes, and had the kind of bone structure that would have inspired Brâncuși.

"Hello, Ting," she said.

I put my phone down on the seat with care. "Hello, C. G.," I responded.

"We need to have a chat," she said. She was speaking in her American-accented English, something she had picked up when she'd attended Middlebury.

"Okay," I said.

She picked a piece of lint off her pants and flicked it idly away. "I don't care if you sleep with Chet," she said. "Frankly, I'm relieved. But if you think I'm giving him an annulment, you're out of your mind."

I had never considered the annulment seriously. I had thought it Chet's decision, beyond my range of influence.

"Claro," I said. I don't know why I said claro, because neither C. G. nor I spoke Spanish.

She looked mildly interested at my response, but after a thought, dismissed this too. "Ting," she said. "I've always liked you. You know that. And do you know why? You're no bullshit. But you are a force for evil."

"Evil's a bit much."

"Is it?" She returned her gaze to me, analyzing my face with a studied languor. "You just wander around as if nothing matters. What's the word for that?"

"Gormless?" I offered.

She considered and shook her head. "I don't even know what that means. You're like a black hole. Everything is fine and then you walk past and everything is destroyed. And you can stand there and say you didn't do anything, but you did."

"Maybe I'm cursed."

"Maybe. But even if you went to Aling Ligaya and had it lifted, you would still be like that."

It occurred to me that Chet had said much the same thing about me and my lack of accountability. I had the uncomfortable sensation of seeing what was good in their marriage.

"Why don't you just go back to the States and leave us alone?"

I did not have a good comeback for that, and C. G. did not expect one. The trunk of the car had been opened and Mannie was loading in the boxes. C. G. got out of the car and Cherry, who was standing behind her, got in. Cherry was carrying a paper bag that smelled of meat.

"It's siopao," said C. G. She looked up and away, presenting me with the perfect line of her jaw. "From Ma Mon Luk. We had extra. I thought you might need some lunch."

Bibo's apartment had been sealed shut for some time. No one wanted to be there. I felt as if I were entering the tomb to find her gone. On the table was a vase with devastated lilies, browned and broken, the water faintly reeking even from where I stood by the door. Cherry looked at me with alert eyes, already assessing the work ahead. I walked to the window unit and turned it on. It responded with a shudder as it woke up, displacing the silence.

"Ano po?" asked Cherry.

"First clean out the fridge," I said. "Kitchen things go in boxes, then to the sari sari store." Bibo's belongings for the family would be picked up there. "I'll pack the masks." These I would bring to Inchoy. There was a picture of Bibo and Inchoy framed on the bookcase. They were at a beach restaurant smiling together behind a platter filled with prawns. The picture must have been taken by one of those people who snap pictures at tourist areas and then sell them to you. I turned the picture facedown on the shelf and shot Cherry a challenging look, but she was already eyeing the kitchen area, breaking it down into the necessary tasks. Bibo had kept the place neat and although the apartment was packed with stuff, the walls groaning with Igorot masks and shields, it was small. We would be done with this final task in a matter of hours.

When the majority of the boxes were filled and organized, I lit a cigarette, taking in how the emptied place seemed even smaller. Mannie, who had been carrying the boxes, was sitting at the table eating siopao. "When you're finished," I said, "the aircon comes out and that goes to the sari sari store with the other things."

"Yung banyo po," said Cherry from the bathroom, which I had forgotten.

I stood with her in the tiny space—a toilet, a shower stall, a sink with a small shelf above it with cheerful cosmetics, lotions, and a picture of Mariah Carey grinning madly, something clipped from a magazine and framed in gold plastic. "Just throw out what you don't want," I said. I picked up Bibo's hairbrush, which, like her other things, was carefully maintained, but still had a few strands of Bibo's stick-straight, iron-strong hair. Inchoy would want it, so I put it in my handbag.

I sent Cherry home in a GrabCar, which would be considered ridiculously extravagant, but I didn't care. I just wanted to get back to my aunt's house and take a bath, put on pajamas, and go to bed even though it would only be eight or nine. I could almost feel my head on the pillow. I picked up my phone and texted Inchoy that I would be dropping boxes by in about two hours and then checked my phone. There was a text from Ann.

Publisher pulled Kent J. Baxter book.

I read it twice. Was this text really meant for me? Who was Kent J. Baxter? I knew the name but couldn't place it. I decided to brave the spotty, expensive cell service and looked up "Kent J. Baxter book pulled."

Kent J. Baxter, I remembered as his picture slowly materialized, was the writer of erudite and surprisingly best-selling histories. He had won a Pulitzer Prize for his study of the banana industry, *Mister Tally Man*, which exposed the exploitation of banana workers in the early part of the twentieth century. When this book appeared in the early nineties I had been plotting my own career. I remembered thinking that if one looked at the plight of workers at any time in history and had something appealing, like bananas, to focus the research, one would likely expose some horrific exploitation in an interesting way and that this might be a good model for a future book. Apparently a photograph from the late seventies had been unearthed of some frat party at the University of Virginia. Senator Norlund Boom of Alabama had been the first suspect for the person in blackface, but he had protested—truthfully—that he was not the man who had chosen to costume himself as Harry Belafonte (an identity suggested by the Hawaiian shirt) but was actually the man in the gorilla suit. It was Kent J. Baxter who was in blackface, and his newest book, *The Sad Menagerie*, already out in advance review copies, was being withdrawn from publication. It was Kent J. Baxter's book that had been seen as the competition for mine. Baxter had made a sincere-sounding apology, saying that his admiration for Belafonte had inspired the costume, that Belafonte's song "Banana Boat" had led him on his quest to tell the stories of the banana workers, but the damage was done. Baxter had been knocked out of the game after generating a significant amount of interest in the plight of the human zoo participants.

I inhaled and groaned and considered, then texted back:

First draft close.

My response sounded so confident that I almost believed it.

III

Mannie and I reached my aunt's house shortly before ten. The lights were all still on, although Tita Rosa usually had only the vestibule and library lit at this hour. I thanked Mannie and gave him some extra money for his help. He tried to refuse, and we went back and forth a few times, pantomiming politeness, because we both knew that he deserved it and would eventually take it.

Tita Rosa and Tito Iñigo were waiting for me, the former with her hair unpinned in preparation for sleep, the latter dancing at my return.

"Tita," I said. "You shouldn't wait for me if you're tired."

"I'm not tired. I'm old. Beng is heating food for you."

"I'm not hungry."

"Not hungry?"

"I'm not hungry. I'm old."

"Don't play games with me, Ting." She shook her head but then smiled. "Okay, I am tired. I just want to be with my children, my grandchildren, and my great-grandchildren, and if I can't be with them, I want to be with God!"

"Don't you want to be with me?" I placed my hands on her shoulders and kneaded a couple of times.

"If you start listening to me, I want to be with you. Otherwise, you're just another trial."

"Maybe you're still here because God doesn't want the competition," I said.

She considered that but kept her answer to herself. "Let's eat," she said. She headed to the dining room. "I already had dinner, but this could be my last meal."

Beng shuttled out with a platter of fried fish and a bowl of rice. As soon as I began to eat, I realized how hungry I was. I ate seconds. And then thirds. Tita Rosa called to the kitchen for atis, which must have just started appearing at the market. "Your favorite," she said. Atis was not my favorite, but Tita Rosa tended to say that anytime she presented fruit that had just come into season. An atis looked like a grenade, dark green and bumpy. When it was ripe, the rind would break along the segments easily. Inside, the fruit was white and had a sweetish, milky taste. There were big black seeds hidden in its meat. It was a fruit that married the mild and the potentially violent.

"Ate Ting," said Beng. She was holding my phone, lifted off the side board, which was buzzing and ringing. I thanked her and looked at the screen. It was José Martin and I swiped immediately.

"Here," I said.

"Ting, I'm sending you a link. Watch it now."

"What?"

"I don't know how long it will be up. I think it's Bontotot."

"Wait. What?"

"I have to go. I'm going. Ting, I'm working." And he hung up.

"Ting! Ting!" said my aunt. I had no idea how long she had been calling my name. "Ting, what's wrong?"

"We need internet now."

"Just go upstairs."

"No, I need to stream something. Is there any good internet? That was my friend the journalist. It's something about Laird."

My aunt got up from the table. "We'll go to Baby's apartment."

"Isn't there a tenant? That Norwegian guy?"

"He's Dutch," my aunt said. "Beng!"

Beng was already standing close by and my aunt was at first startled then relieved by her proximity. "Bring the atis." Beng picked up the bowl and the three of us made for the front door. My aunt held tight to my arm and we exited the house, carefully down the front steps, and then, walking as fast as could be managed, along the driveway. "What did your friend say?"

"Nothing," I said. "He just sent me a link for a video." We were now at the gate. I was trying my phone, now that we were closer to the internet, but the link wasn't opening. "I should get my computer."

"Don't worry about that. Yoren has a computer."

"Who is Yoren?"

"Ay naku, Ting. The tenant. Yoren is the tenant."

My aunt had a few words for the guard, who appeared drunk, slurring and unsteady as he opened the gate. She told him we would be back shortly. We crossed the street, empty at this hour, although the sounds of traffic on E. Rodriguez echoed from the end of the block. The security guard in the apartment building recognized my aunt and was very polite, insisting on getting the elevator and punching in the floor number. As we ascended, I wondered how Yoren would greet our visit, my thoughts of Laird momentarily displaced as I looked at Beng, who was considering the bowl of atis with complacent confusion. My aunt pressed the buzzer at my cousin's apartment. When the door swung open revealing a shirtless, sarong-wearing white man somewhere in his sixties, she was nonplussed.

"Yoren," she said. "Good evening. This is my niece, Christina Klein. And I think you know Beng. We brought you atis, the first of the season."

"Good evening, Mrs. Rivera," he said politely. I didn't know why he was wearing a sarong. People in the Philippines, even the Dutch, did not wear sarongs. He must have been one of those Europeans who were posted all around Asia and picked up this sort of habit in Malaysia or Indonesia.

"Yoren, we are imposing, but we need to use your internet."

Tita Rosa dragged me around him and into the apartment. Beng followed with the fruit. Baby's apartment was furnished with the cast-offs of a number of my relatives. I recognized the chrome-and-plush beige dining chairs from my mother's house and a rocker that had, at one stage, been my tita Dom's.

"And Yoren," said my aunt, "we need to use your computer. Where is it?"

Yoren gestured to the table, where he had clearly been working.

"Ting, give him the link."

Yoren was sensing the importance of the situation and to his credit was making it seem suddenly normal. I remembered my aunt telling me that he was a diplomat. He sat by his computer and gestured for my aunt to sit, which she did. I pulled out my phone. "Can I send you the link?" I asked.

"Yes, of course," he said.

He gave me his phone number and I sent a text, which he picked up on his laptop. We waited for the video to come up.

"Ladies," he said, suddenly grave. "Where did you get this link?"

"A friend of mine," I said. "A journalist."

"I've already seen the video. I don't think you should watch this."

"Let me be the judge of that, if you would be so kind," I said coolly. "If I wasn't supposed to see it, my friend wouldn't have sent it to me." I went to stand behind him.

The video was poor quality, the sound scratchily wavering in and out. The first view was of treetops and moved unsteadily until it panned down to show a number of men, faces concealed with black scarves and ski masks, standing around a kneeling figure, his head bowed. As soon as a man's voice was heard to start speaking, Yoren muted his computer, looking pointedly at me. The men, all in black and uniformed, were also carrying machetes.

"I don't think you should be watching this," Yoren said again. "This video was pulled off the internet several hours ago. I only saw it as an embassy officer. I'm not sure who reposted it."

I watched the kneeling figure, feeling a buzzing sensation, as if I were getting a migraine. My mouth was dry and I realized that I kept shaking my head uncontrollably. The sound muted, I could only assume that there were people yelling. One of the black-clad men kicked the kneeling figure, and then, grabbing a handful of hair, pulled the kneeling man's face into view. It was Laird.

Yoren shut the screen of his computer, pushing it downward.

"If you want to know what happens, I will tell you," he said.

"What is this video?" said my aunt. "Ting, what is this video?"

"Tita," I said. "Give me a minute."

I looked at Yoren, at his pale-blue eyes, inquisitive yet composed.

"Why," he asked, "do you think your friend sent you this video?"

"Because we know this man. His name is Laird Bontotot." The silence resonated around the room. Beng was still holding the bowl of atis. I asked, "Is he dead?"

Yoren nodded several times, slowly, carefully. "Yes, it would seem that way." My aunt had bowed her head, and I could see her lips begin to move in silent prayer. Yoren patted my arm. "I am very sorry."

Two days later the head was dumped in front of Baclaran Church. It was hard to think of the head as belonging to Laird, because that was a horror beyond comprehension: what I knew to be true just seemed impossible. A week after that, a bomb went off inside the church on a Sunday morning, killing twenty churchgoers and injuring two hundred more. These actions mimicked others in Jolo township, deep in the south, in the heart of the Bangsamoro. Nationwide martial law was declared that evening. I tried to get hold of José Martin, but he wasn't answering his phone. Zackito told me that he had gone into hiding. The papers were still printing the news, but many of the journalists had disappeared, while others had been picked up and incarcerated, their reporting against the government seen as treasonous, although the charge was most often libel. There was now a curfew and everyone had to be off the streets at 9:00 p.m. or run the risk of being arrested.

Abu Sayyaf had made their way into the capital and the outrage at the declaration of martial law was somewhat offset by genuine fear as we considered what to do when confronted with this new reality.

IV

I sat at the dining table with Tita Dom and Tita Rosa, who had nodded off after the heavy meal. Tito Ben was stuck at the retirement center at Ateneo because, until we had the curfew completely figured out, it seemed unwise to bring him to New Manila for the weekly dinner. We thought we might have to reschedule for the weekend or for lunch, but everything was so new that no one really wanted to move.

Pictures of Laird were now circulating internationally. Two were in constant rotation. One was of him in the jungle surrounded by masked gunmen. The other was another taken at Jim's house, this one with Cha Cha in the frame. She had been taken unaware, looking off to the side as she adjusted the front of her blouse. Laird was standing beside her, presenting himself in a formal way.

Jim was making phone calls to try to get the picture withdrawn. Couldn't they just crop Cha Cha out?

"Ay naku," said Tita Dom. "Cha Cha has become the cover girl of martial law."

"This is not a joking matter," said Tita Rosa. Her eyes remained closed, but even in a state of deep repose, she could still monitor our behavior.

"I'm not joking," said Tita Dom. "But what can Jim do? The picture has already been sold to Reuters."

"But why do they want Cha Cha in the picture?"

"The way that Rikki explains it is the picture implies that now Manila's finest are also at risk. If Cha Cha's relative can be kidnapped and beheaded, then no one is beyond reach. This has greased the way for martial law. There is still protest, but it's muted. And you've read the news. Gumboc keeps reminding everyone of how his drug policies have reduced the presence of drug crime. And now he's saying that if the politicians just let him have his moment, he'll fix this problem too."

"And if he killed off half the population in Manila, we would also have no traffic," I said, dryly. "This is a nightmare."

"Did you read about the LRT?"

"No," I said. The Light Rail Transit, if it worked, would solve many of the traffic problems, but there weren't enough trains running. The lines for the LRT at high traffic times were ridiculously long. And the trains often broke down. New tracks needed to be added, but with traffic the way it was, it was hard to see how to do it without bringing the entire city to a halt.

"He's saying that the curfew is creating the opportunity to update the LRT. They can build it at night. Construction crews are already being hired. Didn't you read the interview with Rocco Basilang? It was in the *Philippine Telegraph* this morning." Tita Dom gave me a concerned look. "Don't you think you should book a flight back to the States?"

I had thought about this and then dismissed it. I could not bring myself to leave. "I'm finishing my book." I shrugged. "I can handle a curfew."

"You should still get a ticket now," she said. "Rikki says that flights to the States are full for the next two months."

But in my mind, I had crossed the Rubicon. I had already begun to envision a life here, a life with my family. A life with Chet in the belly of the snake. And how could I leave when Inchoy needed me? He and I were headed to Baguio the following week. Martial law had initially dissuaded us, then made it seem as good a time as any to escape Manila. We had decided to stick to the plan that Bibo had arranged, although now we would celebrate Inchoy's birthday in honor of Bibo's life. In another circumstance, we would have scattered Bibo's ashes, but in this Catholic country, ashes had not been an option. I wondered if we could do something with Bibo's hairbrush, which I had been carrying around in my bag, strangely unwilling to part with it.

I hadn't been to Baguio in years. In my college days, when all Manila's finest fled the city and the heat at Easter time, I had stayed at Jim and Cha Cha's ten-bedroom chalet, heading every night to the Goldmine Disco at the Hyatt. The Hyatt was a five-star hotel, an opulent standard, with a great echoing lobby and a glass-and-brass elevator that would shoot one to the heavens with dizzying speed. Or maybe I was just dizzy, since at that time and in that place I was reliably drunk. This is how we spent the days leading to Easter. I remembered appearing on the edge of the dance floor, still hungover from the previous evening, and Chet saying to me: "Ting is risen!"

Jim and Cha Cha's house, perched on a ravine with broad verandahs and views into the pine-strewn slopes, had slid into the valley in the earthquake of 1990. Much of Baguio had been destroyed in the 7.7 temblor, including the Hyatt and the disco: the setting of so many White Russian–soaked nights reduced to beam and rubble. For weeks, recovery crews had pulled bodies from the site. I remembered that two people had been rescued after being trapped for eleven days, their survival a reason to praise God. Of course, this was the same God who had buried them alive.

V

Top Gun had picked me up from my aunt's house and we were now heading to Ermita to pick Chet up from the Manila Hotel. For once, I had overestimated the traffic and as we made the final stretch of Roxas Boulevard, I realized Top Gun and I would be a half hour early. I did not know who Chet was meeting nor why they were meeting, and this seemed an odd choice of venue. Old Manila was far from Makati, which had its own watering holes. I texted Chet to let him know that we'd arrived, on the off chance that he was wrapping things up.

He responded:

> See you Tap Room. Order me V&T.

I hadn't been in the Manila Hotel in years. The Tap Room was much as I'd remembered it, all wood paneling and expensive whiskey. When we dated, Chet and I had often started our evenings here and it did seem a room that was frozen in time, with the same American businessmen and Australian development consultants perched on the stools, deciding the future of the Philippines, although now there were more Koreans and Chinese filling the seats. I chose to sit in a lounge chair and ordered two vodka tonics, Ketel One, although in my youth I'd been partial to Absolut.

Chet appeared when I was halfway through my drink. His had sweated on the table, but with the chill of the air-conditioning, the ice cubes were mostly intact. Chet sat opposite me on the red velvet chair. He looked around the room and said, "You are the most beautiful woman here."

I took a quick glance at the other tables, noting that the ratio of women to men was about five to one. The odds were in my favor. "Did your meeting go well?" I asked.

"Yes," he said. He was unwilling to say more. "It's like old times."

"These are times, and we are old," I responded. This was one of few occasions we'd been in public together, maybe since the movie theater at Robinsons, which seemed like an eon ago. He took a slug from the drink and smiled. Chet was not a big drinker, never had been, although that seemed influenced more by his workaholic habits than by some tendency toward abstinence. We began to chat about a bathroom that was being renovated in the apartment—he had yet to select the tile for the floor—and then we had another drink, because sitting and doing so seemed celebratory, although we had nothing much to celebrate. And then it occurred to me that this drink with Chet was not accidental, as nothing in his life really was. He was setting the scene for a conversation, and I began to wait to see what exactly that conversation would be.

There was a moment of silence, which felt like an intentional lapse as Chet shifted gears. He said, "Have you heard from your husband?"

Ah, I thought. I said, "Not in a while."

"Why not? What's happening with the divorce?"

"I really don't know." I realized I was slightly drunk. "Maybe you can get one of your New York spies to find out." I smiled at him wryly.

"I find it strange that you don't hear from him. That things aren't moving forward."

"Really?" I said. "I don't."

"But he must know that it's over between you. It's been months."

"It has been close to four months and he knows no such thing. Let me explain my husband to you. Better yet, let me be my husband." I prepared to drop my voice an octave and to soak the words in privilege. "Well, you know Christina, she's fiery," I said, in an imitation that had Chet known my husband, he would have found spot-on. "It's going to take her a while to admit she wants to come home. She's hiding out in the Philippines and who can blame her? Collin's back with Magda, and a lot of us are feeling betrayed. But this time apart? It's good for us. It's what we need." Chet watched me, impressed but also uneasy. "Christina was just trying to get back at me for Blaire, which was a mistake." I realized, as I said this, that there had likely been other mistakes. "So now she thinks she's even and she's just licking her wounds. We're taking some time apart because that's what we need to do." I paused and took a sip of my drink. "Of course Christina's not staying in the Philippines. Seriously? The Philippines? That backwater? Good God. We're fixing things and she'll be here by the holidays. Go easy on her. Don't ask her about it. I mean, hasn't she been through enough?"

Chet leaned back in his chair. "You sound like you hate him."

"No. I actually don't . . . hate him. And no matter what you think, he does love me. This is just how he's justifying that weakness." It was true. I was probably the only person he'd ever felt that way about, and regardless of my feelings for him, being the object of such devotion left one indentured, because few people ever felt the full force of such a thing. On some level, I thought I should be grateful.

"He's forgiven you for the affair," said Chet.

"He would say he's being a feminist." Because my husband would say something like that, something false to diminish the betrayal. Affairs were never forgiven. The most one could hope for was that the transgression was logged and then ignored. But despite the talk of us now being even, we weren't. He might have thrown some punches in the course of our marriage, but my blow had landed in his kidneys.

Chet said, "I would like it if you followed up on the matter of your divorce."

"And if I don't, will you do it for me?"

"Do you want me to?"

I sat back in my chair, watching him watching me, his eyes tracking over my face. "Do you really think if we'd gotten married back then, as children, that we'd be happy now?"

"Why not?"

"Do you think I would be happy, happy in C. G.'s life?"

"Ting," he said. "You're never happy. And you're never really sad, not for long. You just are like that." Chet made a sweeping gesture that took in the whole of my being. He rocked back in his chair. "Can you say that you don't love me?"

I looked at him, at his defenseless eyes.

I said, "What is love?"

Chet laughed. "You're tough, Ting. You always were. But I can handle it. Just you see."

With the curfew, I was often stuck at Chet's overnight. Tita Rosa had mentioned a cousin who had gotten an annulment, which was an unsubtle hint that I move in that direction. And Tita Dom, who was not so concerned with appearances, had advised, "If you're in Makati, stay there if it's getting late." One only traveled in the daylight hours, which you would think would have made the traffic even worse. But it hadn't. The traffic was actually better. People were nervous and nervous people stayed close to home.

Chet was standing at his dresser, selecting cuff links. "What did you decide about the curtains?"

"I decided no curtains. I have nothing to hide."

Chet sighted me in the mirror. I was still in bed. "Since when?"

I pulled on his bathrobe. It was almost nine and I had to get going. I was having lunch with Zackito as he was headed back to Hawaii the following day, having managed to get a flight. "Why can't you come with us to Baguio?"

"What, with you and Inchoy?"

"It's only a few days. You can make your calls from there."

"You know I don't like mixing business and pleasure."

"What pleasure? Have you been around Inchoy recently?" Chet, having trouble with his cuff link, extended his arm for me to fix it. "Otherwise we're on the bus both ways."

"Your aunt can't lend you a driver?"

"Mannie? For four days?" I regarded Chet carefully. "I think you're up to something."

"Yeah. It's called work." Chet tugged on his sleeve, checking the cuff. "When are you leaving?"

"Tuesday."

His face grew weary. "Put it off."

"I can't put it off. It's Inchoy's birthday."

He sighed and then nodded to himself a couple of times, working out the agenda in his head. "C. G. and the kids are going to Bangkok for the long weekend. You can take her car on the way up, but you and Inchoy will have to take the bus back."

"Won't C. G. mind?"

"Yes, she'll mind." Chet checked his reflection in the mirror and found nothing to adjust. "But I pay for that driver, and he works for me. Where are you staying?"

"We're staying at the convent."

"You're not staying at the convent." He put on his jacket. "You're staying at Camp John Hay."

"But I like the convent."

"So what? I don't." Chet put his hands on my shoulders. "This is martial law."

"But it's okay for me and Inchoy to take the bus back?"

He gave me a look to let me know that I was pushing my luck, although I didn't know how I was doing so. "Ting, you stay where the Americans stay. You stay where I know it's safe."

My first thought was to remind him that Laird had been an American, and Ridsdel and Hall.

"Ridsdel and Hall were Canadian," said Chet, unprompted, and then summoned to action by the ringing of his phone, he left the room.

VI

Timicheg, chief of the Bontoc tribe, awoke early that morning. His ears were ringing. The previous evening, his wife (wife's name?) *had cracked an egg for the evening meal* (do Bontocs eat eggs for dinner?) *and found a spot of blood, a dark clot with tendrils of red circling into the yolk. "An omen," she had said. Good or bad? Who knew? But in the chill air of morning, he was overwhelmed with a sense of expectation. He rose from his bed* (bed? Sleeping mat? Sleeping platform?) *and went to stand on the threshold of his hut. Stretching out beneath him was the spectacle of the Banaue Rice Terraces, often called the Eighth Wonder of the World* (POV—in Timicheg's world, there was only one wonder, and he was staring at it), *the terraces that he and his tribesmen had carved over two millennia* (they must have been very old) *and maintained with care, a system of such engineering genius and irrigational know-how that it was on par with the Roman aqueducts* (who's to judge?). *But still, that feeling of apprehension was impossible to shake. Perhaps today a signal would be sounded and he and his brothers would hear the call of the gods, prepare with dance and chant, arm themselves with ax and shield, and march the well-worn tracks, so often traversed in pursuit of deer, but on this morning perhaps they would be inspired to hunt that delicate prey* (too Bowlesian?) *and follow the trail to the east in pursuit of heads.*

I read through as Tito Iñigo stirred by my feet. It sounded like other books. Is that what writing was? I highlighted the paragraph and tapped hard on the Delete button.

Perhaps I would be better served by opening pages that located Timicheg geographically or historically or both. I could start with whatever volcanic event first launched the Philippines from beneath the sea and then narrow in on the region. I could talk about the early engineers of the rice terraces. I could write about how their knowledge of irrigation and excavation and the turn of the planets showed a sophistication worthy of pride and how when the Spaniards showed up, the Bontoc and their neighbors were not the simple barbarians they were thought to be but rather an ancient culture on par with the Mayans. I could get the great wheel of history rolling along and then shove Schneidewind into the mechanism, bringing the gears to a screeching halt.

Or maybe I could think about our human fascination with curiosities: Timicheg as elephant man. Did we all need the weirdos in order to make ourselves feel normal?

"Ate Ting," said Beng, from the doorway. "May bisita para sa yo."

"Sino?"

Beng shrugged. "Babae."

I got up from the dresser that served as my desk and went into the vestibule, Tito Iñigo following at my ankles. There was a young woman by the phone stand looking at herself in the mirror in absolute stillness. She was dressed in jeans and a white blouse. Her hair was loose about her shoulders and perfectly styled. She wore small diamond earrings and a gold necklace. Her leather sneakers were immaculately white. I cleared my throat to let her know that I was there as it seemed that she could have stood transfixed by her own reflection indefinitely.

"Christina," she said, awoken.

"Yes," I responded.

"You weren't expecting me," she added, suddenly dismayed. Her accent was unadulterated American, the *r*'s hard, the consonants soft, a lack of questioning politeness in the delivery.

"Well, no, but it's quite all right." I gestured to the dining room, wondering how to politely find out who she was but somehow feeling guilty for not knowing.

"I spoke to Tita Rosa and she said she'd left you a message." She fished her phone out of her bag, a large yellow Kate Spade tote, as if there were something contained there that would vindicate her presence.

I looked over at Beng, who was suddenly wide-eyed with guilt. "Well," I said. "I didn't get the message, but you have found me here."

"I would come back later, but we're leaving tomorrow, you see. My parents are with his parents, fixing the paperwork for the transportation." She stopped, unwilling to supply details, and turned her enormous eyes—doll eyes with heavy lashes in a doll face—to me.

It was Laird's fiancée. Who else could it be?

"I am so sorry for your loss," I said.

She nodded and followed me into the dining room. I motioned for her to take a seat and she did and I took a seat and we sat in unproductive silence.

"Have you eaten?" I asked.

"Thanks, but I'm not hungry."

"Perhaps some fruit?" I looked over at Beng, who turned quickly for the kitchen. "How can I help you?"

"I'm not really sure. I would have come earlier, but I didn't know what to say. It's just that he was so grateful to you for your help. He thought you were one of the people who really understood."

"Understood?"

"What he was working for. His great dreams for the future."

Had Laird really spoken of me in this way?

"Laird said that you were one of only a few here that he thought of as a friend."

"He did?" Maybe he had. The woman, her eyes a parody of earnestness, were desperately sincere. "Well, he wasn't one for small talk. And neither am I. I suppose friendship comes easy—"

"For him, yes, and admiration. He inspired us all. You couldn't know Laird without feeling that power, that force. He understood what truth was."

She was clearly gripped in grief, but instead of overwhelming her, it seemed to be giving her strength. The fan tracked by, disturbing a stack of napkins, but I couldn't find the energy to fix or move it. The napkins scattered, dancing end over end, unobstructed across the table. I found this girl a strange choice for Laird. She was very pretty but as American as one could be in accent and movement, in her directness, which was veiled but not concealed by her grief. She didn't seem to fit his stern posturing. She was the kind of Filipino American who in high school was on student council, a valedictorian, a blond football player's girlfriend. And in college, a straight-A student trained in the rhetoric of social justice, someone who went to rallies but who paid with her phone at Starbucks. "You met Laird at an anti-Gumboc rally," I said, remembering.

She nodded. "He was a leader."

I thought I owed it to her to tell her that Laird and I had not been friends but couldn't figure out how to do it. At this point, did it matter? Maybe the polite and generous thing to do was to hear this woman out, offer her condolences, and send her into the world with whatever falsehoods offered comfort.

She shifted her gaze to me, signaling intent. "Laird's truth, his way, you see, he found it in your article."

"My article in *Vice*?" I remembered what he'd said in the car ride. Laird had been disappointed that I hadn't taken a stand.

"He felt that there was a role for him. You gave that to him." She reached across the table and held my hands. Hers were very cold and smooth. "When he spoke," she said, "one had to listen. At that first rally, he was addressing a crowd, but his words seemed made for me. Somehow, everyone felt that way. We were all riveted."

I looked at my hands in hers, unsure of how to gain them back. "And what did he say?"

At this she smiled and nodded at me, as if we shared a secret. I was grateful to see Beng walking out from the kitchen carrying a tray with Coke, an ice bucket, and a bowl of atis, of which there seemed to be an inexhaustible supply.

What had Laird and I talked about on that long-ago car ride to Café Adriatico? I remembered I'd accidentally quoted Machiavelli—a hitherto unknown imperilment—and that he had pounced on it. I had felt judged by him, but it was more in his eyes and attitude than anything he'd actually said. I remembered the sight of his back as he entered the offices of the *Philippine Telegraph*. And I knew that at some point he had told me the name of this woman, my tita Remi's granddaughter, who he had intended to marry before things had gone so sublimely wrong. But what was it? What was her name?

"I am here," she said, releasing my hands, "because of your friendship, which meant so much to him." She reached into her bag and produced a small laptop, which she extended to me. "I know he would want you to have it."

She kept the laptop extended into the space between us until I finally took it. The laptop, a MacBook Air, was cold in my hands. I didn't want to hold it. It was as if the thing were soaked in blood. "I don't know if he really would want me to have it," I responded.

"His ideas are in there, his legacy. And you are the writer in the family."

I felt a mercenary tingle.

"You will make his thoughts known to the world. I see your hesitancy. This is why he admired you."

I exhaled dramatically, I think for my own benefit, and then gingerly lifted the lid of the laptop. It was still charged at fifteen percent. "Do you have the password?" I asked.

She shook her head.

"Any ideas?"

She shook her head again. And then I remembered the exchange with Laird from so many weeks ago, as if he were whispering in my ear. I typed the letters carefully, using the capital, and hit Enter. Stunned, I watched the laptop come to life.

"Are you in?"

I nodded.

"What was the password?"

"Do you not know?" I had entered "Cheryl." "The password is your name."

* * *

I went to bed that night fully intending to turn Laird's laptop over to the American embassy or some other authority. I wasn't sure who would be able to make use of it. Perhaps I could ask Yoren, who seemed to be plugged in to that world, but I was unsure. A part of me felt that the computer had been willed to me, that Laird wanted me to have it.

My charger worked with the computer and I sat in bed, looking at the screen saver—a picture of Laird and Cheryl on a California mountain in hiking gear—then turned to the email. There were two accounts, a Gmail that hadn't been used much since his arrival in the Philippines and a Hotmail that had a different password and I couldn't open. I tried "Cheryl" again and then "Machiavelli." Neither worked.

He had only a few photos, and none were recent except a cluster of ten taken at Jim and Cha Cha's house. Laird's documents were unenlightening, papers from grad school and social justice pieces for the *Daily Californian*. I looked over a syllabus that he had constructed for an introductory poli-sci class: it required an unreasonable amount of reading, particularly of Marx and Gramsci. A file titled "Personal Directives" was a hodgepodge of inspirational quotes that I guessed was some sort of book or essay that Laird was pulling together.

There was also a draft of a forty-page document, likely his master's thesis, "Martial Law Under Batac." I clicked on it, fully expecting to learn about the various human rights violations that had occurred at that time, but it was a much stranger read. Although the opening started with a clear-eyed look at life under Batac's iron fist, the paper soon shifted, bizarrely, to an analysis of Caesar's dictatorship in Rome. It was not a final draft, and there were notes in the margins: *What is moral? Kant?* And: *Reread Mill's* On Liberty. What did seem apparent was that as Laird worked out his thesis, he was taking issue with Batac's implementation of martial law but finding less to fault with martial law itself. I wondered what his thesis adviser had had to say, and then I realized that I was unsure if Laird had actually received his master's degree. As I read through, it appeared that Laird was, at best, confused, but also someone flirting with a dangerous ideology. I shut the screen.

Nothing I found seemed important, and for the first time, I felt a genuine wave of sorrow that Laird, with all of his ambition and intelligence and unhinged sense of purpose, had left nothing behind but the sort legacy pulled together by any student of promise who had failed to realize his potential.

The following day Inchoy and I would leave for Baguio. Outside, the rain passed in waves, clattering against the pane with sudden bursts of wind. I hoped that the weather would improve, that everything would improve, and then I fell asleep.

VII

The following day the rain had cleared but there was something ominous in the wind that was bending the tops of the trees, rattling the gate at the end of the drive. Inchoy and I sat in the chairs set at the head of the steps at my tita's house, facing each other but at a distance that discouraged conversation. He'd lost weight and his shirt was baggy on him, his face drawn, with large circles beneath his eyes. We'd made a pact to try to be happy for the trip, to do the fun things that Bibo would have wanted to do, both of us knowing it would be a worthy struggle. I had promised to leave all work behind and Inchoy had cleared his grading and prepped for the next week's class. Everything would have been right if it hadn't been so wrong.

On the driveway, Miggie was piloting her Hello Kitty car with Nini following at a quick pace behind. It would likely be the only car she ever learned to drive.

"Where's the driver?" asked Inchoy. "He was supposed to be here an hour ago."

"I'll check," I said. I dialed C. G.'s landline, safe in the knowledge that she was in Bangkok, probably trawling through the stalls at Mabungkrong, striking some bargains because bringing the price down was what the rich did for fun. Cherry answered the phone. "Cherry," I said. "Nasaan ang kotse? Umalis na ba?"

The car had left three hours earlier and was likely stuck in traffic somewhere. As I rang off, I saw the gate swing open. I gestured with my chin in the direction of the car, which was now entering the drive.

"Our chariot awaits," said Inchoy, which was something he would have said in the days when he was happy. I appreciated the effort.

I stepped into the house to say goodbye. Tita Rosa was pulling herself up from behind her desk. "Tita, don't get up," I said, but she was already on her way to me, brandishing a piece of paper.

"Okay, anak," she said. She handed me the list.

"Four jars strawberry jam. Four boxes peanut brittle." This was all standard. "Six walis." I looked at her. "Six walis?" Walis was the native broom. "Why? You can get that in Kamuning."

"It's better made in Baguio."

"And why six?"

"Two for me, two for your tita Dom, and two for Carmi." She thrust an envelope in my direction, which I knew contained a careful allotment of pesos.

"I can pay for it," I said.

"Yes, you can. But you won't." She smiled. "Have a good time but don't go riding horses. It's not good for your uterus."

The trip to Baguio took three and a half hours. Inchoy had fallen asleep as we'd left Manila, then revived for the traditional stop on the outskirts of Angeles. The driver pulled in beside a vulcanizing shop displaying racks of worn tires. Inside, a man in a Ned Kelly mask was welding, and sparks shot out, flashing in the dim interior. A wiry Filipino Vulcan was banging out the dent of a disembodied car door by the entrance. We walked past a vendor, who was working a grill made from a repurposed oilcan. A cheerful cardboard sign announced CHICKEN ASS, a skewer with this part of the bird lined up along it, basted lovingly. The cooking meat sent a smell of sugar, fat, and salt wafting in clouds along the road. I would have eaten one right there, but I had to use the bathroom and convinced Inchoy we needed a restaurant, my treat.

I sat before my plate of pancit palabok and Inchoy before his binagongan. The tables were ramshackle and there was an odor wafting from somewhere that we were both too polite to acknowledge. Inchoy took a spoonful of rice and meat, chewed thoughtfully, then raised his eyebrows in an approving way. "Not bad," he said. "Yours?"

I tried the noodles. "A bit salty, but other than that . . ."

He set his spoon down and looked at me with seriousness. "Ting," he said. "Have you looked at Laird's computer?"

"I did. There's not much there, although he does have some photos taken at Jim and Cha Cha's house. The documents are mostly academic papers."

"So nothing of interest?"

"Well, there's this one document, 'Personal Directives,' that is all disjointed sentences. The one phrase I remember is: 'There is an immeasurable distance between late and too late.' Another is something like: 'Always seek out the seed of triumph in every adversity.' He must have been working on some sort of inspirational book."

"Was another: 'Tomorrow is only found in the calendar of fools'?"

"Yes. How do you know that?"

"It's not Laird's writing," said Inchoy. "It's Og Mandino."

"Og Mandino?"

"Yeah, you know, the inspirational writer. He wrote *The Greatest Salesman in the World.* Didn't you read him? We were all reading him in the eighties."

"My tita Dom has all his books. Maybe Rikki was reading him in high school." Og Mandino had been unbelievably popular. "Why was everyone into Og Mandino?"

"Ah. He was the greatest salesman. He made it seem that one could find one's way to financial gain through belief in God. If you were a true believer, you didn't have to be poor. He gave value to the empty faith of the Filipinos, filling us all with hope." Inchoy laughed. "And he's an easier read than Lacan." He thought for a moment, probably comparing Lacan to Mandino and finding Mandino lacking. "Is that all you found on Laird's computer?"

"I looked at his master's thesis or at least a draft of it. Did you know his thesis is on martial law under Batac?"

"No, but that's not surprising."

"What is surprising is that it wasn't exactly critical. He does take issue with torturing students and journalists, but much of the paper is, weirdly, devoted to Caesar. He talks about how Caesar restored order to Rome, of how it was in complete chaos after the dissolution of the triumvirate and deaths of Pompey and Crassus, of how Caesar was correct to establish himself as dictator. That the people needed it and loved him for it. He goes on at length about Caesar's building projects, about how all those roads and aqueducts and temples employed the poor and gave every Roman a stake in society. He says something about them literally building the state. Then there's a predictable reference to gladiators and Bakhtin's theory of carnival—bet his adviser made him put that in—and then it goes right back into how Rome again descended into chaos after Caesar's assassination. And there's some stuff about Machiavelli in this weird tone, as if we all love Machiavelli. And then he quotes a lot of 'strongman' philosophers that I've never heard of. Laird was a complete lunatic."

"How was the writing?"

"Good, actually, weirdly convincing. I had to keep reminding myself that I was a staunch believer in democracy."

"People who really believe in democracy should keep questioning the various practiced forms of democracy," said Inchoy. "But there's nothing about Marawi or why he would go there?"

"Not so far. I know that the interesting stuff must be in the emails, but it feels weird to read them. And there's an account I can't get into. I don't know. The whole thing creeps me out. I'm not sure how to handle it. I haven't even checked his search history."

"You'll get through it eventually," said Inchoy. "You have to. It's all that's left of him."

We reached the outer limits of Baguio at five. The atmosphere thinned as we ascended the switchbacks of Kennon Road and the landscape began to bristle with pine trees. The sharp cliffs rose rough and jagged, scattering rubble onto the roadway. Boulders were occasionally dislodged and, when they fell, would crush cars with the accuracy and complete devastation of a *Road Runner* cartoon.

"Nearly there," said Inchoy.

Slowed in traffic by the Lion's Head monument, I watched a man in traditional Igorot costume texting on the side of the road. He was dressed for the tourists. You could probably pay some pesos to have your picture taken with him, and in that, he was truly the descendant of Timicheg.

Chet had booked a suite at the Forest Lodge at Camp John Hay. The room was far more extravagant than anything Inchoy and I would have booked on our own. I preferred the cheaper accommodation of the convent, the narrow bed with its stiff little mattress, the pillows hard as a sack of flour, the scratchy blanket that was so exciting to use because this was the only place in the Philippines cold enough to require it. Here we had two huge beds, a bathroom with a tub and water both thundering and hot, and a balcony that gave out to a view of the Cordilleras, at this time shrouded in cloud. I felt manipulated by Chet. He wanted to keep track of where I was and now had done so.

Inchoy's mood was holding. He wasn't wildly joyful, but his stable, reasonable demeanor functioned as a kind of levity.

He was unpacking the contents of his small suitcase into the drawers in the closet. I stood by the window, looking at the view that was quickly fading in the evening light. "I'm going to take a shower," he said.

While he was showering, I ordered a bottle of Johnnie Walker Black from room service, because that's what Inchoy liked to drink. The bottle arrived swaddled in a napkin, perhaps to impart fanciness. It wasn't Inchoy's birthday until the next day, but I felt the need to celebrate something. Or to have something to celebrate in order to drink. I poured myself a glass and went to sit on the balcony with my cigarette as Inchoy got dressed and then came and joined me.

"So?" he said.

"So?" I repeated.

"What are you thinking?"

"I'm thinking about Chet." I was actually thinking about Bibo and how happy she would have been in this hotel room, and I knew that was also what Inchoy was thinking, and he was counting on me to come up with something else. "I wonder what he's up to?"

"Are you so in love with him?" Inchoy found this funny.

"Of course not. You know, he's been back and forth to Baguio." The whiskey was loosening my tongue, but I found it unlikely that Inchoy would share the information. "José Martin thinks he's up to something interesting, some sort of business deal."

"What's interesting about it?"

"Emails go to Rocco Basilang, also Gumboc."

"Chet's in with Gumboc?"

"Chet says he's not."

Inchoy looked at me sternly.

"I asked him and he denied it. Chet hates Gumboc." I took a sip of the whiskey, considering. "Maybe Chet's in with Basilang and Basilang is up to something. José Martin has yet to connect the dots."

"Shady business deal? A resort?"

"That's what I said. And José Martin says no. There are no building permits and there's no money to track."

"Maybe it's Chinese money."

Which would have made sense. Gumboc had a lot of deals going with the Chinese, who had cash to spare and apparent generosity, but of course China would get it all and more in the end with concessions on territory in the South China Sea. Chinese investment was a short-term solution to problems, but a lot of these short-term solutions made great sums of money for Filipinos who happened to be connected to the projects. There was still a lot of rebuilding that needed to be done in Baguio but also fear that all the construction would be quickly erased as soon as another earthquake occurred. "Wouldn't José Martin have figured that out by now, if that were the case? He thinks it's something more interesting."

"And it has to do with Baguio?" Inchoy pursed his mouth, a sign of real thought. "What is there in Baguio? Igorots? Strawberry jam? Peanut brittle? Horseback riding?"

"You forgot walis."

"And ube jam." Inchoy poured himself another finger of whiskey. He gave me an appraising look. "You don't think they're going after Yamashita's gold?" General Yamashita was believed to have buried treasure around Baguio in the final days of World War II.

"I don't think it's the gold," I said. "That doesn't sound like Chet. Or Gumboc." But I had lost Inchoy to his thoughts. His face had grown still and he was swirling his whiskey with a disquieting intensity. "Inchoy," I said. "We promised to stay cheerful. We promised to do that for Bibo."

"For Bibo? Yes, of course, stay cheerful for Bibo. Easier for you. You didn't kill her."

"What, and you did?"

"Oh, no. I didn't kill Bibo." Inchoy chuckled sarcastically. "That was Gumboc and his drug policy." He strung out *drug policy* with chilling sarcasm.

"Inchoy, it was an EJK. No one is disputing that."

He shook his head. "Do you know what Bibo wanted?" Inchoy raised his eyes to me. "She wanted to be my wife, to live with me all the time. To be recognized. She wanted to clean house and cook and be there to make my pipe in the evening. It wasn't much to want, but I didn't give it to her. And you know why?"

"Your mother."

"I can't blame this on her. Yes, ignorance makes her happy, but I left Bibo in Tondo, far from me and on her own, because I didn't want a scandal. I didn't want my family to know. I wanted to keep my perfect standing at the university. I wanted a private life, to have it both ways."

"What else would you have done?"

"You say that, Ting, because you're blind like everyone else here. What I could have done is brought Bibo to Quezon City and set us up in a little apartment, lived cheaply. Bibo wouldn't have been wandering around in the same neighborhood where people knew she had once been a drug dealer. I could have taken her love and given it its due. But I didn't. And you know why?"

"Because you were scared?"

"Because I am a coward. Because I was happy to live a lie. Because I could claim that it was a sacrifice that I was making and you and Chet and Zackito all felt bad for me, that I was making this great sacrifice for my family. And you know who made the ultimate sacrifice?"

"Bibo wouldn't want you to blame yourself, Inchoy. Try to make peace with it."

"Peace? There is no peace in this kind of grief, Ting, I feel . . . this grief is a rage. And I know no one will pay for Bibo's death, that Bibo died for nothing. We all die for nothing here. It's as if . . ."

"What?"

"Nothing. Bibo's death should matter."

“It does, Inchoy. It does matter. We are remembering her. What else can we do?”

“Have another drink?” he suggested, pouring himself more whiskey.

“Yeah,” I said, extending my glass.

We were getting monumentally drunk. I was already anticipating the hangover.

Later, we decided that to honor Bibo we would sing Mariah Carey songs, but the only one we knew was “All I Want for Christmas Is You,” so we stood on the balcony belting it out into the chilly mountain air.

VIII

How do we remember days that start so inauspiciously yet manage to turn a metaphysical corner, leading to a new reality? I awoke to the door being opened. We had forgotten to put the DO NOT DISTURB sign out, but whoever came in quickly apologized and left. I was lying under the blankets fully dressed. I opened one eye, careful to enter slowly into the day, and saw that Inchoy was curled on his bedspread, his feet resting on the still-covered pillow.

"Inchoy," I whispered. "Happy birthday."

"Am I alive?" he asked. He did not sound hopeful.

"If Bibo were here, she would get us coffee," I said.

"If Bibo were here, we could get our own coffee," he replied.

I sat up slowly. On the table, the bottle of whiskey was significantly diminished but not empty. I reached for my phone. It was noon. The previous evening was coming back in flashes, some of which I doubted as real. I remembered Inchoy going through his drawer as I exited the bathroom, him shutting it with drama as if caught at something. And then me rifling through his underwear when he was in the bathroom, because he'd seemed so suspicious.

There had been a gun. Was I making this up? I had taken the gun and switched it with Bibo's hairbrush. If this had indeed happened, the gun was now in my handbag. "I'll order room service," I said. "We should eat before we start to sober up. What do you want?"

"What are you getting?" He still had not moved nor opened his eyes.

"Tapsilog?"

"Okay," he said. "Do you think they're still serving breakfast?"

"I'll ask nicely," I said, which was a joke with us, because in situations like this I didn't ask nicely because it didn't work.

Inchoy soon managed to crawl out of bed and into the bathroom. My bag was on the floor beside the nightstand and I peeked inside. Yes, there was a gun in there. I wondered if it was loaded but wasn't sure how to check and was worried that if I messed with it, the thing would go off. I held it gingerly. The gun was small, couldn't have weighed much more than a pound, and looked as if it were designed to fit in a pocket. This was nothing like the competition pistol Inchoy had back in college when he was on the shooting team. This other must have been the gun that Inchoy had wanted to give to Bibo back when it still might have mattered. But would it really have made a difference? Would Bibo have had time to fish it out of her knockoff Louis Vuitton? Would she have had the stomach to use it on her assailants?

I pulled a tissue out of the box on the nightstand and wrapped the pistol and zipped it into a compartment of my bag, worried that if I were going for my phone I might somehow shoot off my hand. Later, I would address the gun with Inchoy, but now, as it was in my possession, it seemed fine to let it slide until an opportune moment. I would say something droll like: "I understand you might want to kill yourself, but if so, can you please wait until I'm not around?" Or: "This is not how I envisioned our vacation." Ridiculous statements that would pave the way for more direct discussions about the black hole of his despair. I wondered how Inchoy had acquired the gun, but this was the Philippines, and all he had to do, more than likely, was to stand on the sidewalk outside his house waving a wad of pesos, calling: "Baril, baril." My duty was to keep Inchoy occupied, to remind him of the many things that were still capable of diversion. I called for room service, demanding the tapsilogs and also two pots of very strong coffee.

Inchoy and I had originally planned to spend the morning at the BenCab Museum. Benedicto Cabrera was a painter of international reputation who, as a child, had sold comic books and cleaning rags on the streets of Tondo. We had thought, because of the presence of Tondo in both BenCab's and Bibo's history, that it would be a good place to start the holiday. But neither of us felt up to art and, as Inchoy pointed out, the morning was already gone.

"We can go tomorrow," he said. "We'll appreciate it more when we're not hungover."

"Okay," I said. Breakfast was now done and I was feeling surprisingly human again. "Why don't we go to the market, you know, Session Road, and wander over to Burnham Park. And then we can come back and have a nap. And then get dinner. That's the day."

"Not overly ambitious," said Inchoy.

"It's a vacation."

We took a taxi to Session Road and got out by the market. Other than the cooler temperature, this could have been any large provincial town. It was bustling. The last time I'd been to Baguio had been in the pre-earthquake days, when it was very popular. The rich of Manila didn't really come anymore. Baguio was said to be too crowded and the post-earthquake building projects made the town less old-fashioned, which had been part of its charm. It was easier to get to Batangas, where there were also beaches. But Baguio was the only place where you could escape the heat. It was the Philippines' Simla, although standing on the sidewalk in front of a Jollibee and a store that seemed to sell nothing but large women's panties and reflector sunglasses, I, too, was having a hard time feeling the town's mystique. The music was a sputtering of jeepney engines underscored with the occasional blast of disco radio romance. Up the street a policeman was tweeting plaintively on a whistle, trying to manage the onslaught of vehicles.

"Now what?" said Inchoy.

"We only have two full days, and this full day is half gone, so we should get our shopping out of the way," I suggested. "Although I don't really feel like shopping."

"Ting, you never feel like shopping."

But Inchoy did. He was a socialist who loved to shop. I had once spent forty-five minutes in Kamuning Market as he searched for the Platonic pair of rubber flip-flops, even though—to me—they were all the same.

The Baguio Market was, even by the standards of Filipino markets, immense. It stretched in an enormous network of alleyways as far as I could see, an acreage of dry goods, produce, and sweets, clothing and bags, the spoils of the rich soil and cool climate on show in pyramids of strawberries, the finery of the factories of China blanketing the walls of the stalls with T-shirts and bags that shifted in the breeze. Brooms displayed their plumage, bundled in endless racks, alongside vendors of enormous rosaries and three-foot wooden spoons. All of these were traditional Baguio purchases, although who could say why?

"Big or heavy first?" asked Inchoy.

"What do you mean?"

"Do you want to carry jars or brooms?"

"Jars," I said.

"So ube first."

"I don't have ube on my list. Just strawberry jam and peanut brittle."

"Your tita probably left the ube off her list so that you could bring it as pasalubong." He smiled. "Ube is always a welcome gift."

Inchoy was probably right. Ube, also readily available in Manila, was purchased most often as a jam made from purple yams, one of those root-based sweets that, along with bean-based sweets, wasn't much appreciated by Americans. Inchoy sauntered over to a counter and began to look at jars, his face drawn into concentrated disdain. He was a hard bargainer and I could tell from the quiet of the shopgirl that he had flagged his resolve.

Inchoy made some selections and then grouped my selections, which he had also made, in with his. He went back and forth with a series of rapid-fire questions, shifting the quantities and the prices with such speed and clarity that I could almost hear an invisible abacus clacking in his head. The salesgirl looked at me, her eyes wide with dismay.

"Ma'am," she said. "Best price, good quality."

I raised my hands, showing the futility of her appeal.

But the purchase was made to the satisfaction of both, and then we moved on.

"I wish we had someone to help with bags," said Inchoy. He was looking at the packed stalls, their endless variety, and seeing a potential bargain wherever he turned.

"Don't worry, Inchoy," I said. "We'll take turns." My hangover was lifting. Or was it just seeing the old Inchoy—happy, engaged, his energy focused—that was clearing my head? As we made our way to the peanut brittle stall, I felt some hope creeping back. Yes, Inchoy would mourn Bibo, but that didn't mean he had to be alone forever. He would probably meet someone else, maybe one of Bibo's relatives who would already know how kind and generous he was. And maybe with this new love, having learned from the mistakes of the past, he would get the apartment in Quezon City and have the wife, the slippers, the pipe. His mother would make peace with it. She could complain every day to her Santo Niño of the glass dome, and the Santo Niño would listen and bless all with his ever-raised and approving hand.

The last item on the list was the brooms. Inchoy gazed up and down the stalls, which were uniform in nearly every way. Finally, with purposeful strides he approached the chosen stall. The woman—Inchoy preferred doing business with women as he thought them to be more honest—seemed to recognize the oncoming challenge but smiled invitingly. The prices were set on neat squares of cardboard and were the same as all the other prices at the other stalls. Brooms ranged from P135 to P200, based on quality, I assumed, although some brooms were made of a rainbow of fibers, and those cost slightly more than the others. Inchoy's first volley was to ask the woman why her brooms were so expensive, for which she had a ready answer, and soon she was pulling different brooms from the wall, digging others out from beneath a table, explaining the virtues of each with expertise and passion as Inchoy nodded on, mentally calculating the cost with precision, ease, and speed.

"How many brooms do you need?" he asked me.

"Six," I said.

"Get ten. It's a better price."

"I don't need ten. Just six, please. Remember, we're getting the bus back."

We were struggling under all our loot. The jars were heavy and had necessitated the purchase of some woven shopping bags, bargained for without mercy. "We're going to have to go back to the hotel," I said. "There's no way I'm lugging this to Burnham Park."

"True," said Inchoy. "Well, if we're headed back, maybe we should just get everything now."

"Everything?" I looked at the two bags filled with jars, the bundles of brooms, and the two ornamental salakot woven hats, an impulse purchase, because Inchoy had managed to get a good price. He'd even been fingering the packages of betel nut, which was only enjoyed by old people, who chewed it, got red teeth, and were then photographed by National Geographic. "First we go to Chowking and get halo halo."

"But it's too cold for halo halo," said Inchoy.

"You can get something else," I said. I was already headed out of the market, toward the Chowking I'd seen on the way in.

We were seated at an upstairs table that offered a good view of Session Road. I had worried that there would not be enough to fill our days, but already we were running out of time. Tomorrow would be the BenCab Museum, and then there was an antique dealer on the outskirts of the city who had good quality Kalinga and Bontoc traditional carvings. Even though there were boxes of this stuff shoved in the corner of Inchoy's Scout Castor living room, I knew he would not leave Baguio before selecting another few items. And I knew that my birthday gift for Inchoy would come from this store as well. We had also planned to hire a car to go outside the city to view the rice terraces, where we would get lunch. But right now, a snack seemed a good idea, as did a nap.

My halo halo came in a tall glass with shaved ice, all the various ingredients stacked within it. There was a scoop of ube on the top, as well as a piece of leche flan. I chopped away at the ice. Inchoy, who had ordered pork chow fan, was tallying my purchases so that I would have a good accounting for my aunt.

"How many jars of ube do you want?"

"Two," I said. "But don't put that in the accounting. That's pasalubong, remember?"

"Right." Inchoy nodded.

I looked idly out the window. The sidewalks were clogged with a predictable selection of humanity—mothers holding the hands of children, children holding balloons, men with fanny packs. A woman was running down the sidewalk with a T-shirt held in front of her. I thought of the shirtless, G-string-wearing man by the Lion's Head monument and imagined her bringing it to him. I imagined that it was her who he had been texting: Bring me a T-shirt. I looked over at Inchoy, who was using the calculator on his phone, then back to the street. A sleek black Mercedes was slowly inching its way along with the jeepneys and taxis. I wondered if I knew who was in it and was chiding myself for thinking that I might when a man walked quickly to the car, opened the door, and got in. It was Rocco Basilang.

"Inchoy," I said. "I think I just saw Rocco Basilang."

"Maybe you did," said Inchoy. "There's a lot of real estate development in the area."

"I wonder if Chet's here," I said.

"Why don't you call and ask?" asked Inchoy.

"Because he didn't tell me. He knows I'm here. If he's also here, he's keeping it from me."

Inchoy did not seem impressed by this and was looking at a handwritten receipt. He held it out to me. "Ting," he said. "Is this a four or a seven?"

I looked at the wavering pen lines, squinting. "It's a four." I stabbed at my halo halo. "Why wouldn't Chet tell me he was here?" I said.

"Because he doesn't want you to know," said Inchoy. "He doesn't tell you lots of things."

"Do you think he's here?"

"If you really want to find out, why don't you track his phone?"

"Track his phone?"

"Yeah. I have an app. I used to like to see where Bibo was."

"Can anyone do that?"

"Unless he's blocked it."

"Is it legal?"

"Legal where?" asked Inchoy, for which I had no answer. "Here. I'll try his number."

I waited as Inchoy made various moves, touching his screen, and then waited. "Well?"

"Hm. Predictable. It's blocked." Inchoy shrugged. He moved his paperwork to one side and took a fork to his plate of noodles.

"Try this number," I said. I read off the number that was given only to me and C. G.

Inchoy maneuvered around on his screen and we waited. "What number is that?" he asked.

"Wife line," I said.

Inchoy smiled and waggled his eyebrows. "If this is right, he is here."

"I knew it."

"So you knew it and now you still know it." Inchoy chewed thoughtfully. "Ting, if Chet doesn't want you to know he's here, he probably has a good reason. I mean, he is a capitalist pig, but he's not stupid. You should probably leave it alone."

"True," I said. "But where is he?"

"Look, you can see the dot." He held the phone for me where Chet glowed in a small red circle, signaling from somewhere in Baguio.

"Where is that?"

Inchoy tapped the screen and enlarged a map. "Just outside of town. Amu, no, Ambuklao. Ambuklao Road. I don't know it. Must be residential."

We had already instructed the driver to bring us back to Camp John Hay when I had a change of heart. "Let's just take a peek. We can drive by."

Inchoy considered, then addressed the driver. "Kuya, are you familiar with Ambuklao Road?"

"Oo po," said the driver.

"What kind of street is this?"

"Maganda po. There aren't many houses yet, but the ones they are building are very big."

Inchoy raised his eyebrows to me. The only thing that Inchoy liked more than shopping in the market was looking at real estate, especially houses that he would never be able to afford. Perhaps this is why it did not create a conflict with his socialist values. "Okay, Ting," he said. "We'll just swing by and take a look."

Ambuklao Road curved along the side of the cliff. For a road that had few houses, its condition was very good—smooth concrete, no rubble dusting, no dislodging boulder. I began to wonder if Chet's presence was connected to real estate and then, as my mind spiraled into fantasy, if he was building a house for us. Maybe he was constructing a summer residence, a three-story building anchored to the side of the cliff with terraces on every floor, each room poised over the gorgeous dive of valley. Maybe he wanted to surprise me.

"Okay, Ting," said Inchoy. "It's coming up on the right."

If this was a building project, the work had been completed. There was an adobe wall wrapped around an improbably large area, snaking down the cliff in a feat of extreme engineering. All the trees in the surrounding area had been cleared, which made the house, rising above the wall, seem spotlit, sitting in too strong a square of sunshine in an otherwise shady region. On the opposite side of the street was another cleared area and in the middle of this sat a helicopter—big, much bigger than Jim's. It looked official, military.

"I want a closer look," said Inchoy.

"How? I'm not calling Chet, especially not now that I'm tracking him using some KGB software."

Inchoy pursed his lips in an exaggerated way, looked at me, then at the house. "We probably can't get in, but maybe we can get a peek." Inchoy instructed the driver to go back down the hill a short way, so the presence of a taxi did not arouse suspicion. We parked on the shoulder of the road. "Wait here," Inchoy instructed the driver.

I hesitated. "What if Chet sees us?"

"I'm willing to risk it," said Inchoy.

"Two minutes," I said. "And if he catches us, I'm blaming it on you."

"Fine," Inchoy said. "After all, I am deranged with grief. How would I even know where I am?" He checked again that the driver understood that he was not to leave, giving a nervous look to the purchases crammed between us on the back seat.

The peace of the street was disquieting. Inchoy and I were the only people here. I had grown accustomed to the constant crowdedness of Manila life. On the sidewalk, you had to fight for your square of pavement. You crowded around to buy tickets and ice creams and permits, casually bumping the people around you, feeling their inoffensive warmth invade your own. You sat in cars jammed along Ermita and Edsa, Aurora and Morato. Here, the sky was not chopped into corridors of smut-tinged blue but rather a vast expanse interrupted by a few branches: a circling dot in the distance that must have been a bird, a plane dividing with casual exactness one half of sky from the other.

The gate was closed tight and presented a face of impenetrable, impassive steel. A stack of cinder blocks—left over from the construction—was already being overwhelmed with vines. I wondered when the house had been completed.

"Maybe we can get a better look if we walk around," said Inchoy.

"Around? Around where? This place is a fortress and this wall is like the Great Wall of China."

Inchoy said wryly, "Maybe it was built by the Chinese."

At close range the wall was even more obscuring of the house than it had been when we'd driven past. There wasn't much to look at.

"Satisfied?" I asked Inchoy. He nodded. We turned back and were heading down the road when we heard the iron jaws of the gate being opened. Inchoy grabbed my arm, pulling me behind the stack of cinder blocks. Together, we crouched in its shadow. The cinder blocks reeked, as if soaked in urine, and I wondered if this was where the workers had relieved themselves when the building was in progress.

"This is ridiculous," I whispered. Inchoy gestured for me to be silent. The first person out of the gate was Top Gun. He looked both ways, then waved to the others, still hidden by the wall, to follow. The second out was Rocco Basilang, who quickly crossed the street in the direction of the helipad. The helicopter had just stirred to life and the blades were churning the air, drowning all the silence. Rocco's heavily lacquered hair lifted in the artificial wind like the lid of a trash can, revealing the smoothness of his bald pate. The next person out of the gate was Chet, who was looking at his phone, but before I could react to this, Gumboc walked out right behind him. I had never seen Gumboc before. He looked bloated with what might have been power but also might have been illness—some slow rot poaching his innards. What was Chet doing with Gumboc? I wanted to head to the taxi but knew I should stay put, that whatever it was we were doing was no longer fun but undeniably stupid. After Gumboc, the next person out of the gate was a woman who I recognized as an actress of some notoriety, believed to be Basilang's mistress. She was wearing Prada sunglasses and a low-cut Grecian sundress that was blown around by the chopper blades. And then there was a man—tall, with good bearing—who followed with careful steps behind her. It took me a minute to register that it was Laird. Or maybe it was someone similar, but no. He had his shoulders thrown back, a posture that I'd always thought was defensive, but that I now read as arrogance. Yes, it was Laird, very much alive, hazarding a quick look up the street and then hurriedly donning a pair of sunglasses.

"Oh my God, Inchoy," I said. "Laird's alive."

But Inchoy ignored me. He had stood up and was no longer hidden. He pushed off my hands as I made a grab for his arm and then was walking to the chopper and the people gathered there, walking with his right hand raised. He was holding the gun. I opened my bag and unzipped the compartment. Bibo's hairbrush was there again. I saw Gumboc and the others register Inchoy, and then I saw Chet, who had looked for and found me, as I was now standing in full view. His face paled with fear and he mouthed "run" at me, "run." I stumbled back two steps, then, as Inchoy began to fire, started running in the direction of the taxi.

The taxi driver must have heard the gunshots and had already started the engine. I threw myself into the back seat on top of the bags and brooms. I sat there for a moment, my heart pounding. I could feel my pulse in my temples. The driver did not ask where my companion was, just watched me nervously in the rearview mirror.

"Saan po?" he asked. Just then I got a text from Chet.

Take the next bus. Do not go back to your hotel.

I texted back:

What about Inchoy?

I waited for an answer.

Next available bus.

I instructed the driver to take me to the bus station and would have added that he should hurry, but he pulled away from the side of the road with his foot hard on the gas pedal, as eager to get me out of his car as I was to reach my destination. My mind began to swing wildly between wondering how Laird had managed to still be alive and panicking about what might be happening to Inchoy. I held my phone, waiting for some missive. At least Chet was there for him. Inchoy must have been arrested, detained in some way, locked in a room in that fortress of a house, guarded over by one of Gumboc's thugs. He must have been scared. I felt dizzy and alert, cold as well. This was fear, pure fear, as I knew the danger was real.

We were approaching the bus station, but I asked the driver to drop me by the McDonald's on the corner. Chet wanted me out of town, away from my hotel, and that meant he thought someone would be looking for me. I got out of the car nervously, aware that my height and light skin made me easy to pick out. The area around the bus station was bustling with large family groups, people moving boxes, a few American backpackers. Vendors crowded the sidewalk outside the door. I took one bag of the day's shopping and left the other on the back seat.

"Yung banig po," said the driver, gesturing to the bag. I shook my head in response, overpaid, and then made my way quickly across the street.

There were several buses pulled up in the bays. The first was to Pangasinan, the second to Vigan. Behind these two was a bus to Caloocan, which was at least headed in the right direction. A queue had formed, which meant it was leaving soon. I stepped quickly to the front of the line. No one complained. I was adopting that regal bearing that was so false but was the privilege of my class. I was the kind of person you did not want to anger. A young woman, the bus attendant, both uniformed and in heels, asked for my ticket.

"I don't have one," I said. "Which seat is free?"

"Ma'am, you need a ticket," she said.

"Then you will sell me one," I said. I took out my wallet. "Which seat is free? Or should I sit anywhere?"

I chose a window seat near the back of the bus. The overhead compartment was stuffed with brooms, as were many others. A young woman sat beside me playing *Candy Crush* on her phone. Every now and then, her eyes would flicker over at me, but if she was curious how I had ended up on a bus alone, she kept it to herself.

We were reaching the outskirts of Baguio, beginning our descent on the winding switchbacks. I was beginning to make sense out of the chaos. It was as if a corrupt flower had finally bloomed and was now releasing its perfume into the air. José Martin had been right that something was up. Maybe he'd figured it out, which explained why he had gone into hiding. Eagle's Nest was not a resort but some sort of alliance formed with Gumboc to bring on martial law. Laird had wanted to be a part of something, had presented himself as useful—a martyr with a narrative: he was a naïve American, the kind of person who would go to Marawi to understand its devastation, the kind of fool who would be kidnapped, whose connections to Manila's elite would terrify the oligarchs into compliance should Gumboc declare martial law. He had seen an opportunity to make a difference, and he had leapt at it. I thought, *Tomorrow is only found in the calendar of fools.* And in this saw a second meaning, because it was possible that Laird—now that I had seen him—might not survive the night.

Chet had known this and must have gone along with it, because he wanted to tame the general disorder and thought martial law the best way to achieve that end. This was not the Chet I knew. Chet would never be involved with Gumboc. But he had been.

We were just entering San Fernando when Chet called. I watched the ringing of the phone, unwilling to pick up, even though I knew I needed him.

I finally answered. "Chet," I said.

"Where are you?"

"I'm on the Caloocan bus, just outside San Fernando."

"That gets in at, what, around nine?"

"Something like that."

"Listen. Don't worry. You're going to be all right."

He had meant this to be reassuring, but I felt my adrenaline surge, a pulse thrumming in my ears.

"I have a plan. All you have to do is look for Top Gun."

"Okay. I'll text when I'm getting close."

"Don't text me anymore. Radio silence after this, Ting. Understand?"

"Okay."

"You get in to the bus terminal. You look for Top Gun. Okay?"

"Yeah."

"Okay. Don't worry. Bye."

It was only after I'd let him go that I realized that I hadn't asked after Inchoy or Laird or even Gumboc, who must have been Inchoy's target. I hadn't asked why it had taken him so long to call. And I hadn't asked him what the plan was beyond my finding Top Gun.

The bus pulled in at San Fernando, a break in the journey, as the restroom on the bus was out of order. In the terminal, a television was set high in the crook of the ceiling blasting a news broadcast, but if the president had indeed been assassinated, it had yet to be released to the public. The story was about the murder of a Cebuana teenager who had been brutally killed, her body mutilated, organs cut out and the skin stripped from her face. The suspects, a pair of brothers, were thought by the locals to be in a cult, to have murdered another in a similar way. They were also thought to be cannibals, and funds had been raised among the locals as a reward for their capture. But Gumboc was convinced that it was drugs. He used the bizarre killings to again push his strategy for rendering the country safe. He said he would kill any drug users and anyone who sold drugs. He said plainly, "I will kill you." And then he followed with a brief explanation of how martial law was making the country safer. I wondered when Gumboc had been recorded making this statement, probably several days ago, right after the murder, although it was claiming to be a live feed. Maybe Gumboc was in Manila. I wondered how long the helicopter took to get to Manila from Baguio. I bought an orange soda from a boy, who poured the contents of the bottle into a plastic bag, expertly rubber-banding a straw in place while sealing the contents, and handed it to me. It was dinnertime, but I was not hungry.

We had reached the outskirts of Manila. As the roads became more glutted and the bus decelerated in the final stirrings before the curfew, everyone was hurrying and speeding, like molecules compressed and slowly turning to liquid. I saw the people rushing along the sidewalks, their hearts keeping time as their slippers pressed along the dirty concrete. I took my phone from my bag and thought of Tita Rosa and Tita Dom. I thought that I should call, but what would I say? And they would not be worrying. I was supposed to be in Baguio for two more nights and for all they knew, I was sitting at Camp John Hay drinking a beer with Inchoy or finishing up dinner at the hotel.

Top Gun was waiting when I descended the bus. He took my bag in silence. I still had the half-full bag of soft drink in my hand. The car was parked close by, watched over by a young man in a singlet and shorts, one of those people who patrolled the parking lots claiming to watch over cars for the rich.

I got into the back seat, at first wondering if I should lie down, but I remembered that the windows were heavily tinted and that I would be sufficiently obscured for safety. We had pulled out of the terminal when I realized that I had no idea where we were going.

"Top Gun, saan tayo pupunta?" I asked.

"To get your passport po," he replied. "Just rest."

"My passport? Does my aunt know?"

"She is packing your things. She knows that you are safe."

As we approached my aunt's house, I wondered how much she knew. No doubt, she had not been told about Laird but probably instead some vague truth that I had to make a hasty departure, that Chet had learned something that made it in my best interests to leave. She knew well that martial law occasioned such departures. I was, after all, a journalist. I imagined Tita Dom making a joke about it: *Ting's not big into letting people know her travel plans.* It was what she did when things were serious. I would explain it all later, when I knew enough to do so. I could not tell them about Laird. I would keep his life to myself. And then I realized, with a chill that extended all over my body, settling in my bowels, that no one would think me capable of keeping such a thing a secret. There was only one way to make sure of my silence.

Outside a light rain had begun to fall, spattering in large drops on the windshield. I looked out on the sidewalk as a man pushed a cartload of bottles and old newspapers. A child in shorts and slippers jumped into a puddle, annoying his mother. And then on the corner I saw my coat—the pink fur coat—moving in slow circles at the corner of Twelfth Street. Beng was wearing the coat, looking up at the sky and the inconvenient rain with benign resignation. She was carrying a backpack and a tote bag, no doubt following orders with her usual cheerful solicitude. Tita Rosa must have put her in the coat so that I would be sure not to miss her on the crowded sidewalk. Chet had surely called my aunt, knowing it likely that Gumboc's people would head to the house, and they must have beaten me there.

"Pull over," I said to Top Gun. "That's Beng."

Top Gun quickly navigated across a lane of traffic and brought the car to a stop. A chorus of horns blared in protest. Alerted by this, Beng came quickly to the car.

"Ate," she said. "There are men at the house looking for you." She handed me the backpack and then the tote bag and, slipping off the coat, pushed that through the window of the car as well. "Your things are in the backpack," she said.

"Thank you, Beng," I said. "You should go."

Top Gun had gotten out of the car and placed the bag of jars and the brooms on the sidewalk, but now back in the driver's seat, was shooting me nervous looks in the rearview mirror.

"Ate Ting," said Beng.

"What?"

"When are you coming back?"

"Very soon. Don't go to Dubai." I reached my hand out the window of the car and she held it squeezing hard with both of hers.

Top Gun said, "We have to go."

I released Beng and then watched her pick up the brooms and bag, turning to make her way back to the house. I wondered if my aunt would be safe. But she didn't know anything, and that would quickly be determined. I didn't even know what was going on and I was sure that Chet had kept this from me so if something did transpire, I would be convincingly clueless.

We tracked the emptying streets, switching lanes, sometimes swerving into opposing traffic before ducking back in. I unzipped the backpack. Inside were my passport, a plastic bag with a few shirts and some underwear, and a brown paper envelope that had three rubber-banded bundles of bills. A piece of paper in my aunt's wavering, emphatic hand stated it was three thousand dollars.

There was a satin bag with my jewelry in it and a heavy string of pearls the size of cough drops that I had never seen—a gift from my aunt, who never sent me off without some extravagant piece. The tote bag had my notebooks and whatever papers had accumulated on my desk. Also a computer, but here Tita Rosa had been uncharacteristically mistaken because the computer was not mine: it was Laird's. My computer was stashed in the bottom drawer of the chest in my room. I would have to make sense of this later, just as whoever was now going through my things would have to make sense of what was on mine: inane emails to Inchoy, pictures from my failed marriage, a history of fabric swatches for the curtains, and the first draft of *The Human Zoo*, just a ridiculous mishmash of meaningless activity of value to no one but me.

Top Gun pulled into the dark quiet of a garage, circling downward and downward until he came to a stop by a metal door. I didn't know what building this was and, to my recollection, had never been there. The metal door opened and Chet stepped out, resulting in the usual Chinese fire drill rearrangement. Top Gun got in the back, I got in the passenger seat, and Chet sat behind the wheel. He took a moment to compose himself, looking straight ahead, before he turned to me. I said nothing. He took my hand and held it for a moment, then put the car in gear and pulled quickly away.

Neither of us spoke a word for the first fifteen minutes. I had so many questions racing through my head and was hoping he would speak first, but Chet probably had little that he wanted to say and was willing to prolong the luxury of silence for as long as he could.

We sat waiting at a traffic light that finally turned. "We need to get Inchoy," I said. "If I'm leaving, he needs to leave too."

Chet shook his head.

"What?" I said. "Damn it, Chet, say something."

He looked over, mouth pursed, then back at the road. "Ting, we cannot help Inchoy."

"We can't or we won't?"

"We can't."

I asked, "What happened to him?"

"What happened to Inchoy," said Chet, his voice controlling both anger and sadness, "is that he pulled a gun on the president."

I saw again Inchoy running up the street, his arm extended, firing off one shot, all the rest of the events swallowed up in the noise of the chopper blades. Of course they had killed him. The worst had already occurred. "And what happened to Gumboc?"

"A scratch, his arm. He found it funny."

Inchoy was dead, picked off by some armed person, someone used to carrying a gun. I nervously checked the rearview mirror and caught Top Gun's profile as he looked out at the passing storefronts and packs of children, always vigilant, always ready. I thought back to that moment when Inchoy decided to kill Gumboc, intent on revenge. It was the fire of liget, but also that long-burning hatred at the suffering of his people. Had he really thought he could kill Gumboc? In the end, it was an act of self-immolation.

IX

I didn't know what time it was or how much time was passing. We were now taking back roads and I had lost my map entirely. We were in a part of Manila where I had never been. The buildings were all one story, the road a strip of concrete with deep ditches on either side. A pack of dogs skittered across our path, the barking diminishing as we sped away. Chet would occasionally confer to ask Top Gun questions, usually inquiring if Top Gun had heard back from some person that I'd never heard of. The answers were either simple affirmatives or negatives. They were keeping me in the dark.

"Chet," I said. "You told me you weren't in business with Gumboc."

He replied without hesitation. "Business is business. This is something else."

"I don't understand."

Chet gave me a weary look. "It's true. You don't understand, and you won't, because you think you've figured it out and aren't willing to make the effort."

"Inchoy is dead," I said. "I want to know why. Maybe I was stupid to look for you, but Inchoy should still be alive. Some—" I wanted to say thug but couldn't with Top Gun sitting there. "Some *person* killed him and you owe me a real explanation."

"I owe *you*?" Chet's face hardened and he shook his head, which I knew meant he was controlling his temper. For the first time, I saw how angry he was. He was blaming me. This was all my fault. "What's this, Ting?" He had reached down to the console where the empty plastic bag from my soft drink was resting.

"It's a bag. I bought a Mirinda to drink on the bus."

"And who did you buy it from?"

"Some kid selling soft drinks."

"And how old was he?"

"I don't know. Twelve?"

"And he's selling soft drinks now and has probably been working since he was eight. He should be in school, but he's not. And you buy a drink from him and don't even see him." Chet put the plastic bag down. "Ting, if you are not the solution, then you are part of the problem. I am tired of being part of the problem."

I said, "You wanted martial law."

Chet composed himself. "I wanted the contract for the LRT and expansion of the highway system in the provinces. I wanted to cut through the red tape."

"Gumboc is a murderer. He's killed over ten thousand people and—"

"Ting, I know that," Chet said. He had dropped his voice to a soothing level and was talking to me as if I were a child. "Gumboc would have won the next election anyway, maybe not in a landslide, but handily. So what harm has been done? He's old and sick. Another couple of years, he's dead, his party flames out because the infighting has already started. Again, we swing the other way. Next president's probably your guy, Lijé, or someone like him. Someone who deals in the old ways, where nothing gets built and the wealth of the country is spread among the cronies."

"You're a crony," I said. I didn't mean it as an insult but merely to point out an irrefutable truth.

Chet gave a sad laugh and said, "But I will get my highways to the provinces, I will get the LRT, I will improve the traffic."

I thought of the long lines snaking down the steps of the LRT terminals, of the hours we all spent stalled in the traffic, of the overflowing sewers that flooded the houses of the poor every time it rained. The LRT was, to Chet, a modern-day aqueduct, a source of employment for the many workers who would no longer have to go overseas and leave their families, who could now live cheaply outside the squalor of Manila's poor neighborhoods. If the whole thing wasn't so corrupt, it would have been admirable.

"But why did you involve Laird?"

"Involve Laird? This was his idea. He sold it to Rocco. The guy's crazy, but he's smart. Laird knew what the video would have to look like. That was easy. And then he just needed to find a head."

I wondered how they had made it look like Laird or if the head had been decomposed, which would have been convenient. Or if they had simply found someone to sign some document saying that this head had been identified when it hadn't.

I asked, "So whose head?"

"Ting," said Chet. He looked hurt. "I'm a businessman. I don't deal with that. But no one was killed." Although I felt certain that he was not sure of this. Chet's eyes flickered over to me, then returned to the road. "You remember when Batac declared martial law. There was the bomb that went off in Plaza Miranda."

I said, "I was three, and you were five, so no." But I knew the Plaza Miranda bombing had been a false flag, the whole thing arranged by Batac, who blamed it on the communists. We had all known it was Batac, but the power of his story had overwhelmed the truth.

"Do you know how many people died that day? Nine, one of them was a five-year-old. Ninety-five people were injured. This was an incident without bombs. No blood was shed."

But blood had been shed. There had been the bomb in Baclaran Church, now conveniently forgotten or downgraded to collateral damage. Chet had blood on his hands, and so did I.

We were quiet for some time. The air-conditioning was on full blast and the joints of my arms were beginning to ache, reminding me that I was still alive. Chet was following my thoughts. He did blame me. He blamed me for my stupidity. In the great machine of his plan, there had been but one faulty circuit, and that had been me. Or his inability to control me. He was now blaming himself.

"And what will happen to Laird?" I said.

"The plan is that he goes to Shanghai for a few months. After that, who knows?"

"Is that still the plan?"

"Now you're worried about him?" Chet laughed coldly. He had a harsh smile in his eyes and for the first time I saw the wrinkles forming. "He's the one who said you were with Inchoy. He knew from your aunt. It's his fault they're looking for you."

We pulled up to a gate that opened to an enclosure encircled by a chain-link fence. A wiry old man with his cap pulled low over his eyes undid a padlock, pulled the chain, and let us through. Another man in jeans and sunglasses stood at a distance, an Armalite held casually in his hands. There was a hangar of rusting iron, a gas tank, a corroded water tower that was standing at a tilt and looked ready to collapse. The area was paved with deteriorating concrete, broken by uneven earth and young trees that burst through its seams. A rooster ran across the busted tarmac, flapping its wings but unable to take flight. We sped along, bumping across the rutted terrain, heading—now I saw—to a four-seater plane, its propellers going, the grumble of its engine reaching through the tinted windows and air-conditioned hum of the car.

Chet pulled over by the plane. Top Gun shot out of the car and immediately began talking to a man in a leather jacket.

"Get your things," said Chet. "We need to move quickly."

I got out of the car, shouldering my backpack and tote bag. Chet grabbed my coat and nodded at it approvingly. "Good thing you have this," he said. "It's going to be cold."

I put my bags down and let Chet help me into the coat. "Chet," I said.

"What?"

"Where am I going?"

Chet looked around nervously. He put his hands on my shoulders. "You're flying to Macau, then Hong Kong. Your flight to New York leaves early tomorrow. Gumboc thinks you left Baguio this morning, that you found a last-minute seat on the two p.m. Manila–Hong Kong flight. Records here will support that. Your aunt is also of the same opinion or is at least convincingly presenting the story."

"But I was seen at the hotel—"

"Also taken care of." No one had noticed me in the mayhem of Ambuklao Road. I was now a part of another story that would hold against the truth. Chet took an envelope that had been folded in the pocket of his shirt and handed it to me. I looked at it, realizing it was the itineraries, then shoved the envelope into my coat pocket.

Chet nodded a few times in a way that I knew was supposed to inspire confidence. Maybe he was composing some parting words, but the engines of the plane were growing louder. We were running out of time. Just then, my phone beeped with the signal that I knew meant it was a text from my husband. I ignored it.

"You'll be fine," Chet said. "We'll just wait for things to quiet down. And then . . ."

"And then I come back?" I asked. I could feel a heaviness in my chest and I sensed immediately what it was, my heart, that quiet machine, and from its subtle ache, I knew that we were over. There was no future for us.

"Yeah. Just let me . . ."

"Let you fix things."

Chet nodded. "You, Ting," he said. He looked at me directly, accusingly. He was angry at himself, at his weakness. He said, "You."

I stepped to Chet and he embraced me. I rested my head against his chest. I could feel him warm through the fabric of his shirt. I could hear his heart beating in there.

By the time we took off, Chet was already speeding away across the concrete, working hard to maximize the distance between us. My pilot was Chinese, as was the copilot, who spoke some English and seemed very excited at this opportunity to use it.

He asked me, "How was your day?"

"Very nice," I replied. "Thank you for asking."

Both my companions on that flight looked to be about twenty years old.

We left the ground shortly after that, hurled brutally into the sky as if tossed by some colossus. The engine screamed with effort as the plane shuddered upward, and even though the motor of the plane was deafening, beyond it I sensed an infinite silence. We were moving through an even darkness that made progress in any direction seem improbable, as if we had lifted off the earth and into a state of benign stasis from which we might never emerge.

When we had been aloft for some time, I took my phone from my bag. There were three messages from my husband.

The first said:

I cannot sign these papers.

The second said:

We need to talk.

The third said:

Christina, we both have done things that we regret.

ACKNOWLEDGMENTS

I would like to extend my gratitude to my family, all of you, Filipino and American, who are my country. And particularly to those members who helped with this book through inspiration, generosity, and love. You know who you are.

This book would never have happened without the support of a Samuel F. Conti Faculty Fellowship Award from the University of Massachusetts.

I would also like to thank Katie Raissian, who read so many versions of this manuscript and responded with her usual tough love, and Elisabeth Schmitz, for her unflagging faith in my work. Also thanks go to Morgan Entrekin for his support for this and through the years.

I would also like to thank Jessica Friedman, my agent, for her energy, imagination, and vision.